romancing the workplace series

The Maine Event

alia smith

BAL
KON
media

ALSO BY ALIA SMITH

ROMANCING THE WORKPLACE SERIES

The Plus-One Clause (Novella)

Bookish with Benefits

The Maine Event

The Midnight Meet-Up

THE MAINE EVENT

Published by Balkon Media

Paperback edition ISBN: 978-1-916970-10-6
Also available as an E-book

Edited by Hanna Elizabeth

Cover Design: graphichouse 123

www.balkon.media

*To the optimists and dreamers,
the coffee-fueled overthinkers...
and everyone who's ever accidentally fallen in love
when they least expected it.*

ONE

I take a deep breath and stride into the conference room, my heels clicking sharply against the polished floor. The air is thick with the scent of expensive coffee and barely concealed skepticism. A dozen fast food executives sit around the sleek glass table, their arms crossed, their gazes expectant. They don't think I can sell them on this. That's adorable.

I flash my best boardroom smile and place my portfolio on the table with a crisp *thud*.

"Gentlemen. Imagine a plant-based burger that not only tastes amazing, but also aligns perfectly with your brand's commitment to sustainability," I say, my voice clear and strong. "Our campaign will position your new offering as the go-to choice for health-conscious and environmentally aware consumers."

A pause. One executive raises an eyebrow, as if I've just suggested they start serving kale milkshakes.

I hold their gaze and continue. "It's not just another burger —it's the burger that changes the conversation."

As I delve into the details of the proposed marketing strategy for their new healthy choice menu item, I can see the executives nodding along, any objections they had planned to raise melting away. I highlight the key selling points—the burger's delicious flavor, its nutritional benefits, and its potential to attract a new demographic of customers. You get a sixth sense about whether your pitch is landing right with an audience and, not to toot my own horn too hard... seven minutes in, I have everyone in the room eating out of my hand.

"By partnering with influencers in the wellness space and leveraging social media, we'll generate buzz and drive demand for your plant-based option," I explain, gesturing to the colorful slides projected behind me. "This is an opportunity to establish your brand as a leader in the fast food industry's shift toward healthier, more sustainable offerings. In a nutshell, my team and I will position your product as a burger that's good for you, good for the planet, and good for business."

The lead executive, a silver-haired man with a perpetual frown, clears his throat. "That's... impressive."

Damn right, it is.

The polite applause tells me I've nailed it. I field questions with ease, keeping my responses tight and strategic.

This is my playground, and I own it.

Just as we're wrapping up, a man I hadn't paid much attention to—a tall, dark-haired exec with the confident ease of someone used to getting what he wants—steps forward, smiling.

"Great presentation." He offers his hand. "Lyle."

I shake it, firm but brief. "Rachel Holmes."

"You clearly know your stuff. I'd love to discuss it further. Maybe over dinner?" His smile is smooth, like he already knows the answer.

I return it, but mine is professional, unwavering. "I make it a policy not to mix business with pleasure."

His expression falters for a split second before he recovers.

"Well, that's a pity." He hands me his card. "But either way, I look forward to working with you."

I tuck the card into my portfolio, already moving on. As I stride down the hallway, the familiar rush of success hums in my veins. One step closer to landing this account. One step closer to making partner. My personal life might be a barren wasteland, but my career? *On fire.*

The truth is, I've always been better at managing brands than people. Crafting narratives and selling ideas come as naturally to me as breathing, but building relationships? That's where things get messy. At work, everything follows a strategy —objectives, deliverables, measurable outcomes. If a pitch doesn't land, I can pinpoint why, learn from it, and try again. But in my personal life? There's no tidy PowerPoint presentation to guide me through the chaos of human connection.

I've spent years perfecting my professional image—the competent, confident, always-prepared woman who can sell anything to anyone. I know how to make an impression, how to leave a room buzzing with ideas and possibilities. But after hours, when the office lights dim and I'm alone in my immaculate, lonely apartment, I feel the weight of that polished veneer crushing me.

I think of my old friends, the ones who slowly drifted away while I was climbing the corporate ladder. Birthday texts that went unanswered, dinner invites declined because of deadlines and meetings. Now, even if I wanted to rekindle those friendships, I wouldn't know where to start. I've wrapped myself in my ambition like a safety blanket, convinced that I don't need anyone.

But sometimes—just sometimes—I catch myself scrolling through social media, pausing on photos of people I used to know. Laughing in crowded bars, holding hands on beach vacations, watching their kids take their first steps—living their best life. And it hits me, sharp and unexpected: I've built a life so perfectly curated that I don't really fit into it anymore.

I shove the thought away, focusing instead on the rush of victory from the pitch. There's no room for self-pity today. I won them over, and that's what matters. I'll celebrate later—maybe with a glass of something expensive and a quiet toast to myself. After all, who else will?

As I stride down the hallway, still riding the high of the successful presentation, I catch sight of Helen through the glass walls of her office. My boss is the picture of effortless authority, well put together in a tailored navy suit, her mani-cured fingers laced together. But her expression is unreadable, and that—*that*—is unsettling.

"Rachel, sit down."

I lower myself into the chair opposite her desk, still riding the post-pitch high. "What's up? The meeting went well."

"It did," she agrees. "In fact, it went so well that I'm forcing you to take a vacation."

I blink. "I'm sorry. You're *what?*"

Helen leans back, studying me like a puzzle she's just figured out. "You haven't taken a single day off in eighteen months. You need a break before you break. Two weeks. No arguments."

"But—"

She holds up a hand. "Non-negotiable. Go read a book, reconnect with your family. Hell, get a hobby."

I open my mouth, then close it. Helen is one of the few people on earth who can out-stubborn me. I could fight this, but I'd lose. And the truth is, there's no one in my life demanding my time. No partner. No kids. Even my friend-ships have faded under the weight of work.

A convenient excuse not to face that reality.

"Fine." I exhale. "But I'm not happy about it."

Helen smirks. "I don't expect you to be. Now get out of my

office before I start to suspect you *like* being here. And who knows? Maybe you'll surprise yourself and actually enjoy yourself."

I let myself in with the key my sister Claire keeps hidden under a plastic rock that is, frankly, an insult to camouflage. Technically, it's Claire and Richard's house—a big, modern place they bought after Lily was born. They invited Mom to move in with them soon after. She'd been on her own for decades, still living in the little house we all grew up in, and they didn't like the idea of her rattling around in it alone. This place had the space, and the logic was simple: more help with childcare for them, more company for her.

Still, the moment I step inside, it smells like Mom's house —lavender and freshly baked cookies. A scent so deeply nostalgic it nearly knocks me sideways.

A familiar warmth wraps around me, tugging at memories I'd thought long buried. The layout's different, sure, but the feeling is the same. And Mom's touch is everywhere—the floral cushions, the knitted throw on the back of the couch, the armchair where she still reads the newspaper with her tea, just like she did back when we were kids.

Back then, I'd convinced myself that being the best—at school, at track, even at the annual science fair—was the only way to matter. Mom never pushed me to be perfect, but I craved the reassurance of straight As and trophies as proof that I was doing something right. Once, after winning the regional debate championship, Mom had hugged me so tight I thought I'd break, whispering how proud she was. But all I could think about was the kid who came second, the way his face fell when they called my name.

In my mind, there was no room for mistakes or second

place. I thought that if I just worked hard enough, controlled every variable, I'd never have to feel that gnawing sense of inadequacy again. Even now, standing in this familiar hallway, it's hard to shake the compulsion to be the best—to outwork, outperform, and prove to everyone, including myself, that I'm worth the effort.

Maybe that's why I never stopped pushing—why I buried myself in work instead of forming lasting relationships, why success became synonymous with self-worth. If I let up, even for a second, it might all unravel. And that's a risk I've never been willing to take.

"Mom? Claire?" I call out.

Mom's voice cuts through my thoughts, bringing me back to the present. "Rachel? You okay?"

I force a smile, shaking off the remnants of old insecurities. "Yeah, Mom. Just... had some time to spare."

I find her in the living room, curled up in her armchair, eyes glued to the TV.

"Hey." I move some toys out of the way and plop onto the couch beside her.

"Oh! Perfect timing. You have *got* to see this show I'm watching."

I glance at the screen. A ruggedly handsome man with piercing blue eyes is engaged in a heated argument with an equally beautiful woman. *Malibu Lagoon*, the title graphic reads—I've never heard of it, but that doesn't mean much. I barely have time to switch on the television, so major zeitgeist shows pass me by all the time. A quick search on IMDb reveals that this telenovela-type soap opera ran for four seasons before being abruptly canceled eight years ago. It has a surprisingly high rating and judging from the comments, a legion of fans just like my mom.

I arch an eyebrow. "Really? A soap opera?"

Mom waves me off. "It's *very* well done. And the lead actor? *Ugh*, so talented."

I study the screen. The guy *is* striking, all brooding intensity and movie-star good looks. If I were casting a campaign, he'd be a marketing dream.

"Isn't he handsome?" Mom gushes, as if reading my thoughts. "So good."

I nod absentmindedly, my mind already drifting back to work. Instinctively, I reach for my phone to check my emails, but a breaking news alert catches my eye.

"Mount Spurr erupts again in Alaska," the headline reads, accompanied by a dramatic image of a massive ash cloud billowing from the volcano.

I feel a knot form in my stomach. I can't imagine living next to such a frightening force of nature that could erupt at any time. I'm not sure how those who do can possibly sleep at night.

"Rachel, are you even listening to me?" Mom's voice snaps me back to reality.

"Sorry, Mom. Just catching up on world events. I'm all ears, promise."

Mom sighs, shaking her head. "You're always glued to that thing. Even when you're supposed to be relaxing."

I feel a pang of guilt, knowing she's right. I've been so consumed by work lately that I've barely had time for anything else, including visiting my mother.

I sink back, allowing myself to relax for the first time in what feels like months. I haven't been to visit in ages, and it feels... strange. Almost like I don't belong here anymore.

I moved out of Mom's house as soon as I could, desperate to make something of myself. Even back in high school, I was the girl with the color-coded planner and the stack of textbooks bigger than my head. The girl who stayed up until midnight finishing extra credit assignments just to make sure no one could beat me to valedictorian.

God, I remember the feeling of opening that acceptance letter to Northwestern, my hands shaking so badly I almost ripped it in half. It wasn't even about leaving—no, I was ready for that. It was about proving I could do it. That I could be the best. That all the late nights and stress-induced migraines meant something.

Mom used to worry about me back then, always saying I was pushing myself too hard. Claire, on the other hand, just thought I was nuts. "You're like a hamster on an espresso drip," she once joked when I was cramming for finals. "Chill out, Rach. You're already a shoo-in."

But chilling out never felt like an option. Not for me. I couldn't let myself be just good enough. I had to be the best. I had to make something of myself—something big, something important.

Maybe Mom was right all those years ago. Maybe I have been pushing myself too hard. But the thought of slowing down, of stopping to take stock of my life, terrifies me. Because what if, when I stop, I realize that none of it is worth anything at all?

"I know, I know," I concede, putting my phone away. "I'll try to unplug more, I promise."

"You'd better. You're not too old for the flying slipper, you know."

To be fair, my mom's ability to nail someone with a slipper from across the room is legendary. When Claire and I were growing up, she could hit your arm or your leg, or whatever appendage was offending her, from thirty feet. It was never thrown with particular malice, but the accuracy was astounding.

"Still think you've got it, Mom? You're not in your thirties anymore, and I'm not eight."

"That's true, but *you* are in your thirties now, and luckily for me, you're a much bigger target. I like my chances."

Mom hovers a hand near an ankle, fingers twitching over her slipper like a gunslinger ready to draw.

"Okay. Okay." I concede and place my phone face down on the coffee table, out of sight, out of mind.

As soon as I do, Mom smiles and turns off the television. "So, what's going on?"

"Nothing's going on."

"It's four o'clock in the afternoon. Have you been fired?"

"No!" I squeak, horrified at the thought. "I'm... I'm on vacation."

"Since when?"

"About an hour ago."

I fill Mom in on my forced sabbatical and foolishly admit that I don't really know what to do with myself. But even as the words leave my mouth, I know it's a mistake.

With the lithe grace of a mountain cat, she's up and out of her armchair, dialing my sister's cell phone before I know what's happening.

Thirty minutes later, my life is ruined.

"Claire will pick you up at ten on Sunday," Mom announces, far too pleased with herself. "Pack warm."

I stare at her. "Mom. No."

"Oh, come on. A cabin on Lake Michigan! Fresh air! Family time! You *love* your nieces."

"I love them in small doses," I mutter. "Preferably when they're asleep."

Mom grins. "Then think of this as character-building."

"I *don't* need character. I need Wi-Fi and a coffee machine that doesn't require manual labor."

Mom pats my cheek. "You need to live a little, sweetheart."

"Thanks for the support."

"Don't mention it."

"I was being sarcastic."

"I know. Well, I think it's lovely you're all going away together," she says and turns back to her program.

I stare in disbelief at my mom's beaming grin of self-satisfaction. I don't like vacations. I certainly don't like camping. And I'm more of a "here's your birthday gift, now run along and play" kind of auntie, at least until they're potty trained and can string a sentence together.

Somehow, I'm now signed up to spend ten days cooped up with my sister, her husband, and their two rambunctious toddlers at their log cabin on Lake Michigan. It's not that I don't love my sister and her family, but the idea of being away from work, from the city, fills me with an unsettling sense of dread. Somehow, I'm signed up for a trip to the wilderness, hunting elk, and drinking from streams—or whatever it is people do when they're in the great outdoors.

I groan.

This is going to be a disaster.

Or, at the very least, deeply, *deeply* inconvenient.

Two weeks away from work? Away from my team, my clients, my *progress*? I've been working toward a partnership for years, and I can't impress the powers that be if I'm off roasting marshmallows and pretending to enjoy nature.

They say out of sight, out of mind. What if someone else steps in and wows them in my absence? What if I come back to find that all my hard work has been quietly shuffled onto someone else's plate?

I'll make it work. I *have* to. Because the last thing I can afford is to be forgotten.

TWO

❤

"Woohoo, we made it to Wisconsin!" Richard cheers as we pass the sign announcing the state border. Claire, sitting shotgun, grins and gives him a high five.

The road trip to the cabin is already an exercise in patience and we've only been on the road for ninety minutes. I'm crammed into the back between two car seats, my nieces babbling and giggling on either side of me. The air is thick with the scent of strawberry yogurt and baby wipes, and I can already feel a headache forming behind my eyes.

"Rach, Rach, look!" My older niece, Lily, thrusts a sticky handful of chips towards my face. "I'm sharing with you!"

"Oh, um, thanks, Lily," I manage, gingerly accepting a soggy chip and trying not to grimace. "That's very nice of you."

Claire catches my eye in the rearview mirror and grins. "Isn't this fun, Rach? Just like old times, hitting the road for a family adventure."

"Sure, if by 'old times' you mean 'never,' since we definitely didn't take many road trips growing up," I mutter, shifting uncomfortably as Lily's baby sister, Anna, lets out a piercing shriek.

"Oh, come on, where's your sense of adventure?" Claire teases. "This is going to be great, you'll see. Quality family bonding time!"

I open my mouth to retort, but suddenly there's a clatter and a splat, and I look down to see a blob of purple yogurt dripping down my blouse. *Versace. Ruined.*

"Oopsie!" Lily giggles, waving her now-empty yogurt cup. "Auntie Rachel is wearing my snack!"

I close my eyes and count to three, reminding myself that this is just temporary, that I can handle a little mess and noise for the sake of my family. But as I feel the cold yogurt seeping through to my skin, I can't help but wonder what the hell I've gotten myself into.

This is a mistake, a voice warns in my head. *You should be back in Chicago, focusing on your career, not playing babysitter in some backwoods cabin.*

But then I remember my promise to Mom, and the wistful look in her eyes as she urged me to find something more than just work. And I think of Claire, who's always been there for me even when I've been too busy to return the favor.

No, I tell myself firmly. *This isn't a mistake. This is an opportunity. A chance to reconnect with what really matters, to figure out who I am beyond just my job title.*

I open my eyes and smile at Lily, who's now happily smearing yogurt on her own face. "You know what, Lil? I think purple might just be my color after all."

Claire laughs from the front seat, and I feel a flicker of warmth in my chest. Maybe this trip won't be so bad after all.

"Okay girls, what should we do first when we wake up at the lake house tomorrow?" Richard asks Lily and Anna.

"Make s'mores!" Lily exclaims.

"Go swimming!" Anna counters.

They chatter on excitedly, while I try to tune it out. I clear my throat.

"So, um, Lily... how's kindergarten going?" I ask, attempting to make conversation with my five-year-old niece.

She turns and blinks at me. "I don't like it." An awkward pause. "They make us do work. Writing letters and numbers. Boring."

"Oh, uh, wow. That sounds... fun." I force a smile.

I'm saved from further small talk when my cell phone rings. I frown at the caller ID—it's Helen, my boss. This can't be good.

"Sorry, I have to take this. Work emergency," I say, relieved at the interruption. "Helen, what's up?"

"Rachel, I have huge news," Helen says breathlessly. "Guess who was just on the phone inviting us to pitch?"

"Don't do this to me. Who?" I knew immediately if Helen was playing coy, it was big news. "Who?!"

"You've been trying to poach them for months?"

My pulse quickens. "GreenShoots?"

"Yep. They're looking to go in a new direction. But here's the rub—they've put the account up for tender. Four agencies, including us."

A thrill runs through me, followed by steely determination. I've worked too hard on landing GreenShoots to lose them now. Nearly eighteen months of subtle but constant engagement, and it's finally paid off.

"A pitch is fine; I can handle the competition. When do they need the proposal by?"

Helen exhales. "That's the kicker. They want pitches tomorrow."

"Tomorrow?!" The word explodes out of me, making Richard glance back in concern. I wave him off.

"I know, I know. They're doing it on purpose, to see how we react to pressure. They want fresh ideas, not a polished dog and pony show," Helen explains.

My mind races, already envisioning the key messages,

tactics, case studies I'll need to wow them, jetlag be damned. I'm their woman and they need to know it.

"Okay, I'll make it work," I say firmly. "Text me all the pitch details, I'll start strategizing. Tell GreenShoots they'll have the most persuasive damn proposal they've ever seen, even on short notice."

"That's my star closer," Helen says proudly. "I knew I could count on you."

I hang up, adrenaline surging through my veins. This pitch could make my career. I have to win it. I have to get to Portland, fast.

But as I look up, I suddenly remember where I am—wedged in my brother-in-law's SUV, zooming farther away from the airport with each passing mile. My stomach sinks.

What the hell am I going to do now?

I steel myself for the conversation I'm about to have. "Richard, I need you to turn the car around. I have to get to the airport."

"What?" Claire twists around in her seat to face me, her eyebrows knitted together. "You can't be serious! We're literally going on vacation."

"I know, I know." I hold up my hands placatingly. "But this is a huge opportunity. I've been trying to land a huge client for over a year, and the pitch is tomorrow. I have to be there."

"Unbelievable." Claire shakes her head, her lips pressed into a thin line. "You're really choosing work over family? Again?"

I wince at the accusation, but I don't back down. "If I win this client, I'm a shoo-in for partner. It's everything I've been working towards. I promise, once I close this deal, we can take a proper vacation, my treat."

Claire scoffs and turns away, her arms crossed tightly over her chest. The girls have gone silent in the back, their earlier excitement fizzled out. They have no idea what we're talking about, but they can sense it's not good.

"Richard, please." I lean forward, my voice urgent. "I wouldn't ask if it wasn't important."

Richard meets my gaze in the rearview mirror, his expression conflicted. After a long moment, he sighs. "Alright, Rach."

Relief floods through me, followed quickly by a pang of guilt as the girls start to whine.

"But Mom, that means it'll take even longer to get to the lake!"

"I don't want to spend more time in the car!"

I tune out their complaints, my mind already whirring with ideas for the pitch. This is my chance to prove myself, to show everyone at Channing Gabriel that I have what it takes to be a partner.

As Richard navigates the car through the traffic, heading back towards Chicago, I pull out my phone and start typing furiously. I have a presentation to plan, and I'll be damned if I let this opportunity slip through my fingers.

The airport bustles with activity as I hurry through the sliding doors. I spot my assistant, Emily, near the check-in counters, her red hair a beacon amidst the crowd.

"Emily!" I call out, waving to catch her attention.

"Rachel, there you are!" She rushes over, handing me my ticket, a small carry-on, and a garment bag. "I picked out the blue suit, hope that's ok. You're going to crush this pitch."

I take the items gratefully, a smile tugging at my lips. "You're a lifesaver, Em. Truly."

We navigate the throngs of travelers, making our way to security. As we wait in line, Emily fills me in on the latest office gossip, but my mind is already on the pitch, running through key points and anticipating potential questions. Em waves me off as I show my ticket to the TSA agent.

Once in the air, I pull out my laptop and immerse myself

in the presentation, refining slides and practicing my delivery. The hours slip by, and as the plane touches down in Portland, I feel a surge of confidence. I've got this.

Disembarking, I reach for my suitcase in the overhead bin, my mind still running through the opening lines of my pitch. As I step onto the airbridge, a deep, mellifluous voice breaks through my thoughts.

"Excuse me, miss? I think you might have my suitcase."

I turn to find a striking man with chiseled features and a charming smile. There are jawlines... and there's him. He gestures to the bag in my hand, and I glance down, noticing a small red ribbon tied to the handle. Heat rises to my cheeks as I realize my mistake.

"Oh my gosh, I'm so sorry!" I hand him the suitcase, flustered, and he hands me mine.

His eyes sparkle with amusement. "No worries, it happens to the best of us. I take it you're here on business?"

We fall into step, chatting easily about the trials and tribulations of corporate life. There's an undeniable spark, and I find myself drawn to his wit and warmth.

But as we exit the airbridge, a beautiful woman with flowing blonde hair rushes up to him, pulling him into a tight embrace. "Honey, I missed you so much!"

Reality comes crashing down, and I laugh inwardly at my foolishness. Of course, a man like him would be taken. I offer a polite nod and turn to head towards the exit, my focus shifting back to the task at hand.

And that's when I see it. The sign that stops me dead in my tracks.

"Vacationland, welcome to the State of Maine."

No!

This.

Is.

Not.

Happening?

My heart plummets as the realization hits me. I'm not in Portland, Oregon. I'm on the wrong side of the country.

No. No, no, no. That can't be right. I blink hard, as if willing the sign to change. I dig into my bag, nearly ripping the zipper off as I yank out my ticket and unfold it with trembling hands. My eyes scan the fine print—Portland International Jetport (PWM).

Oh my God. PWM. Not PDX.

My heart thunders so loudly in my ears that I barely hear the chatter of the other passengers around me. I stare at the letters, trying to force them to rearrange themselves, to magically morph into the correct airport code. But they don't. Because they can't.

I clutch the ticket like a lifeline, my brain scrambling to piece together what the hell had just happened. How did I not notice this? How did I let this happen? I'm always so meticulous, so organized—I double-check everything, triple-check, even.

I feel lightheaded. I look around, as if someone might pop up and tell me it's all a joke, that I haven't just flown to the wrong damn side of the country—it's just a hidden camera, YouTube prank channel. But there's no one to laugh with me, no friendly face to reassure me it's not as catastrophic as it seems.

Frantically, I pull out my phone and scroll to the confirmation email from Emily. There it is, plain as day—Portland, ME. My stomach lurches. How did I miss that? How did neither of us catch it? I thumb through the flight information again, as if somehow the words will change, but they're still the same damning coordinates pointing to Vacationland instead of the West Coast.

My knees go weak, and I stumble toward a bench, collapsing onto it. The gravity of my mistake hits me like a freight train. I'm in Maine. I'm supposed to be in Oregon. I'm supposed to be pitching to one of the biggest potential clients of my career tomorrow morning.

I can't breathe. I press my palm to my forehead, trying to calm down, but it's no use. The reality is suffocating me, stealing the oxygen from my lungs.

"Oh, my good God." The words escape my lips, disbelief and panic rising simultaneously in my chest. "What have I done?"

Frantically, I rush to the airline's service desk, my mind reeling with the gravity of my mistake. The line seems to stretch on forever, and every passing second feels like an eternity. I tap my foot impatiently, my eyes darting to the departure boards, hoping against hope that there's a flight that can get me to Oregon in time.

As I wait, the TVs above the desk flash with breaking news. The anchor's grave tone fills the air. "The ash cloud from the eruption of the Alaskan volcano is rapidly spreading across Canada and the Northern United States, causing unprecedented disruptions to air travel. Experts predict massive delays and cancellations in the coming hours."

My stomach churns as I watch the departure board flicker, the word "DELAYED" morphing into "CANCELED" next to flight after flight. The reality of the situation crashes over me like a tidal wave. I'm stranded, and there's no way I'll be flying to the pitch.

With shaking hands, I pull out my phone and start searching for alternative routes. Train schedules, bus timetables, anything that could get me to Portland, Oregon. But deep down, I know it's futile. The distance is too vast, the time too short.

I step out of the line, my legs feeling like lead. The bustling airport seems to fade away as the weight of my failure settles on my shoulders. I find a quiet corner and sink into a chair, burying my face in my hands.

"Think, Rachel, think," I mutter to myself, desperately trying to come up with a solution. But the more I rack my brain, the more apparent it becomes that there's no way out of this mess.

The disappointment is a bitter pill to swallow, but I know I have to accept the reality of the situation. The pitch, the partnership, the future I've worked so hard for—it's all slipping through my fingers, and there's nothing I can do to stop it.

With a heavy heart, I pull out my phone again, my fingers hovering over Helen's number. I hesitate, dreading the conversation that's about to unfold. But I know I can't put it off any longer.

As the call connects, I steel myself for the inevitable fallout. "Helen, it's Rachel. I have some bad news..."

While I explain I'm in Maine, she mostly remains calm, although it would be fair to say her choice of language is zesty. However, the magical solution I was hoping she could conjure from thin air isn't forthcoming.

"TSA is shutting down all flights. There's no way you're getting to Oregon."

My heart sinks. "But the pitch—"

"Don't worry about it. Given the circumstances, Zoe will handle the presentation instead. She can drive from Seattle."

"Zoe?" I feel a surge of frustration. "But I've been working on this for months, Helen. GreenShoots is *my* client."

"Not yet, they're not, Rachel. I don't have a choice. The pitch is happening tomorrow, we have to be in the room."

I pace, my mind racing. "What if I use my influence with GreenShoots to change the pitch day? I'm sure they'll understand, given the situation."

"No, Rachel," Helen says firmly. "They've set the date, and we have to comply. We're sending Zoe."

"But Zoe doesn't have my *green* credentials," I argue, desperation creeping into my voice. "She primarily works on Big Oil accounts, for God's sake. And she drives a 5-liter Mustang GT. Wouldn't it be better to Zoom into the meeting, to reduce our carbon footprint?"

My arguments fall on deaf ears. "Rachel, this is not up for discussion," Helen says, her tone leaving no room for debate. "Zoe is the next-best closer in the company, and GreenShoots is a must-win client for Channing Gabriel."

I feel my anger rising, but I try to keep it in check. "So, if Zoe closes the deal, does that mean she'll get the partnership?"

There's a pause on the other end of the line. "Rachel, I suggest you enjoy your two-week vacation in Maine and forget about work for a while."

"But Helen—"

"That's an order, Rachel. Send your presentation and notes to Zoe. Now."

The line goes dead, and I'm left staring at my phone, seething with frustration. I can't believe this is happening. I've worked so hard, and now Zoe is swooping in to steal my thunder.

I want to scream, to throw my phone across the airport, but I force myself to calm down. Losing my cool won't solve anything.

I glance out the window, watching planes that were supposed to be departing return to the terminal to offload their passengers. None of us are going anywhere.

Two weeks in Vacationland. You'll have to forgive me if I'm not jumping for joy.

♡

The taxi swerves through the crowded streets of Portland, and I lean forward, scanning the buildings for any sign of a hotel vacancy. I try looking again at the multitude of travel apps I have on my phone, but everything is grayed out, mocking me with a 'sold out' banner. The driver glances at me in the rearview mirror, his eyes sympathetic.

"Tough luck with all these flight cancellations, huh?" he says, shaking his head. "Seems like everyone's stranded."

I nod, my attention still focused on the passing storefronts. "You wouldn't happen to know of any hotels with available rooms, would you?"

He chuckles. "Wish I could help, but I've been driving folks around all day, and every place is booked solid."

I slump back against the seat, my mind racing. I can't spend the night wandering the streets of Portland. I need a plan.

As if on cue, my phone rings. It's my mother. I hesitate for a moment before answering, bracing myself for the inevitable barrage of questions.

"Rachel, honey, are you alright? Your sister told me what happened with your flight."

I sigh, rubbing my temple. "I'm fine, Mom. Just trying to find a place to stay for the night."

"Oh, sweetheart, don't be like Mary and Joseph and end up in a manger. Why not just rent a car and come join us at Lake Michigan? We'd love to have you."

I'm not sure Mom fully comprehends just how far I am away from Wisconsin. "Mom, it would take me days to drive back to... Hang on? You're with Claire?"

"Yes, when they dropped you off at the airport, Richard drove over and asked if I'd like to take your spot. So here I am. Between you and me, I think they just wanted a babysitter, but I'll not look a gift horse in the mouth. Come on, join us."

The thought of spending the rest of my vacation with my family is tempting, given that the alternative is spending it alone in a strange city. I'm about to give Mom's suggestion some serious consideration when the taxi passes a massive industrial complex, the sign reading "Harcourt Foods" in bold letters.

Suddenly, an idea takes root in my mind. Harcourt Foods is one of the largest frozen food manufacturers in the country. If I could land them as a client...

"Rachel? Are you still there?"

I snap back to the present. "Yeah, Mom, I'm here. Listen, I appreciate the offer, but I think I'm going to stay in Portland for a bit. There's something I need to take care of."

"Are you sure, honey? We'd really love to see you."

"I know, and I promise I'll make it up to you. But this is important."

There's a pause, and I can almost hear the wheels turning in her head. "Well, alright then. I can't say I understand you at all. Promise you'll call if you need anything?"

"I will. Thanks, Mom. Love you."

As I hang up, I lean forward, tapping the driver on the shoulder. "Actually, could you take me to the nearest car rental place?"

He nods, merging into the turning lane. I sit back, my mind already formulating a plan. Partnership or not, I'm not leaving Maine empty-handed.

Harcourt Foods, here I come.

The car rental place is a hive of activity, with frazzled travelers scrambling to secure vehicles. I join the line, tapping my foot impatiently as I scroll through my phone, gathering as much intel on Harcourt Foods as I can. Their CEO, Jonathan Harcourt, has something of a reputation as a die-hard traditionalist. Referred to as 'Old Man Harcourt' by friend and foe alike, he's certainly not known for his commitment to innovation and sustainability. A poultry industry stalwart, it's going to be a hard sell to convince him to diversify from the frozen chicken nuggets that built his empire.

But... thanks to my market research for GreenShoots and IncrediBurger, I have data. Lots of it. Compelling, detailed facts and figures that show a shift in eating habits and a growing demand for plant-based alternatives. If I can pitch CGPR as the agency to revamp their public image and convince him that plant means profit, it could be a game-changer.

Lost in thought, I startle when the clerk calls, "Next!"

I step up to the counter, flashing my most charming smile. "Hi there. I need to rent a car, preferably something electric, compact, and efficient."

The clerk, a young man with a name tag reading "Ethan," looks at me apologetically. "I'm sorry, ma'am, but we're pretty much out of everything due to the flight cancellations. The only vehicle we have left is a pickup."

I blink, processing this information. A pickup truck? That's about as far from my sleek, urban, green lifestyle as it gets. But beggars can't be choosers, right?

"I'll take it," I say, handing over my credit card.

Minutes later, I'm staring at a behemoth of a truck, its red paint gleaming under the lot lights. I clamber into the driver's seat, adjusting it to accommodate my shorter stature. The engine roars to life, and, truth be told, I can't help but grin. There's something empowering about being behind the wheel of this beast. It pains me to think it, but maybe, just maybe, I can understand why Zoe chooses to drive her Mustang despite the societal pressure to drive electric.

As I navigate the unfamiliar streets of Portland, my mind races with ideas for a potential Harcourt Foods pitch. I'll emphasize CGPR's track record with green initiatives, our innovative social media strategies, and our ability to connect with younger, eco-conscious consumers. Driving almost on instinct, I've left the city and find myself in the quieter suburbs.

Signs for Biddeford start to appear and as I'm approaching the city limits, I find a quaint motel on the outskirts of town, its neon 'vacancy' sign a beacon of hope after a very trying few hours. The owner, a gentleman in his early forties, introduces himself as James, insists on carrying my carry-on case to my room, and hands me a key with a knowing smile.

"Just call down to the front desk if you need anything," he says kindly.

I nod gratefully, suddenly feeling the weight of the day catching up with me.

"Thank you. I will."

THREE

The motel door clicks shut behind me and I let out a heavy sigh. I kick off my heels, not caring where they land, and strip off my blouse and skirt, tossing them onto the faded armchair in the corner.

As I settle into the cozy room, I can't help but feel a flicker of excitement amid the disappointment. Sure, not being the point woman on the GreenShoots pitch is a major setback. But landing Harcourt Foods? That could be the key to everything I've been working towards.

I pull out my laptop, firing off a quick email to Emily to gather more information on Harcourt Foods. We're going to have a serious talk when I'm back in the office about that little ticketing screw-up, but right now I need her on her A-game, not worrying about if she's going to be fired. If she can get me the information I need, and quickly, it will certainly put her in a better light. Tomorrow, I'll try to reach out to Jonathan Harcourt directly.

But for now, I need to rest and recharge. I have a feeling I'm going to need all my energy for what's to come. The wrinkled floral comforter isn't exactly inviting, but all I want right now is to close my eyes and forget this train wreck of a day ever happened.

I sprawl out on the lumpy mattress in just my bra and panties, too exhausted to even slip under the covers. Maybe if I rest my eyes for a bit, I can rally enough energy to find a decent meal and figure out my next steps. I allow my eyelids to flutter closed...

BAM! The door flies open and my heart leaps into my throat as I bolt upright. A man in a motel uniform backs into the room, awkwardly dragging a cleaning cart behind him. Earbuds dangle from his ears, a tinny beat pulsing from them. He's humming off-key as he turns around.

Our eyes lock and his jaw drops, mirroring my own shock.

"Oh my gosh, I am so sorry!" he stammers, averting his gaze. A blush creeps up his neck. "I thought this room was vacant."

"Do you make a habit of barging in on half-naked women?" I snap, scrambling to yank the comforter over my exposed body, my face burning.

His blush deepens, and he runs a hand through his hair, the tension visibly knotting his shoulders.

"No, no, I swear I don't. This was just... a massive screw-up. Room was listed as vacant, and I didn't hear anything from inside."

There's something about the way he talks—his words are casual, but his delivery is strangely deliberate, like he's choosing each one with more care than the situation calls for. I can't help but notice how quickly he adjusts, how his voice evens out, tone confident but not overbearing. It's like he's used to performing calm, even when he's mortified.

For a second, I think maybe it's just some kind of customer service charm—the way he stays relaxed, apologizes so smoothly. But it's more than that. He's not just smoothing over a mistake; he's stepping into a role, like he's done this a hundred times before, memorized his lines.

Before I can analyze it further, he clears his throat. "Look, I'm really sorry. I'll make sure it doesn't happen again." He ducks his head and practically bolts out the door, nearly tripping over the cleaning cart in his haste to exit, leaving me alone to process whatever the hell just happened.

I let out a shaky breath, trying to get my heart rate under control. It's probably nothing. Just a guy embarrassed out of his mind and doing his best to cover it. But still... There was something about the way he carried himself, the way he delivered his apology, that didn't quite fit with his cleaning uniform.

It's probably nothing. I push the thought away and focus on calming down. I've had enough surprises for one night.

I collapse back onto the bed with a groan, my heart still racing. I have to admit, he was kind of cute, in an awkward, embarrassed sort of way. But after the day I've had, cute isn't going to cut it. I need a strong drink and a hearty meal to erase this memory.

I can't possibly sleep now, so I slide off the bed, ready to pull myself together and salvage what's left of this disastrous day. One thing's for sure—this is a motel check-in I won't soon forget. Although, for both our sakes, I kind of wish I could.

Glancing at the clock, I realize with a start that I've been out cold for nearly two hours. Eight p.m. already? My stomach growls in protest, reminding me that the last thing I ate was a stale bagel before boarding my ill-fated flight.

I drag myself to the bathroom, catching a glimpse of my disheveled reflection in the mirror. Raccoon eyes, courtesy of my smudged mascara. Hair sticking out at odd angles from my haphazard nap. Lovely. With a sigh, I turn on the shower, hoping the hot water will wash away the stress of the day and revive me enough to venture out in search of sustenance.

As the steam fills the small space, I step under the spray,

letting it soothe my tight muscles. My mind drifts back to the man who barged in earlier. Dan, was it? There was something vaguely familiar about him, but I can't quite put my finger on it. Probably just one of those faces.

I lather up, the scent of the generic motel soap filling my nostrils. It's a far cry from my usual coconut-infused body wash, but it'll do. As I rinse off, my stomach lets out another insistent rumble. Time to stop daydreaming and focus on the mission at hand: food.

Toweling off, I rummage through my suitcase for something presentable. Jeans and a cozy sweater will have to suffice. I'm in no mood to dress up, and besides, who am I trying to impress in this quaint little town?

A quick blow-dry and a swipe of lip gloss later, I'm as ready as I'll ever be. I grab my purse and room key, steeling myself for the chilly Maine evening. As I step out into the parking lot, the crisp spring air nips at my cheeks, a stark contrast to the stuffy motel room.

Now, to find a decent meal in this unfamiliar place. I pull out my phone, hoping for a little culinary guidance. "Come on, Siri," I mutter, "don't let me down. I need some comfort food, asap."

With a few voice commands, a list of nearby restaurants pops up. I scroll through the options, my mouth watering at the thought of a warm, hearty dish. Seafood, maybe? When in Maine, right? I settle on a diner that boasts the best clam chowder in town, according to the glowing reviews.

As I navigate the quiet streets of Biddeford, my mind wanders back to the chaos waiting for me back in Chicago. The PR crisis, the demanding clients, the endless emails. But for now, at this moment, my only concern is filling my grumbling stomach and maybe, just maybe, finding a glimmer of peace in this unexpected detour.

But first things first—bring on the seafood.

The bell above the door jingles as I step into Julie's Diner, a wave of warmth and the aroma of sizzling bacon enveloping me. It's a cozy little spot, all checkered floors and vinyl booths, the kind of place that feels like home even if you've never been before.

I slide into a booth, the red cushion squeaking beneath me. Before I can even reach for a menu, a waitress with a smile brighter than the neon sign outside appears at my table.

"Well, hello there, sugar!" she chirps, her blonde ponytail bobbing with enthusiasm. "What can I get started for you tonight?"

I blink, taken aback by her energy. It's nearly nine o'clock. How can anyone be this chipper at this time of night?

"Oh, um, I read your clam chowder is the best in town," I manage, mustering a tired smile.

"You betcha! One bowl of our famous chowder, coming right up!" She winks, jotting down my order. "Anything else, hon?"

I shake my head, and with a nod, she whirls away, leaving me to take in my surroundings. It's then that I spot a familiar face five tables across.

It's him. The guy from the motel room. Dan. He's sitting in a booth, sharing what looks like an enormous sundae with a young girl, maybe eleven or twelve years old. She's giggling as he dabs a dollop of whipped cream on her nose, and the affection between them is palpable.

I watch as they interact, the easy banter, the inside jokes. It's clear they have a special bond, the kind that comes from years of love and trust. A father and daughter, I surmise, noting the way he looks at her like she's the center of his universe.

It's undeniably sweet and I can see the appeal—the laughter, the love, the sense of belonging. But having kids is the death knell of careers. At least for women. And I have so much more I still need to achieve.

As I sit there, lost in thought, the waitress returns with a steaming bowl of chowder. "Here you go, darlin'," she says, setting it down with a flourish. "Careful, it's hot."

I nod my thanks, inhaling the rich, comforting aroma. It smells like home, not my home, but it oozes warmth and safety, and all the things I didn't realize I was craving.

As I take my first spoonful, savoring the creamy, briny flavor, I can't help but steal another glance at Dan and his daughter. They're lost in their own little world, oblivious to the rest of the diner, to the rest of the world.

And for a fleeting moment, I wonder what it would be like to be a part of something like that. To have someone look at me the way Dan looks at his daughter, like I'm the most important person in the room.

I shake my head, pushing the thought aside. I don't have time for silly daydreams or small-town sentimentality.

I have a job to do, a life to get back to. This is just a temporary detour, a blip on the radar. Nothing more.

Or so I tell myself, as I focus on my chowder, trying to ignore the nagging feeling that maybe, just maybe, there's something more to life than market research and late-night conference calls.

Dan catches my eye, and I quickly look away, suddenly fascinated by the patterns in my chowder. But it's too late. He's already making his way over, his daughter trailing behind him.

"Hey, I thought it was you," he says, his voice warm and friendly. "I just wanted to apologize again for earlier. I really didn't mean to startle you like that."

I wave him off, forcing a smile. "It's fine, really. No harm done."

But Dan's daughter isn't so easily dismissed. She peers at me with those big, curious eyes, her head tilted to the side.

"You look really pretty," she says, her voice so earnest it catches me off guard. "But you also look really sad. Are you okay?"

I blink, taken aback by her perceptiveness. How can this little girl see right through me, when I've spent years perfecting my poker face?

"I'm fine, sweetie," I assure her, my voice a little too bright. "Just a long day, that's all."

Dan touches her shoulder, gently steering her towards the door. "Come on, Chloe. Let's let the lady enjoy her dinner in peace."

I nod, grateful for the reprieve.

Just then, as Dan reaches for the door handle, there's a commotion near the counter. An elderly woman, her face pale and drawn, sways on her feet, then crumples to the ground.

"Go take a seat, sweetie, I just need to take care of something." Dan indicates an empty seat and Chloe follows the instruction.

Instinctively, Dan and I both rush to the woman on the floor. I check for a pulse while Dan calls out for someone to dial 911.

The elderly woman barely has time to gasp before he's kneeling beside her, his voice low and steady.

"You okay, ma'am? Just stay still for a second, alright?"

There's something about the way he says it—calm, but firm —that immediately makes people trust him. She nods, breathless, clutching his arm as he carefully helps her sit up. The diner staff rush over with concern, offering napkins, ice, the kind of mild panic and random offerings that come when no one's quite sure what to do.

Dan, though? He's already taken care of it.

It's such a small moment. Nothing dramatic, nothing particularly heroic. But as I watch him smooth down the woman's coat, making sure she's steady before letting go, it hits me.

This is who he is. The guy who steps in. The guy who cares. Not because there's anything to gain, not because he expects recognition—just because that's what you do when someone needs help.

Something tightens in my chest, unexpected and unfamiliar.

I spend my life impressing people. Convincing boardrooms full of skeptical men that I'm worth listening to. Selling ideas, crafting strategies, making sure that when I walk out of a meeting, no one forgets my name.

Dan doesn't have to do any of that. And yet, somehow, in this tiny, insignificant moment, he's managed to impress the hell out of me.

Together, Dan and I work to make the woman as comfortable as possible, our movements synchronized and efficient. With her back now resting against the counter, I roll up a sweater the waitress hands to me into a makeshift pillow and place it behind the woman's head. Dan takes one of her hands and holds it in his, letting her know that help is on its way and everything's going to be okay.

As we wait for the paramedics to arrive, I catch Dan's eye over the woman's head. And in that moment, I see something I recognize, something that mirrors my own determination, my own need to help, to fix, to make things right.

"Is she going to be okay?" Chloe asks, her brow furrowed with concern as she looks across from the booth.

"I hope so," I reply, unsure. "We'll let the paramedics decide what to do next."

We lapse into silence, the weight of the moment hanging heavy. Around us, the diner buzzes with anxious energy, the other patrons looking on with worried expressions.

"You know," Dan says suddenly, his voice cutting through the tension, "I never thought I'd be playing hero in a diner on a Sunday night."

Despite myself, I feel a smile tug at the corners of my mouth. "Yeah, well, I never thought I'd be stranded in Maine, but here we are."

Dan chuckles, a low, warm sound that seems to ease the tightness in my chest. "Funny how life works out sometimes, isn't it?"

I nod, my gaze still fixed on the woman's face. "It's been a hell of a day, that's for sure."

"Tell me about it," Dan says, shifting to a more comfortable position. "I woke up this morning thinking the biggest challenge I'd face today would be getting Chloe to eat her vegetables."

I can't help but laugh at that, a real, genuine laugh that feels foreign and wonderful all at once.

At the sound of her name, Chloe's head shoots up from her phone like a meerkat. She hops up from the booth and into Dan's warm embrace.

"Love you, pumpkin. You did good."

There's something in his voice, a warmth and sincerity that catches me off guard. I glance over at him, really seeing him for the first time. The exhaustion etched into the lines of his face, the love and pride shining in his eyes when he looks at his daughter. Maybe there's more to this guy than meets the eye. More than the harried single dad, more than the small-town motel cleaner.

Dan turns back to me, his eyes crinkling at the corners. "I'm Dan, by the way. This is Chloe."

"Hi, Dan, yes, you introduced yourself earlier in my room. I'm Rachel."

"I'm really sorry–"

"It's ok. Really." I offer Dan my hand. He smiles and shakes it.

That's when the sound of sirens fills the air, growing louder with each passing second. Dan and I exchange a glance, relief and anticipation mingling in the space between us.

"Looks like the cavalry's here," he says, rising to his feet.

I nod, my heart racing as the paramedics burst through the doors, a flurry of activity and purpose. They take over, their movements practiced and precise, and I step back, letting them do their job.

Dan approaches me as the paramedics wheel the elderly woman out on a gurney and the remaining patrons all settle back down at the tables, now that the show's over.

"Thanks for your help tonight. You were incredible."

I brush off the compliment, suddenly feeling self-conscious. "Oh, it was nothing. I'm just glad she's going to be okay."

He shakes his head, a smile tugging at the corners of his mouth. "It wasn't nothing. You stayed calm under pressure. That's pretty cool."

I feel a blush creeping up my neck, and I glance away.

He huffs a quiet laugh, and Chloe manages a small, wobbly smile. "You were really brave," she says, her voice soft.

"You too, kiddo. You did great."

Dan squeezes her shoulder and gives me a nod. "Well... we should probably get going. I need to get her home and settled. But... I hope to see you around?"

I can't help the small smile that tugs at my lips. "Just remember to knock."

He lingers for a second longer, like he wants to say something else, but then he just nods again and steers Chloe toward the door. I watch them go, a strange mix of emotions swirling inside me—relief that the elderly lady is in good hands, and something softer, something I don't quite know how to define when it comes to Dan.

I turn back to my table, my unfinished chowder now stone cold and completely unappetizing. I sink onto the seat, letting the adrenaline ebb away, and glance at the mess of napkins and half-eaten food. I push the bowl away, resting my chin in my hands, but the scene keeps replaying in my mind—the old woman, so pale and fragile, crumpling to the floor.

The waitress reappears with a small smile, breaking me out of my daze. "Hey," she says gently. "How are you holding up?"

I force a smile, though I'm sure it's more of a grimace. "Fine. Just... worried about her, I guess."

She nods, wiping down the table, her movements slower than usual. "You did good, you know. Helping out like that."

I glance at her, then back at my chowder. "Thanks. Although I think Dan did most of the heavy lifting. I just... followed his lead."

"Still counts," she says, giving me a reassuring nod. "You two made a good team."

I don't know what to say to that, so I just nod and reach for my purse, fishing out some cash to cover the meal. But when I set it down on the table, she waves it off.

"Don't worry about it. This one's on us. Least we can do after what you did for Marjorie. She's a regular here, known her for years. Tough old bird, but her heart's been giving her trouble lately."

I push the money toward her anyway, but she just shakes her head firmly. "Keep it. We couldn't possibly accept."

With a resigned nod, I slide the cash back into my purse and gather my things. As I head for the door, I glance back at the now-empty spot on the floor where Marjorie had collapsed. It's like it never happened. Just a normal evening at Julie's Diner.

Outside, the night air is crisp and cool. I start down the quiet street, heading back toward the motel. My footsteps sound too loud, like they're interrupting the calm of the night.

I should go to bed. I'm exhausted—mentally and physically—but there's a nagging knot in my stomach that won't let go. I can't just walk away and forget about Marjorie, not when I don't even know if she's alright. What if she's alone in the hospital, scared and confused?

I pause on the sidewalk. I'm not going to be able to sleep until I know. I dig through my bag until I find my phone and look up the nearest hospital with an emergency room. There's one about fifteen minutes away.

Without giving myself time to overthink it, I pull out the keys to my rental and head back to where it's parked. The beast of a vehicle is still obnoxiously red, still absurdly large, but at this moment, I don't care. I just need to make sure Marjorie's okay.

As I slide into the driver's seat and start the engine, I can't help but think about how utterly exhausting today has been. Nothing's gone the way I expected. The universe seems hell-bent on throwing curveballs at me, and I'm struggling to keep up.

But at least I can do this. At least I can check on her.

Pushing open the glass doors, I'm met with the unmistakable scent of antiseptic and the low murmur of voices from a TV playing a nature documentary in the waiting area. A bored-looking receptionist glances up from her computer as I approach.

"Hi," I start, trying to keep my voice steady. "I'm looking for a patient who was brought in earlier. An elderly woman named Marjorie. She collapsed at Julie's Diner."

The receptionist's face softens a little, and she nods. "Are you family?"

"Uh... no. Just a friend, I guess. I just wanted to make sure she's okay."

She hesitates, clearly weighing the rules against whatever empathy she's managed to hold on to during the night shift. Eventually, she offers a small smile.

"Hang on. I'll check for you."

As she types something into the computer, I fidget with the strap of my bag, my mind still racing. What am I even doing here? Am I overstepping? But I couldn't just go to bed without knowing.

After a few moments, the receptionist glances up. "She's stable and awake. Room 204. Visiting hours are technically over, but... if you're quick, I don't think anyone will mind."

"Thank you," I say, relief flooding through me.

I follow the signs down a corridor lined with faded diabetes awareness posters and finally find Room 204. I'm just about to knock when I hear familiar voices inside.

Pushing the door open cautiously, I peek in—and freeze.

Dan is sitting in one of the plastic chairs by the bed, talking softly to Marjorie, who's propped up on the pillows looking surprisingly chipper. Chloe is perched on the edge of the bed, holding Marjorie's hand and nodding along with whatever story she's telling.

Dan looks up when I enter, his eyebrows rising in surprise. "Rachel?"

"Oh," I mumble, feeling suddenly awkward. "I... I just wanted to check on her. Make sure she's okay."

Marjorie's face lights up when she sees me. "Oh, hello."

I step inside fully, offering a hesitant smile. "I just... I was at the diner tonight. Couldn't stop thinking about you. Wanted to make sure you were alright."

Marjorie waves a wrinkled hand, dismissing my concern. "I'm fine, sweetheart. Just a little spell, that's all. Doctor says

I'll be out of here by tomorrow morning. You young folks made quite a fuss over me."

Chloe grins up at me from her spot on the bed. "We brought her some flowers," she says proudly, pointing to a small, slightly wilted bouquet still in a 7-Eleven bag. "Dad said they're good for cheering people up."

"They're lovely," I say, glancing at Dan. "Good call."

He catches my disparaging look. "Choices were limited at this time of night."

Marjorie's eyes flit between us, her smile turning sly. "You two make a lovely couple," she says.

Dan's head jerks up, his mouth opening to protest, but I beat him to it. "Oh, no, we're not—"

He cuts in, clearing his throat. "Just friends."

Marjorie gives him a look that says she doesn't buy it for a second. "Well, you ought to be. She's a keeper, that one."

I feel my cheeks heating, and I glance at Dan, whose expression has shifted to something almost unreadable. He doesn't respond, just looks away, his jaw tightening.

The nurse pops her head in, giving us a stern look. "I'm sorry, but visiting hours are over. You'll have to say goodnight."

Marjorie waves her off, and sees the worry flit across my face at the thought of leaving her alone. "Oh, don't you worry about me, dear. I'll be just fine. You've done more than enough already."

I give her hand a gentle squeeze. "Take care of yourself, Marjorie."

She pats my hand warmly. "You too, sweetheart. Don't let this one get away," she adds, giving Dan a pointed look.

He rolls his eyes, muttering something, but there's a faint smile there too.

We file out of the room, and as we walk down the hall, Chloe pipes up, "See if she's hungry, Dad?"

Dan glances at me. "Did you get anything to eat earlier?" he asks, almost cautiously.

The truth is, I'm famished. But I hesitate, my mind spinning with the implications. Dinner at a stranger's house? It feels too intimate, too personal.

"I don't know. It's been a long day. I've kind of lost my appetite and I should probably just head back to the motel..."

"Of course, I understand. You must be exhausted. I just thought... Well, never mind. Another time maybe."

I chew on my bottom lip, torn. It would be so easy to say no, to retreat to the safety of my solitude. But something in Dan's eyes, in the earnest set of his shoulders, makes me pause.

When was the last time I let myself slow down? When was the last time I just did something for the fun of it?

I think of the endless string of late nights at the office, the bare shelves in my refrigerator, the takeout containers piling up in my trash can.

Maybe it's time to try something different. Maybe it's time to not think about clients and work and pitches, after the day I've had...

I meet Dan's gaze with a tentative smile. "You know what? Sure. I've barely eaten all day."

The grin that breaks across his face is blinding, and I feel an answering warmth blooming in my chest. "Fantastic. It will make me feel like I've made amends for barging into your room. And, just to manage expectations, I make a mean grilled cheese."

I laugh, shaking my head in mock disbelief. "Grilled cheese? You sure know how to woo a girl."

He winks. "Don't mock it until you've tried it.

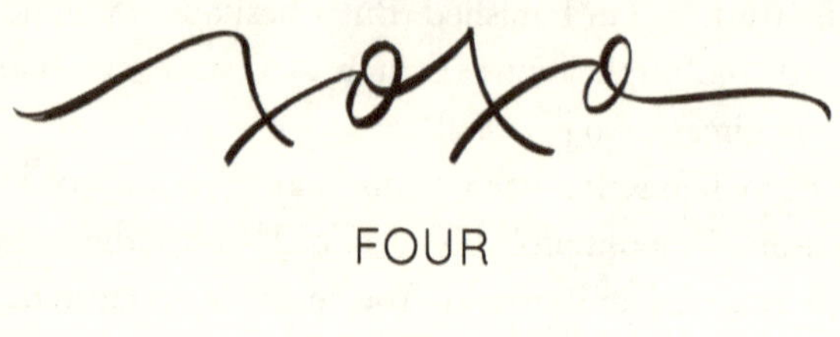

FOUR

As I pull up to Dan's home, I'm struck by how breathtaking it looks against the night sky. The waterfront property is bathed in the soft glow of outdoor string lights, their golden hue reflecting off the water like scattered fireflies. The two-story house stands nestled among tall pine trees, their dark silhouettes swaying gently in the evening breeze. Warm light spills from the windows, illuminating the wraparound porch and casting long, inviting shadows across the neatly kept lawn. It looks like something out of a movie—effortlessly charming, like it's been waiting for someone to come home.

Chloe jumps out before Dan can even put his car in park and runs straight into the house. I step out of my truck, taking a moment to inhale the crisp, salty air. The sound of gentle waves lapping against the riverbank fills my ears, and I feel a sense of peace wash over me, a stark contrast to the chaos of the day. Dan lingers by his car until I catch up, giving me a glance that's both grateful and a little uncertain.

"It was nice of you to check in on Marjorie. She's something of a Biddeford institution. I wasn't sure she was going to make it."

"Someone's got to look out for you stubborn Mainers. Can't have you collapsing in diners every time the chowder's a little too salty."

Dan huffs out a short laugh, but the tension between us still lingers, hovering like unspoken words in the air. Before I even know what to say, Chloe reappears on the porch, waving us inside.

"Come on! I'm starving!" she calls out, clearly unfazed by the chaos of the evening.

"Guess we'd better feed her."

"Yep. You do not want to mess with a hungry tween. Welcome to Casa Rhodes, by the way," Dan says with a smile, leading me up the porch steps. "It's not much, but it's home."

I shake my head, taking in the charming details of the house—the white-painted wood, the nautical-themed decorations on the porch. "It's lovely, Dan. Truly."

As we step inside, I'm immediately enveloped by the warmth and coziness of the space. The living room is adorned with plush, inviting couches and soft, worn rugs. A large stone fireplace dominates one wall, its mantel lined with family photos.

I step closer, my eyes drawn to a particular image—a younger Dan, his arm around a beautiful woman with long, dark hair and a radiant smile. They look so happy, so in love. My heart clenches as I realize he's married. *Of course he is.*

Dan notices my gaze and clears his throat, a flicker of sadness passing over his features. "That was taken on our honeymoon," he says softly. "Becca always loved the ocean. She passed."

I nod, unsure of what to say.

Just then, Chloe bounds into the room. She's already changed into her pajamas, and she bounces excitedly. "You hungry?" she asks.

I laugh. "Starving, actually. And I couldn't pass up the chance to see your dad's famous grilled cheese skills in action."

Chloe giggles, grabbing my hand and tugging me towards the kitchen. "Come on, you can help me set the table."

As we enter the kitchen, Chloe opens all the cupboards and pulls out enough tableware to host a banquet. Dan stands at the stove, heating a large cast-iron skillet, then takes ingredients out of the fridge.

Chloe clearly relishes the responsibility and is meticulous with her placement of dinnerware. We set the table together and I have to admit, it looks great.

With a flourish, Chloe pulls out a chair for me. "Madam."

"Thank you." I take a seat and look over to see how Dan's getting on.

"Smells amazing," I comment, inhaling deeply. "What's your secret ingredient?"

Dan grins, tapping the side of his nose. "Ah, now that would be telling. Let's just say it's a family recipe, passed down through generations of Rhodes grilled cheese connoisseurs."

Chloe rolls her eyes, handing me a napkin. "He puts garlic powder in the butter," she stage-whispers. "It's not that big a deal."

"Hey!" Dan protests, waving his spatula in mock offense. "Don't go giving away all my culinary secrets, missy."

As we laugh and joke, pouring glasses of ice-cold lemonade, I feel a sense of warmth and belonging that I haven't experienced in longer than I can remember. The easy banter, the genuine affection between father and daughter—it's a glimpse into a life I never knew existed and a far cry from my own relationship with my absent, now dead, father.

And as we sit down to eat, the golden, gooey sandwiches almost too hot to handle, I don't think I can remember eating a late-night snack that tasted so good.

I take another bite and let out a satisfied sigh. "Okay, I'll admit it—this really is something special. You've mastered the fine art of bread and cheese."

Dan chuckles, a little bashfully, at the compliment. "I'll take that as high praise. It's one of the few things I can actually cook without burning it to a crisp."

As we dig in, Chloe's face lights up with excitement. "Oh, Rachel! Guess what? I'm going to be in the 'Sing!' Talent Competition next month!"

"Wow, that's fantastic, Chloe!" I exclaim, genuinely impressed. "What will you be performing?"

Chloe beams, her eyes sparkling with anticipation. "I'm singing 'Brave' by Sara Bareilles. It's all about being true to yourself and not being afraid to speak up. I really, really like the song!"

I nod, understanding the significance of the song, if a little surprised that it's her own choice, given the song is almost as old as her. "That's a powerful message, Chloe. I'm sure you'll be amazing."

"I've been practicing every day," she gushes, her grin wide and infectious. "I really think I have a shot at winning this year."

Dan beams with pride, his love for his daughter shining through in every glance, every word of encouragement.

Dan reaches over, squeezing his daughter's hand. "I've never seen her so dedicated to anything before."

Chloe's enthusiasm is contagious, and I find myself caught up in her excitement. "I'd love to hear you sing sometime. If you're comfortable with that, of course."

She grins, nodding eagerly. "Definitely! I could use all the feedback I can get."

I'm impressed by Chloe and love the way she pursues her passion with such fervor. It reminds me of my own childhood dreams, the ones I never had the chance, or encouragement, to realize, and that are now long since buried beneath the weight of adult responsibilities and expectations.

Dan claps his hands. "Now, come on, bed."

"But we have a guest." Chloe groans.

"Nice try. Up."

"Are you gonna come up and listen to the story?" Chloe asks.

I blink. "Oh, uh... I—"

I glance at Dan, feeling instantly awkward. This is *their* thing, their routine, and I suddenly feel like I'm intruding on something private. Like I've somehow stumbled too deep into their world.

Chloe, however, doesn't care about my reservations. She steps forward, arms crossed like she's already decided for me. "You should come," she insists. "Dad's really good at it."

Dan smirks at her confidence in his storytelling abilities. "She's not wrong," he says, tilting his head toward me. "I do voices and everything. If you're lucky, I might even let you read a character or two."

I let out a small laugh, shaking my head. "I don't know... I don't want to interrupt—"

Chloe groans dramatically. "You *wouldn't* be interrupting." She turns to her dad. "Tell her she wouldn't be interrupting."

Dan chuckles, setting his glass down. "You wouldn't be interrupting."

I sigh, defeated by their combined insistence. "Fine," I say, standing. "But if this turns into some impromptu theater production, I'm not responsible for any secondhand embarrassment."

Dan grins. "Oh, trust me, you won't be the one embarrassed."

Chloe groans again, already making her way up the stairs. "Dad, *please* just read normally tonight."

We follow her up, and I feel a little out of place as I step into Chloe's room. It's full of personality—books stacked on a nightstand, fairy lights draped around the bed frame, a few well-loved stuffed animals pushed to the side. The walls have posters of singers and anime characters I don't recognize, wedged in between photos of what looks like school trips and summer adventures.

Chloe climbs into bed, pulling the blankets up to her chin as Dan grabs a book from the shelf. He flips it open and clears his throat dramatically.

I take a seat on the floor by the doorway, trying to stay as inconspicuous as possible, but the second Dan starts reading, I realize *that* is not going to happen.

Because he doesn't *just* read.

He *performs*.

Complete with character voices, exaggerated expressions, and over-the-top dramatics, he brings the story to life like a seasoned stage actor. Even though Chloe is clearly growing out of these bedtime stories, she still adores them.

She rolls her eyes, groaning at some of his sillier antics, but her giggles betray her. *"Dad, come on,"* she mutters when he makes one of the characters sound like they've inhaled helium.

"What?" Dan says, feigning innocence. "This is *how* the royal wizard speaks. It says so right here in the subtext."

Chloe sighs dramatically, but she's smiling. I find myself biting my lip to stop myself from laughing as he goes on, somehow managing to make a generic adventure story sound like an award-worthy performance.

By the time he gets to the final page, Chloe is clearly fighting sleep, her eyes fluttering slightly even as she tries to keep up the pretense of being unimpressed.

Dan softens his voice for the last few lines, closing the book with a quiet *thud*.

I watch as he reaches out, brushing a few strands of hair from Chloe's face, tucking them gently behind her ear.

It's such a small gesture. Simple. Unremarkable.

But something about it makes my chest tighten.

"Goodnight, kiddo," he says.

Chloe hums sleepily in response, already halfway to dreams.

Dan stands, quietly setting the book aside before glancing over at me, a knowing smile tugging at the corner of his lips.

"Well?" he whispers as we step out of the room. "Told you I was good."

I shake my head, still smiling, as we make our way back downstairs.

"You're ridiculous," I say.

Dan and I find ourselves on the back porch, nursing mugs of steaming coffee wrapped in a couple of Dan's heavy winter coats and an unbelievably soft blanket he appropriated from the living room sofa.

"She's a remarkable little girl," I say softly, breaking the stillness. "You've done an incredible job raising her."

He smiles, but there's a hint of sadness in his eyes. "Thanks. Appreciate it. It hasn't been easy, doing it alone. After Rebecca passed, I wasn't sure I could manage. But Chloe —she's been my rock, my reason to keep going."

I nod, sympathizing with his loss. "I can't even imagine how difficult that must have been."

Dan shrugs, staring out at the shimmering water. "We've found our way. I don't always get it right, but it works. Although, I have to admit, I'm dreading the teenage years. But I guess I'll cross that bridge..."

"When you're forced to ground her for life?" I finish, smirking.

He laughs, shaking his head. "Something like that. They

say it gets easier as they get older. It better, because some days I just want to tear my hair out."

"My sister says my nieces have aged her ten years."

"Sometimes it feels like that. I knew being a single dad would be hard, but I didn't realize how relentless it would be. You don't just have to be the provider—you've got to be the chef, the nurse, the chauffeur, the teacher... Sometimes I feel like I have half a dozen jobs, all rolled into one."

I can tell he's not really complaining—just being honest. "I guess you don't get much time to yourself."

He shakes his head with a rueful smile. "Not really. It's rewarding, don't get me wrong. Watching Chloe grow up... nothing compares. But it's just so... exhausting. Sometimes I feel like I'm just keeping my head above water, making sure the right sports gear is in the right bag on the right day and that there's a homemade healthy lunch that won't get traded for a pack of peanut M&M's. All while juggling laundry that somehow keeps multiplying and trying to figure out why certain foods are suddenly unacceptable when they were her favorite last week."

I laugh, imagining the chaos of it all unfold. "I don't know how you do it. Parenting sounds like the hardest—and most underappreciated—job in the world."

Dan glances at me, the corners of his mouth lifting into a grateful smile. "Yeah. It kind of is. You don't really understand it until you're in it. Before Chloe, I thought I knew what hard work was. But it's different when it's your kid. There's no clocking out. No quitting time. You just have to make it work because they're counting on you."

He pauses, almost like he's catching himself before he says too much. I see it in his eyes—the fierce love, the unwavering commitment, but also that gnawing doubt that he's not doing enough. I know the feeling. Different context, same fear.

"Sounds like you're doing an amazing job," I say softly, meaning it. "She's happy. That says a lot."

Dan glances over at me, his expression caught between surprise and something almost vulnerable. He doesn't say anything, just nods, and the weight in the air softens just a little.

There's a comfortable silence, just the rhythmic lapping of the waves filling the space. The air is cool, but not uncomfortably so under the heavy blanket, and for the first time in a long while, I feel... still. Not rushing to the next thing, not thinking three steps ahead. Just here.

Dan takes a sip of his drink, then tilts his head slightly. "What about you?"

I glance at him. "What about me?"

Dan takes a sip of his drink, then tilts his head slightly. "So, what do you do, Rachel?"

I glance over at him. "I'm in PR. Public relations."

He nods slowly, like he's turning the phrase over in his mind. "So you're the person who makes things look good even when they're falling apart?"

"Pretty much," I say. "I tell stories for a living. Spin chaos into narrative. Make people and companies look polished, relatable, reliable—even when they're anything but."

Dan raises an eyebrow. "Sounds intense."

"It can be." I swirl my drink, watching the ice clink against the glass. "But it's also kind of addictive. You get to shape perception. Influence the conversation. It's like being the wizard behind the curtain."

"And you enjoy that?"

I nod. "Most days. There's something satisfying about taking a mess and turning it into something meaningful."

Dan studies me for a moment, then gestures vaguely with his glass. "So is that what you always wanted to do? Be a wizard behind the curtain?"

I huff a laugh. "Not exactly. I didn't even know PR was a real job until I was halfway through college."

He grins. "Then what did younger Rachel want to be?"

"Honestly?" I pause, considering. "I just wanted... more."

"More?"

"Yeah." I roll the glass between my palms, the condensation slick under my fingers. "More than what my mom had. More than what I grew up with. It was just me, my mom, and my sister. No big tragedy or anything—we just didn't have much. Mom was a teacher, but she took on extra work too. We lived paycheck to paycheck. And I saw how hard it was for her, how she always looked tired. Always had to fight for everything."

Dan's expression softens.

"I used to lie awake at night promising myself I'd never live like that. That I'd build something solid, something stable. So yeah... I guess I've always been driven. Ambitious. Whatever you want to call it."

He nods, quiet for a moment. "Makes sense now."

"What does?"

He shrugs. "You've got this... presence. Like you're always in motion, even when you're standing still."

I let out a quiet laugh. "Not sure if that's a compliment or a warning."

"It's a compliment," he says, smiling. "It's... impressive."

We sit in silence for a moment, the comfortable kind. I glance back at the house, the lights from within casting a soft pool of yellow on the decking, the sky overhead already inky with night.

I hesitate, then decide to ask what's been on my mind since we first met. "So... have you always worked at the motel?"

Dan hesitates mid-sip, like the question catches him off guard. He puts his cup down carefully on the table before finally meeting my gaze.

"At the motel?"

I nod.

He lets out a snort of amusement, shaking his head. "No. I just help out when my brother needs me. James, I guess you would have met him when you checked in. He's the one who actually runs it. Took over when our dad passed."

There's something in the way he says it—just a little too casual, a slight weight in his tone that makes me pause.

"So, it was your dad's business?"

"Yeah," Dan says, raking a hand through his hair. "Not really my thing, but my brother wanted to keep it going."

I hesitate before asking, "Were you close?"

His jaw tightens for just a second before he shrugs. "Not really."

His voice is light, but I know enough about deflection to recognize it when I hear it.

"I wouldn't know," I admit after a moment. "About having a bad relationship with a dad." I exhale. "I never met mine."

Dan looks at me then, something unreadable flickering across his face, like he wasn't expecting that.

There's a silence—not awkward, just heavy. Like we're both working through something unspoken in real time.

I glance toward the staircase. And suddenly, things start clicking into place. The way Dan rushed to help that woman at the diner without hesitation, the way he crouched down to talk to her, making sure she was okay before stepping back. The way he always seems so attuned to Chloe, so present in her world.

It's not just because she's his daughter.

"You dote on her," I say softly, the realization settling in as I speak. "Not just because she's your daughter. But because maybe you're trying to do things differently."

Dan exhales. "Maybe." He gives me a small, wry smile.

"Or maybe I just got lucky and ended up with a kid worth doting on."

I smile at that, but don't push.

Instead, I shift the conversation. "So, if you aren't always at the motel, what do you do?"

Dan leans back. "I used to work in television."

That gets my attention. I raise an eyebrow. "Really?"

"Yeah." He smirks, but there's something distant about it. "But that was a long time ago."

"Do you miss it?" I ask, tilting my head.

Dan considers the question. "The money? Sure. But not the long hours. Or the time away from home. To be honest, acting feels like a lifetime ago. Sometimes I wonder if it even really happened, or if it's just this weird story I used to tell."

I watch him for a second, like there's something unsaid just behind his smile. He says it so casually like it doesn't matter anymore. But there's something in the way his eyes linger on the wall, something wistful in his voice that he probably doesn't even hear.

And I get it. I really do.

There's a part of me that wants to press, ask more, prod a little at that closed door—but I don't. Not yet.

Still, I can't help the thought that slips in, uninvited.

He was someone once. Not just someone's dad, or someone's husband, or someone's motel handyman. He was... bigger. Famous and successful, sure, but there was a version of him that stood in front of a camera or a crowd and believed— truly believed—that he had something to give.

I wonder what it would take to bring that version of him back.

He exhales, his gaze flicking back toward me. "And anyway, I have Chloe now. It's just not a life that's compatible with kids."

I nod slowly, letting that sink in.

I've spent my whole life chasing the next big thing—success, recognition, my career-defining moment. Dan, it seems, has spent his, making sure he doesn't repeat the past.

A glance at my watch makes me blink. Somehow, the night has slipped away without me noticing. The warmth of Dan's company, the quiet of the waterfront, the easy rhythm of conversation—it all lulled me into a space I'm not used to. One where I wasn't checking my phone, thinking about my next move, or strategizing my career path.

But reality nudges in. I should go.

I clear my throat, stretching slightly. "I should probably head out."

"Yeah, it's late." He lifts the blanket from his legs and gets up. "You want me to drive you back to the motel?"

I shake my head. "You don't have to do that. Chloe's in bed, it's too much trouble."

"It's no trouble." He shrugs. "Or I could just call you a cab."

I let out a small laugh. "That works too."

We go back inside, and while he taps the app on his phone, I glance toward the staircase. The house is quiet now, the kind of deep stillness that comes when the world outside is sleeping. I can't remember the last time I spent an evening like this—no work emails, no client calls, just... talking.

Dan slides his phone into his pocket. "It'll be here in about eight minutes."

I nod, suddenly feeling like I should say something. Acknowledge something.

"I'll wait outside with you," he says simply, like it's the most natural thing in the world.

And for some reason, I don't argue.

FIVE

The aroma of fresh-brewed coffee swirls around me as I settle into a cozy corner booth at the local café just two blocks from my motel. My laptop glows invitingly, earbuds are secured, light jazz is playing, and a stack of notebooks sits ready for any brilliant ideas that might strike. It's time to get to work.

"One black coffee and a blueberry muffin, please." I smile at the waitress, my fingers already flying across the keyboard. Through a friend of a friend of someone who used to share a gym locker with him, I've managed to get the personal email address of one of the senior techs in the new product development division at Harcourt Foods. He's not the decision maker, but if I can paint a convincing picture of what's possible, he could prove to be an ally on the inside. I've sent a teaser pitch, now it's just a waiting game for his reply.

The real test will be trying to use that meeting to get some face time with Old Man Harcourt himself—a notoriously prickly individual, I'm realizing as I unearth more and more of his previous interviews. I'm beginning to think he may call for my flayed body to be strung up on a flagpole for even suggesting the largest frozen chicken producer on the Eastern

Seaboard diversifies into non-meat alternatives. It's a gamble for sure, but I've done it with a hamburger chain, why not frozen meals? I glance up at the TV mounted on the wall, wincing at the news report.

"...the volcanic eruption continues to wreak havoc on air travel, with all flights grounded indefinitely as the ash cloud spreads further across the US..."

Fantastic. Looks like I'm stuck in Maine for the foreseeable. But I can't let a little thing like a natural disaster derail my career. Harcourt's yet-to-be-invented non-chicken line is counting on me. *Cluck on, Rachel.*

I pull up their current product info and start brainstorming taglines, muttering to myself. "Harcourt Alternatives— always fresh, never frozen...wait, that doesn't make sense for a frozen food company. Okay, how about...Feelin' Peckish? Harcourt's Eggplant Lasagna is Delish! Ugh, that's terrible. C'mon Rach, you can do better."

I nibble on my muffin, tapping my pen against the notebook. This is usually when creative genius strikes, but so far, all I have is a page full of crossed-out scribbles and increasingly desperate doodles of chickens with broccoli florets for legs. I'm just about to give up and order another coffee when my phone buzzes with an incoming call. Unknown number. My heart leaps. Could it be him?

"Rachel Holmes speaking," I answer, attempting to sound both professional and nonchalant.

"Ms. Holmes, this is Jenna from Harcourt Foods Marketing. We received your meeting request from Paul on the product team, and we would be delighted to meet with you. Are you available the day after tomorrow, ten a.m. at our headquarters?"

I do an internal happy dance while maintaining my composed tone. "That would be perfect, Jenna. I look forward to meeting with your team and discussing how we can elevate Harcourt's brand to new heights."

"Wonderful. We'll see you then, Ms. Holmes."

As I end the call, I can't stop the grin from spreading across my face. This is my chance to prove myself, to show everyone at Channing Gabriel that even when stuck in the middle of nowhere, Rachel Holmes always gets results. I have a lot of work ahead of me to prep for this pitch, but I'm ready for the challenge. Harcourt Foods, get ready to meet your future.

Energized by the call, I gather my things and head back to the motel, my mind already beginning to structure how I want to deliver the message. We'll just ignore the small but crucial fact that I have no idea yet what it is I'm pitching. As I approach my room, I notice the 'Do Not Disturb' sign still hanging on the doorknob. Strange, I could've sworn I removed it this morning.

I step inside and my suspicions are confirmed—the bed remains unmade, towels lay strewn on the bathroom floor, and my used coffee cup sits untouched. Sighing, I drop my bag and make my way back to the reception desk to seek out James.

As I round the corner, I spot a small commotion near the elevators. It's Dan, looking slightly harried as a middle-aged woman thrusts a paper and pen at him, gushing excitedly. He obliges with a tight smile, scribbling his autograph before politely excusing himself.

Intriguing. Shaking my head, I approach the front desk and relay my housekeeping issue. The young receptionist apologizes profusely, assuring me the room will be cleaned immediately.

Back in my room, curiosity gets the better of me. I pull out my laptop and type 'Dan Rhodes' into the search bar. My eyes widen as the results flood in—profile pieces in *The Washington Post* and *Wall Street Journal*, fan sites, and tabloid articles. Turns out, Dan isn't just famous, he's soap opera royalty.

I dial my mom's number, still processing this newfound information. She picks up on the second ring

"Hey sweetie, how's Maine treating you?"

"Mom, you'll never guess who I've been running into at the hotel. Dan Rhodes."

There's a beat of silence, then an ear-piercing squeal. "THE Dan Rhodes? From Malibu Lagoon? Oh, Rachel, you have to marry him! Immediately."

I roll my eyes, chuckling. "Slow down, Mom. He may have played the perfect husband on screen, but real life is a different story. Besides, I'm here for work, not romance."

"Well, you never know, darling. Fate works in mysterious ways."

I stare at the error message blinking on the motel's ancient printer. *Fault E17*, amazing, like I know what that is or how to fix it. There's paper in the tray, no visible paper jam, and it's plugged in. I need these copies of my pitch for Harcourt Foods, but it looks like this hunk of junk has other ideas.

"Everything okay?" Dan's voice startles me. I didn't even hear him approach.

"Oh, hey. Yeah, it's just this printer..." I gesture helplessly at the stubbornly silent machine. "I wanted to print some copies of my presentation, but it's not cooperating."

Dan glances at the printer, then back at me with a gentle smile. "I don't think that's worked this decade; I'd hazard a guess you're the first guest to even try. Look, there's a perfectly good printer at my place. I'd be happy to print those out for you."

"Oh no, I couldn't impose like that." But even as I say it, I'm thinking about how much I need those copies.

"It's no trouble at all. Here…" He extends his hand. "I can take your flash drive, print them, and bring them right back."

I hesitate, my fingers tightening around the small drive. It contains all my work, my ideas. Handing it over feels strangely intimate. Dan senses my unease.

"Or, you can always come too," he offers. "I'll even throw in dinner. Nothing fancy. I'm cooking for Chloe anyway, but I make a mean spaghetti carbonara."

Against my better judgment, I find myself nodding. "Okay. Yeah, that would be great, actually. Thank you."

Dan's car is right out front. When I exit the motel and head into the lot, the sky seems…gray. *Is this the ash cloud, or is it just dull and overcast?* The more I stare up at the clouds, the more I convince myself that I can see tiny particles of ash.

"Storm's coming," Dan confirms as he blips the remote to unlock the car.

He turns the engine on, and I'm hit by a blast of loud music. Dan fumbles with the buttons on the dash and turns it down. "Sorry, Chloe's been practicing her song non-stop. I think I know it so well I could perform it myself."

"Why don't you?"

"Gotta give the next generation a chance. As much as I would love to."

"Would you," I push, genuinely intrigued. "Love to, I mean. Do you miss it?"

"Acting?" Dan's eyes flick across to me before he looks back at the road. "No. Those days are gone. Different life. I have Chloe to look after. The house."

"Those sound like excuses."

"They are excuses. Well… they're reasons." Dan looks over again, "Acting is more than just your time on set in front of the camera. When you're filming a series, it's relentless. Ten months of fourteen, sometimes sixteen-hour days. New scenes come in from the writers and you've got like three hours to learn it. Scene after scene after scene. And then there's being so far from home, stuck in a motel room or a trailer. After the fourth week of food delivery from the same restaurant, you've tasted everything off the menu twice. No. Not for me. Not anymore."

I don't know if I've hit a nerve or just sent Dan on a little nostalgia trip back in time, but he drives in silence the rest of the way, and I'm not sure how to segue into another topic.

We pull up in the drive, and as I step out of the car, I get to really see the house properly in the light of day. Dan's property sits gracefully at the edge of a rocky shoreline. Its weathered gray shingles and white trim glow softly under the late afternoon sun. A wide, wrap-around porch offers a perfect view of the Saco River, with the outdoor chairs we sat on last night neatly arranged on the decking. The house itself is timeless, blending coastal charm with rustic elegance. Large picture windows capture the view of the pine forest on the opposite bank, the scent of salt air from the ocean wafts right up to my nose like a welcome embrace.

What I hadn't noticed when we sat outside last night was the gravel path that winds down through the backyard to the boathouse, perched just above the waterline, its faded barn-red paint worn by decades of salt-laced sea breezes. Beyond it, I spot a small wooden dock that stretches out to meet the lapping water. But there's no boat.

The yard itself looks like a work in progress, wild beach grasses sway in the breeze, and clusters of lupines bloom near the house, their vibrant purples contrasting with the rugged landscape. The rhythmic sound of waves breaking on the shore completes the scene, giving the property an air of serene isolation, yet it feels warm and lived in, as though I've known this place all my life. *What the hell is this? I'm nostalgic for a place I hadn't set eyes on twenty-four hours ago?*

"You alright?" Dan asks.

I can't quite believe I agreed to this. Dinner? At his place? Again. I'm here for work, not to socialize. But the promise of a functional printer is too tempting to resist.

"Sorry, yeah, I'm good. You have a beautiful home."

"Thanks." Dan points up to the front door. "Shall we?"

We slip off our shoes in the front hall and head through to the living area. He gestures for me to take a seat at the kitchen island.

"I'll just fire up the printer and get those copies started for you," he says, taking the flash drive.

I sit down and pick up one of Chloe's math textbooks, flipping through the pages. Part of me doesn't want to even attempt any of the questions in case I don't know the answers. If there was one subject that made me nervous in school, it was math. Of course, I use mental arithmetic every day at work. Whether it's budget planning or market research on total addressable markets, I know my way around numbers, but there's something about algebra and quadratic equations that still makes me shiver.

"Three copies of each enough?" Dan shouts down the stairs.

"Yes, that would be great."

Dan skips down the stairs with the printouts in a neat plastic sheet-sized envelope. He places it on the table.

"At a dime a page, you're in nearly two dollars. I don't usually offer credit to new customers."

"Oh. Right, of course. Sorry, let me Venmo you now." Embarrassed that I didn't even think to offer, I pull out my phone and start searching for the payment app.

"I'm kidding, Rachel." Dan laughs.

"I don't want you to be out of pocket."

"I'm not. It's there to be used."

"Thank you."

Dan heads over to the kitchen and immediately starts to fill a pan with water and begins chopping some cured sausage into tiny chunks.

"I hope you're hungry," he says over his shoulder as he starts finely chopping a clove of garlic. "I tend to meal prep on the weekend, so I only seem to be able to cook huge portions now."

"I'm pretty hungry, actually. It smells amazing," I admit. And it does.

Dan smiles as he stirs the ingredients in the pan. He sprinkles the grated cheese with a flourish and then pours in the egg.

"Chloe not around?"

"She'll be back later. Thursdays she goes home with her friend Zara after school. Ostensibly to study, but I'm not sure the textbooks ever make it out of her backpack."

"Ask no questions, get told no lies?" I offer.

"Something like that. They've been friends since kindergarten. Zara's mom will drop her off soon. I think it's important she can, you know, talk girl stuff or whatever. Sometimes dad's the last person she wants to confide in, especially at her age, if you know what I mean."

Dan sets a plate of steaming pasta in front of me, the rich, creamy sauce still bubbling. "Dig in. But just to be clear, this is strictly not a date," he says with a wink.

I laugh, feeling myself relax a notch. "Duly noted."

As we eat, our conversation flows easily, jumping from work to books to ridiculous childhood stories. I'd almost forgotten how nice it could be, just sharing stories, not trying to sell something.

"You confident? About your meeting, I mean," Dan says, looking at my documents in the plastic folder. "Did you want to run through your pitch? I'd be happy to listen, maybe offer some feedback."

I'm tempted, but I shake my head. "Thanks, but I should probably go over it on my own. Back at the motel."

"Of course. I always rehearsed in private too."

I nod, wondering if I should go there. "Why did you stop? Acting, I mean."

A pained expression dances for a second across Dan's face. He stands and reaches to take our empty plates. But he catches himself, and sits back down. "When Rebecca. That's Chloe's mom. When she died, I took a long hard look at myself and knew I needed to make some changes. For Chloe as well as myself."

"But what about the income?"

"No point earning it if you can't spend time with your family enjoying it."

"Rebecca and I were practically strangers by then. She was bringing Chloe up by herself while I was on the other side of the country eating the aforementioned takeout food for the forty-ninth time."

"But what about when you weren't filming?"

"That's just it. As soon as the series wrapped, I'd take on small roles in indie films, voice-over work, anything my agent could sign me up for. I had this arbitrary figure in my head of how much I wanted to earn, and I just went for it. At the expense of everything else."

"What happened? To Rebecca. If you don't mind me asking."

Dan considers the question as he lines the salt and pepper shakers up on the table. "I'd just finished shooting a supporting role in an indie feature. Had been home less than forty-eight hours when the producer called. I needed to do some ADR down in Florida."

"ADR?"

"Sorry, it's when you go into a studio to record some of the lines of dialogue again if they're not clear, or you need to add something new because they've edited something out, which means that scene no longer makes sense. Anyway, it was the week before Thanksgiving, so everyone wanted to finish up before the holidays. Producer was begging me on the phone, really laying on the guilt. If I didn't do it right then, they weren't going to hit their deadline, and the film would miss its release window."

"So, you went."

"Yep. Rebecca was furious. She had planned Thanksgiving down to the last minute. I don't just mean the day itself, I mean the whole week. My mom was coming to stay with us to look after Chloe, and we'd RSVP'd to various gatherings in Portland. And I got on a plane to Tampa."

Dan stands, resting his hands on the table.

"When I landed, I had a missed call from Portland PD. Rebecca had been killed in a car accident on the way back from dropping Chloe at school."

"I'm so sorry." The words sound hollow. Not enough. Sometimes this language of ours simply isn't adequate.

"It should have been me driving that morning. I always took over the school run when I was back. But I wasn't here, I was in Tampa, and my wife was dead."

I let his words hang in the air, thick and heavy like the fog rolling in from the water. Part of me wants to tell him that it wasn't his fault—that none of it was his fault—but I know that's not what he needs. Sometimes, no matter how many times people tell you it wasn't your fault, it doesn't make the guilt any easier to bear.

He glances at me, his jaw tensing, like he's bracing himself for judgment. I surprise myself by moving closer, reaching out to put my hand on his forearm.

"Dan," I say softly, choosing my words carefully. "You did what you thought was right at the time. We all make choices we think we can fix later. Sometimes, we just don't get the chance."

He looks down at my hand, his gaze lingering like he's not quite sure it's real. "I wanted to give them everything," he says. "A good life, a secure future. But I was too focused on being the provider and not enough on just... being there."

I nod, understanding more than I'd like to admit. "You know, I used to think that success meant proving everyone wrong. Proving I could do it on my own. But sometimes, in the middle of the night, when it's too quiet to ignore my own thoughts, I wonder if I've just been running from the things that really matter. Like I'm so scared of standing still that I keep moving just to avoid looking back."

He looks up then, his expression softer. "It's hard to know where the line is," he says. "Between ambition and obsession. Between wanting to do the right thing and losing sight of why you're doing it in the first place."

The weight of his confession presses down on both of us, and I can't help but wonder if I'm just as guilty of letting life slip through my fingers while I chase something I'm not even sure I want anymore.

Dan's lips quirk into a half-smile, but it doesn't reach his eyes. "I never thought I'd end up here, living in my hometown, raising a kid on my own, wondering how the hell I got it all so wrong."

"You didn't get it all wrong," I say firmly. "Look at Chloe. She's amazing. Funny, smart, confident. You're raising her to be exactly the kind of person the world needs. That's no small thing."

He gives a shaky laugh. "Maybe. I just... I don't want to mess her up, you know? She deserves better than a dad who doesn't always have his shit together."

"Join the club," I say, nudging his arm. "None of us have our shit together. We're all just pretending we do."

Dan's laugh this time is more genuine, and something loosens in my chest—like maybe he's not the only one who needed to hear that.

The front door opens. "Hey, Dad," Chloe chirps from the hall as she kicks off her sneakers. "Oh, hey, Rachel."

"Hi. Did you have a good evening?" I ask with a smile, hoping she can't sense the mood in the room.

"The best!" She drops her school bag and starts shedding layers of clothing as she skips towards the stairs, leaving them where they fall. "Dad, can I get five bucks for Toca Boca?"

"For what?"

"For my Toca World account. I need an upgrade."

"I don't know what you're talking about?" Dan looks visibly perplexed.

"Dad!? The app. Zara's got the Bohemian house pack. It's so cool. I think I've moved on from my cottagecore phase, and I'm really feeling the Bohemian aesthetic."

Dan turns to me mouthing *aesthetic* in mock reverence.

I laugh. "I'll leave these very important design decisions in your very capable hands." I take my phone out of my purse and book a Lyft.

"Please, Dad?"

"Fine. Only if you promise to show me what it is I've bought."

"Deal!" Chloe runs to Dan and gives him a huge hug.

When I get the notification that my car is on its way, I sweep my pitch documents off the table and let Dan and Chloe catch up with each other.

Of course, Dan offers to drive me home, which is kind, but it would mean dragging Chloe out of the house and she'd only just gotten home. I may not be a parent, but I know the importance of routine and a good night's sleep on a school night.

I slip into my motel room, still feeling sad for Dan and Chloe. The weight of the day crashes over me as I kick off my heels and collapse onto the bed. My phone buzzes insistently, and I reach over to decline and let it go to voicemail.

I guess my muscle memory needs a bit of a refresh because I accidentally accept the call.

Zoe's face fills the screen, her grin a mile wide.

Oh, great, I'm on a video call with everyone from the office.

"Guess what, team? I know it's late, but I just got the confirmation call. I landed the GreenShoots account!"

A chorus of cheers erupts from the gallery video view, everyone toasting their screens with coffee mugs and water bottles.

I force a smile, trying to muster some enthusiasm. "That's great news, Zoe. Congrats."

She preens under the praise, her eyes darting to mine. "Thanks, Rach. Couldn't have done it without your groundwork."

I nod, feeling the jealousy welling up. It should've been my win, my moment to shine. But here I am, stuck in Maine, while Zoe basks in the glory.

Helen's voice cuts through the chatter. "Excellent work, everyone. But let's not rest on our laurels. Rachel, we're looking forward to having you back in a few weeks. There are a lot more clients out there who need Channing Gabriel... They just don't know it yet."

All eyes turn to me, and I sit up straighter, smoothing my hair. "Absolutely. Looking forward to being back."

Helen nods, her expression unreadable. "Good. That's all, team. Recharge and regroup, we go again tomorrow."

No pressure, then. I push aside thoughts of Dan and his guilt. I can't afford any distractions, not when my career is on the line.

As the call wraps up, I take one of the complimentary bottles of water from the nightstand. I need a break—and ice.

If I'm going to stay up much longer, I'm going to need something cold to keep me from nodding off.

I grab the empty ice bucket and step out into the night air, the hallway dim and silent. The machine is just around the corner, humming like it's working far too hard for its age. I fill the bucket halfway, already craving the clink of cubes in my next drink.

But when I get back to my door and reach into my pocket, my hand hits nothing.

I freeze.

No key.

No. No, no, no. I check again—every pocket, twice, even under the bucket, as if I might've stashed it there.

I sigh, long and loud.

Because of course this would happen. On this day. After that call.

I set the bucket down and make the walk of shame back to the front desk.

To my surprise, it's not the young receptionist on duty—it's Richard, Dan's brother, and the man who checked me in when I first arrived. He looks up from his computer screen and offers a warm but tired smile.

"Lock yourself out?"

I nod, holding up the empty hand that should be holding my key card. "Classic rookie move. I guess my day wasn't quite finished messing with me."

He chuckles and pushes back from the desk, already reaching for the spare keys. "Happens more than you'd think. Coffee in one hand, phone in the other, and the door clicks shut. You'd be amazed how many people leave barefoot."

He hands me a fresh key card.

"Thanks," I say, sliding it into my pocket.

"You holding up okay?" he asks, his tone shifting ever so slightly—just enough to suggest he means more than the key situation. "Must be strange being stuck out here with all the flight chaos. That volcano's throwing a bigger tantrum than they expected."

I smile faintly. "Yeah, I saw the news earlier. I was hoping it would have cleared up by now, but sounds like I'm here for a while longer."

"Well," he shrugs, "you could do worse than Biddeford."

"That's what Dan keeps telling me."

Richard's eyebrows lift slightly, but he doesn't comment.

I clear my throat, keeping my tone as casual as I can. "Speaking of... how is he? Dan, I mean."

Richard gives a little noncommittal shrug, eyes thoughtful. "He's doing alright. Been through a lot, but... he keeps going. He's that kind of guy."

It's not much, but I don't expect more. Still, the way he says it lingers in the air like something unsaid. I nod, letting the silence speak for both of us.

"Well, I'll let you get back to it," I say with a little wave. "Thanks for rescuing me."

He chuckles. "Anytime. And hey—maybe tomorrow's the day everything goes right."

I raise an eyebrow. "That'd be a first."

SIX

The elevator doors slide open, and I follow signs for The Sako Suite. I knock once and push open the door to find a once-grand conference room bathed in morning light. Paint is peeling from one of the walls and the chairs are mismatched. My heart rate increases slightly as I step inside, gripping my briefcase tightly. A dozen expectant faces turn my way. *Quelle surprise*, they're all men.

I feel the familiar rush of adrenaline as I approach the group. I know from the specific click-clack of my heels on the tiled floor that I have their complete, undivided attention. Do I like the feeling of power? *You betcha*. Is it an unfair advantage? *Oh yes*. I've done this so often now that my body and mind are on autopilot. This is Rachel's patent-pending Madonna-Mistress guide to winning new business:

When I'm trying to convince a predominantly male team that I am the right person to take their product or service to market, I need to exude two things before the pitch even begins. I would go so far as to say, the pitch is won or lost before the first rehearsed word leaves my lips. It's all on the entrance. So much needs to be conveyed in so little time. One, that I'm a safe pair of hands to entrust their baby with. They need to be absolutely sure that I will nurture it, feed it and wipe its nose if it starts to run. And two, that I have enough vim and passion to be entrusted with their baby and take it out to the world.

I've gotten good at reading a room and a glance at my audience confirms my suspicions—scuffed, unpolished shoes, standard-issue blue oxford shirts with button-down collars and beige chinos—for a split second, the vinyl scratches on my mental record player, as I realize that my gathered audience isn't the upper echelons of the organization. Nowhere near it. These aren't the decision-makers, they're the doers.

Not a problem, I shall turn them into card-carrying allies before I'm through.

Alright, Rachel, you've got this. Just like we practiced.

I center myself and launch into my pitch. "Good morning, everyone. I'm Rachel, and I'm here to change your mind. As you can see from the data I've compiled, plant-based foods are no longer just a fad or niche market. Consumer demand is surging across all demographics and could represent millions of dollars in annual revenues... If you want it to."

I click to the next slide, displaying colorful graphs and charts. "In the past year alone, sales of plant-based products have grown by twenty-seven percent, outpacing traditional frozen foods by a significant margin. This represents a huge untapped opportunity for Harcourt Foods to expand its customer base, and drive long-term growth."

The room is silent except for the hum of my laptop fan. I scan their faces, trying to gauge reactions. Some nod thoughtfully, jotting down notes. But a few wear skeptical frowns. Here come the tough questions.

"How do we know this trend will last?" one executive asks, leaning back in his chair. "What if it's just a flash in the pan?"

I click to another slide showcasing long-term market

projections. "While no one can predict the future with one hundred percent certainty, all indicators point to plant-based eating becoming a lasting lifestyle shift, not a passing fad. As consumers become more health-conscious and environmentally aware, they're seeking out alternatives to meat. Getting ahead of this curve positions Harcourt Foods as an innovative leader, not a reactive follower."

More nods, a few grudging smiles. They're starting to see the bigger picture. I shift into my closing argument.

"The data is clear—plant-based foods are the future. Harcourt Foods has a choice: embrace this growing segment of the population and thrive, or ignore it and risk being left behind as the market moves on without you. Fortune favors the bold. This, gentlemen, is your chance to lead the next generation of frozen foods into a more sustainable, health-focused era."

The product managers continue to ask questions for another twenty minutes. Crucially, they change in tone from combative and outright scathing, to considered and curious. Satisfied I'm leaving them with a clear route forward, I wrap things up. They're on board. Now the real work begins—making sure my message is passed up the food chain to Old Man Harcourt himself. But after today, I'm pretty confident that I've sown the seeds of a plant-powered revolution at Harcourt Foods. I leave the folder with the printed copy of my pitch for dissemination among the wider team and make my exit.

The energy of the pitch meeting lingers as I slide into the driver's seat of The Big Red Beast, my mind still buzzing with possibilities. I tap *White Pines Motel* into Maps and then find an appropriately upbeat playlist to match my mood.

As I navigate the streets of Portland, I allow myself a moment to savor the victory. The product team's enthusiasm was palpable. It's a major milestone, but it's not a done deal just yet—convincing the higher-ups to take a leap of faith, particularly the patriarch of the company, Jonathan D. Harcourt himself, will be a true test. But for that, I need to get into the room.

Lost in thought, I almost don't notice the elementary school building to my left. But the colorful banner catches my eye: "Sing! Talent Competition - Qualifier Heats Here."

On impulse, I suddenly turn into the parking lot, earning me a long and angry blast of a horn from the vehicle behind me. I give the driver an apologetic wave of the hand, but he's already accelerating hard, no doubt cursing me and all of womankind.

Standing in front of the impressive main building, I shake my head, pulling myself back to the present. What am I doing here? I have a million things to do, calls to make, emails to answer. But something pulls me towards the large double doors. I really do want to see Chloe perform, and this is absolutely not at all about possibly seeing Dan again.

I follow the signs to the auditorium, my heart quickening with each step as the excited chatter of children and parents envelops me. It's silly, I know. I'm a grown woman, a successful executive. But at this moment, I'm also the little girl who once stood on a very similar stage, belting out a slightly off-key rendition of "Tomorrow" from Annie.

Taking a deep breath, I slip inside the auditorium door, and the volume increases tenfold. The air is electric with anticipation, with frantic moms trying to apply a frightening amount of makeup and hairspray to their tween progenies. The stage is bathed in a soft glow, empty save for a single microphone stand, creating a sense of anticipation. I find a seat in the back, settling in just as the lights dim and a hush falls over the room.

As a young performer takes the stage, all nerves and raw talent, I feel a smile spreading across my face. Maybe this unexpected detour is exactly what I needed—a reminder of the joy and innocence that's so easy to lose sight of in the daily grind. For now, I let myself get lost in the music, the worries of the adult world fading away like a half-remembered dream. The boy sings well. When he's done, he politely bows and exits stage left.

There are performances from four more singers and a young guitarist before I spot a familiar figure waiting in the wings. When a teacher pats her on the shoulder, Chloe walks confidently to the center of the stage and pauses in front of the microphone. She takes a moment and then gives a little nod to someone who must be controlling the music.

Chloe's voice is breathtaking. Soulful, sweet, and with bundles of confidence. When I close my eyes, I can't believe it's the voice of the same twelve-year-old girl I saw at Dan's house. Chloe sings the lyrics like they're her own. Bittersweet regret over love lost and an unsure future. I'm mesmerized from start to finish.

The song comes to an end, and everyone in the auditorium breaks into applause. Chloe grins, bows theatrically, and skips off the stage. Dan's there in the wings ready to greet her, and he picks her up into his arms for a huge cuddle, fatherly pride etched onto his face.

One of the teachers approaches the microphone and explains that Chloe was the last of the individual performers and that there will be a five-minute break before rehearsals will continue for the groups.

Dan appears at the stage door, and rushes over to a group of kids between twelve and fifteen years of age, who are getting ready to go up next. He coaches them through their final vocal warm-ups and double-checks that they remember the choreography. I watch, transfixed, as he offers each one a high-five and a word of encouragement.

There's something about seeing him in this element that

makes my heart skip a beat. Gone is the weariness that seems to cling to him like a second skin. In its place is a man who's fully alive, his passion for performance and his love for these kids shining through in every gesture.

I sink down a little lower in my seat, suddenly self-conscious. What would he think if he knew I was here, spying on this intimate moment? But I can't tear my eyes away. It's like watching a master craftsman at work, each movement precise and purposeful.

As the kids take their places on stage, Dan steps back into the shadows, his job done. But even from this distance, I can see he's invested in them and willing them through sheer force of mind to sing their hearts out. This means something to him, I realize. More than just a school talent show. More than being an over-enthusiastic PTA member. It's clearly a connection to a past he can't quite let go of, maybe something of a reminder of the life he once lived.

The music swells, and the kids begin to sing, their voices blending in a harmony that sends shivers down my spine. I glance back at Dan, and for a moment, our eyes meet across the crowded auditorium.

He looks surprised, then curious, his head tilting slightly as if to ask, "What are you doing here?"

I offer a small smile and a little wave in return, hoping it conveys everything I can't quite put into words. That I see him, really see him, and that I understand, on some level, the weight he carries. That maybe, just maybe, we're not so different after all.

As the song comes to a close and the parents and teachers in the room begin to clap, I can't help but join in.

Dan's voice cuts through the applause, warm and genuine as he congratulates the kids on their performance. "That was fantastic, guys! You should be so proud of yourselves." His smile is wide, his eyes shining with a mix of pride and something else, something that tugs at my heart in a way I can't quite explain.

As the kids disperse, chattering excitedly among themselves, I see a woman approach Dan. She's tall and slender, with vibrant red hair that cascades down her back in loose waves. There's a confidence in her stride, a purposeful sway to her hips that draws the eye and commands attention.

"Dan, that was amazing!" she gushes, her hand coming to rest on his arm in a gesture that feels a little too familiar, a little too intimate. "You've done such an incredible job with these kids."

Dan ducks his head, a slight flush creeping up his neck. "Thanks, Veronica. But really, it's all them. They've worked so hard."

Veronica leans in closer, her voice dropping to a conspiratorial whisper that I'm unable to hear.

I feel a sudden tightness in my chest, a pang of something I can't quite name. It's not jealousy, exactly. More like a sense of... loss. Like I'm watching something slip away before I even had a chance to reach for it.

Dan hesitates, his eyes darting around the room as if searching for an escape. For a brief moment, his eyes find mine before he shakes his head and says no to Veronica's request.

But Veronica is persistent, her smile widening as she leans in even closer, one hand tactically placed on his forearm as she continues to talk.

I turn away, suddenly feeling like an intruder in a private moment. My heart is beating too fast, my palms slick with sweat. I need to get out of here, need to clear my head.

As I make my way towards the exit, I catch a glimpse of Chloe out of the corner of my eye. She's sitting alone on the floor, near one of the fire exits, her knees hugged to her chest, her face hidden behind a curtain of hair. Something in her posture, in the slump of her shoulders, makes me pause.

I glance back at Dan, still deep in conversation with Veronica, and then back at Chloe. And suddenly, I know what I have to do.

I square my shoulders and make my way over to where Chloe sits. I lower myself to the floor beside her, my legs crossing underneath me.

"Hey," I say softly, nudging her shoulder with my own. "That was a really great performance. You can really sing."

Chloe lifts her head, her eyes wide and startled. "Thanks," she mumbles, her gaze darting away from mine.

I nod, letting the silence stretch between us for a moment. And then, before I can second-guess myself, I ask, "Do you want to talk about it?"

Chloe shrugs, her fingers plucking at a loose thread on her jeans. "It's just... I don't know. Sometimes I feel like I'm not good enough, you know? Like no matter how hard I try, I'll never be as good as the other kids."

God, how familiar that feeling is.

My heart clenches at her words, at the raw vulnerability in her voice. I sit down next to her. "Chloe, listen to me. You are *so* talented. And not just at singing—at everything you put your mind to. Don't ever let anyone make you feel like you're not good enough. I saw you up there and you were amazing."

She looks up at me then, her eyes shining with unshed tears. "Really?"

I nod, my throat tight with emotion. "Really. And you know what? I bet your mom would be so proud of you if she could see you now."

A single tear slips down Chloe's cheek, and she brushes it away with the back of her hand. "I miss her," she says, her voice barely audible over the chatter of the other kids.

"I know," I say softly, reaching out to tuck a strand of hair behind her ear. "And it's okay to miss her. But she'll always be with you, Chloe. In here." I tap my finger against my chest, right over my heart.

Chloe nods, a watery smile tugging at the corners of her mouth. "Thanks," she says, leaning into me for a quick hug.

I squeeze her tight, feeling a sudden rush of affection for this brave, resilient girl.

"Do you talk to your dad? About missing your mom, I mean?"

"Sometimes. But whenever I do, he starts acting weird. Sort of tries even harder to be perfect. You know? Like he's messed up, and I hate seeing him like that. It makes me feel like I'm the one making things harder for him."

My heart aches for her. For both of them. I think back to how fiercely Dan spoke about parenting the other night, how he seemed almost desperate to get it right.

"Chloe, your dad loves you more than anything. You know that, right?"

She nods, but the doubt is still there, swimming just under the surface. "I know. But... it's like he never takes a break. It makes me feel like I'm the problem."

I reach out and touch her shoulder gently. "You're not the problem. You're his whole world. He just doesn't want to let you down."

Chloe gives me a small, shaky smile. "He never talks about Mom. Like, ever. I feel like I have to be good all the time because... what if he thinks I'm too much? Or that I remind him of her too much?"

"Oh, Chloe." I pull her into a hug, her head tucked under my chin. "You're not too much. You're exactly enough. And I know your dad wouldn't change a single thing about you. He's just... figuring it out as he goes. It's messy, and it's hard, but you're both doing an amazing job. I think he's just scared sometimes. Scared of losing you too."

She sniffles against my shoulder, her arms tightening

around me. "I just wish he'd talk about her more. So, I don't forget stuff. Like... how she used to braid my hair. I don't even remember what her laugh sounded like."

I pull her closer. "Maybe you can ask him to share stories with you. He's really good at stories. I think it would help both of you."

Chloe pulls back and wipes her nose with the back of her hand, giving me a small, determined nod and the hint of a smile. "Yeah. Maybe I will."

"Come on," I say, standing up and holding out my hand. "You ready to join your dad?"

"No," she says, her smile replaced with a frown. "I'm still mad at him."

"Why?"

Chloe sighs dramatically. "I asked him for a new dress to wear to the final rehearsal tomorrow night, something that I could wear at the heats too, but he said I should just pick something from my closet. But it's all baby stuff! He doesn't get it— I'm not a little kid anymore."

I nod empathetically. The frustration of feeling misunderstood at her age is still vivid in my memory. "That's tough. It's a big moment and you want to look and feel your best."

"Exactly! I'm practically a teenager. But Dad still treats me like I'm five." Chloe crosses her arms, pouting.

As I look at Chloe, I'm struck by how she's caught between two worlds right now—not quite a child, but not yet an adult. It's a tricky tightrope to walk. An idea starts to form in my mind... Maybe what Chloe needs is a little old-fashioned girl time to help her find her footing in this new phase.

A smile spreads across my face as the plan takes shape. "You know what, Chloe? I think I have the perfect solution. What you need is a girls' day out—just you and me. We'll go shopping tomorrow, find you a fabulous new outfit that makes you feel like the amazing young woman you're becoming. What do you say?"

Chloe's eyes widen, a grin tugging at her lips. "Really? You'd do that for me?"

"Absolutely! Every girl deserves a special shopping trip now and then." I wink conspiratorially. "Now, let's go talk to your dad and make it official."

We march over to where Dan is chatting with some other parents, determined expressions on our faces. I'm pleased to note that the red-haired interloper is nowhere to be seen. He turns as we approach, quirking an eyebrow at our matching stances—hands on hips, chins held high.

"Dan, Chloe and I have an announcement," I declare, fighting to keep a straight face. "We're commandeering the day tomorrow for a very important mission: Operation Shopping Spree!"

Dan's eyes dart between us, taking in Chloe's hopeful expression and my resolute one. I can practically see the wheels turning in his head, calculating the odds of winning this battle.

"I don't know, Rachel... Chloe, don't you have plenty of clothes already?" he tries, but his heart isn't in it.

Chloe and I exchange a glance, then unleash our secret weapons simultaneously—the dreaded puppy dog eyes. We've got this down to a science.

Dan throws up his hands in surrender, chuckling. "Alright, alright, I know when I'm beat. Listen, Rachel, there's something important I need to tell you."

"Uh oh," I jest.

"You might think us actor types are all super liberal. And I guess we are. I am. But when it comes to Chloe, I'm conservative with a capital C, underlined and in bold. Please, for the love of all that is good in this world, please don't come home with something scandalous. She might think she's all grown up, but she's twelve."

"Dad!—" Chloe is about to complain further, but I interject.

"We won't." I salute him. "Scout's honor."

"Very well. In that case, I'll drop her off at Congress Street tomorrow at ten. Give me your number and I'll send you a pin. And thank you. I'll use the time to work on the boathouse."

SEVEN

At one minute past ten, Dan's car slows and pulls up next to where I'm waiting on the sidewalk.

"Rachel!" Chloe shouts from the open window, all smiles and clearly excited to get started. She hops out, closing the door behind her without so much as a look back.

"Have fun, you two," Dan shouts through the same open window as he pulls away from the curb and joins the traffic.

"I haven't been shopping in like, forever," Chloe beams. "What's the plan?"

I can't help but smile at her enthusiasm. "Well, we have a lot to fit in. First, we're heading to Spring Blossom Boutique to find you the perfect dress for the talent show. Then, it's off to the spa for some much-needed pampering. If we have time, there might even be ice cream. How does that sound?"

"Amazing! I can't wait to try on all the dresses!" Chloe claps her hands together, practically vibrating with excitement.

As we head towards the mall, the crisp ocean breeze greets us, carrying the scent of pine from the nearby forests. The charming streets of Portland's Old Port district bustle with activity as we make our way to the boutique.

The tinkling of the shop's bell announces our arrival. Inside, an array of colorful dresses in various styles and sizes fill the racks. Chloe's eyes widen as she takes in the sight, her fingers already reaching out to touch the soft fabrics.

"Welcome to Spring Blossom Boutique!" a friendly sales associate greets us. "Let me know if you need any help finding the perfect dress."

"Thank you," I respond with a smile. "Go ahead, don't be shy, see what catches your eye."

Chloe doesn't need a second invitation and immediately gets to work browsing the racks, on the cusp of adolescence, eager to assert her own style and identity.

The store hums with the chatter of other customers and the rustling of fabric as dresses are pulled from hangars and held up for inspection. The air is filled with a sense of possibility and excitement, as if each dress holds the promise of a new beginning.

Chloe pulls out a shimmery blue dress, holding it up to her frame. "What do you think of this one?"

I tilt my head, considering. "It's lovely, but maybe a bit too fairy-tale princess. Let's keep looking. We want to find something that really showcases your personality and makes you feel confident on stage. It needs to match the song."

Chloe nods, her eyes sparkling with enthusiasm as she dives back into the racks. I follow suit, running my fingers along the soft fabrics, searching for that perfect dress.

"Oh, Rachel, look at this one!" Chloe exclaims, pulling out a crimson dress with a twirly skirt. She holds it up to her body, swaying side to side. "It's so fancy!"

I chuckle, delighted by her excitement. "It's beautiful, Chloe. Why don't you try it on?"

Chloe dashes off to the fitting room, leaving me to browse a little more. I find myself drawn to a deep green dress with delicate lace detailing. It's not quite right for Chloe, but I can't resist holding it up to myself in the mirror, imagining for a brief moment what it would be like to have a special occasion to dress up for.

"Rachel, I need help with the zipper!" Chloe calls from the fitting room, jolting me back to the present.

I make my way over and help her with the dress. As she steps out and twirls, the skirt fans out around her, and I feel a lump form in my throat. She looks so grown up, so beautiful.

"Chloe, you look amazing," I manage to say, blinking back the sudden rush of emotion.

She beams at me, but then her brow furrows slightly. "I love it, but I'm not sure if it's the one, you know?"

I nod in understanding. "That's okay. Let's have a maybe pile. We'll keep looking until we find the dress that feels just right."

And so, we do, laughing and chatting as we try on dress after dress. It's hard not to warm to Chloe, and I'm pretty sure I'm enjoying this shared experience as much as she is. Finally, she emerges from the fitting room in a dress that takes my breath away. It's a deep blue, like the evening sky, with a sweetheart neckline and a skirt that flows like water around her legs. The fabric shimmers subtly under the lights, and the cut is both youthful and elegant.

"Chloe, that's the one. You look stunning."

She does a little twirl, her face glowing with joy. "I hardly recognize myself in it," she confesses, a hint of shyness in her voice.

I walk over and place my hands on her shoulders, meeting her eyes in the mirror. "You look like the strong, talented, beautiful young woman you are. You're going to knock the judges' socks off," I tell her sincerely.

"You're right. This is the one," Chloe declares, a smile spreading across her face.

I nod, mirroring her smile. "It definitely is."

As we head to the checkout counter, dress in hand, Chloe's practically skipping beside me, her eyes sparkling with delight. Suddenly, she pauses and looks up at me with a hopeful expression.

"Rachel, do you think we could do a makeup makeover, too? I want to look extra special for the talent show."

I hesitate, considering her request. While I want nothing more than to make this day perfect for Chloe, I also know that she's only twelve. Makeup might be a step too far, especially considering how protective Dan can be.

I crouch down to meet her eyes, taking her hands in mine. "Chloe, sweetie, I know you're excited, but I think a full makeover might be a bit much for now. You're already so beautiful, inside and out, and I don't want to take away from that. Not to mention, the talent show is ages away, so the makeup won't last until then."

She looks a little disappointed, but nods in understanding. "I guess Dad might not like it either, huh?"

"He just wants you to enjoy being young," I explain gently. "Tell you what, how about we head to the spa next? We can get pampered with some facials and maybe even a mani-pedi. That way, you'll feel extra special without going overboard."

Chloe's face lights up again. "That sounds amazing! Let's do it!"

With that, I pay for the dress and head out into the bright afternoon sun. The spa I liked the look of is only a short walk away, nestled in a tranquil corner of the bustling city. As we step inside, the serene atmosphere envelops us immediately. The air is fragrant with essential oils, and soft, soothing music plays in the background.

"Welcome," the receptionist greets us with a warm smile. "Do you have an appointment?"

"We do," I confirm, giving her our names.

She checks her computer and nods. "Ah yes, I have you here. Come right this way."

We're led to a comfortable, dimly lit room with two plush massage tables side by side. The soothing scent of lavender fills the air, instantly making me feel more relaxed. Chloe and I change into the soft, fluffy robes provided and settle on the tables, sighing contentedly as the warm sheets embrace us.

Our estheticians enter, their voices low and calming as they explain the treatments we'll be receiving. As they begin to apply the cool, refreshing facial masks, I steal a glance at Chloe. Her eyes are closed, a serene smile playing on her lips. It warms my heart to see her so peaceful and content.

The next hour is a blissful escape from reality. I didn't know how much I needed this as skilled hands massage my face, arms, and feet. The stress of the past week, my worries about work, and about not closing the GreenShoots deal melt away, leaving only a sense of pure, indulgent relaxation.

"This is, like, amazing," Chloe murmurs, her voice muffled. "Can we do this every day?"

I chuckle softly. "I wish, sweetie. But that's what makes it so special, don't you think?"

She nods, reaching out to squeeze my hand. "Thanks so much, Rachel. This is the best."

I squeeze back, my heart full. "My pleasure."

When I look over, there's something comical about Chloe lying there with a grin on her face and slices of cucumber on her eyes. I can't resist taking a photo and sending it to Dan.

As our treatments come to an end, we reluctantly sit up, our skin glowing and our bodies relaxed. We thank our estheticians and head to the nail salon area, where, despite Chloe's incredible attempts at wounded indignation, she finally—if somewhat reluctantly—agrees to clear nail varnish for our manicures and pedicures.

Sitting side by side, admiring our freshly painted nails, Chloe and I chat and giggle like old friends. The spa has worked its magic, not just on our appearances, but on our mood. I could get used to this.

"Come on, I promised you lunch."

"And ice cream," Chloe is quick to remind me.

"And ice cream."

As we pull into the driveway, I can see Dan at the far end of the garden putting the finishing touches to some new guttering on the boathouse. His brow is furrowed in concentration, his movements precise and deliberate. The boathouse has had a fresh coat of red paint and it's looking very grand. It's clear he's poured his heart into this project, just as he pours his heart into everything he does for his family.

Chloe calls out to him, waving enthusiastically with her freshly manicured hand. "Dad! Look at us!"

He looks up, a smile spreading across his face as he takes in our refreshed appearances. For a moment, his eyes meet mine, and there's a flicker of... something. Gratitude, perhaps? Appreciation? I smile back, feeling a warmth that has nothing to do with the spa treatments.

Right then, I realize that this unexpected detour in Maine has given me more than just a break from my fast-paced life. It's given me a glimpse into a world where love, family, and the simple joys of life take center stage. And as I watch Dan and Chloe embrace, laughing and chatting animatedly about our spa day, while that sort of life is not for me, I think I'm appreciating for the first time why it's so important to others.

Dan wipes his hands on his t-shirt and puts an arm around Chloe, guiding her back toward the house.

"Sounds like you two had a blast."

"We did. Chloe's good company." I smile.

"Dad, invite her inside. I want to show you my new dress."

Dan looks embarrassed. "Of course, sorry. Would you like to come in for a drink?"

"Sure."

I follow Dan into the house.

Dan turns on the faucet and scrubs at his hands. "Thanks again for taking her out today. I really appreciate it."

"Happy to help. The boathouse is looking very cool."

The patter of feet running on stairs causes both of us to look up.

Dan's smile falters as his eyes dart over to Chloe. His gaze sweeps over her, taking in the way the dress hugs her developing curves, the hint of maturity in her stance. His expression shifts, a mix of pride and something else—a wistfulness maybe, a longing for the little girl who used to run into his arms without a care in the world.

"Chloe, you look like..." He clears his throat, struggling to find the right words. "You look beautiful, honey. So grown up."

Chloe beams, twirling in her dress. "Isn't it perfect, Dad? Rachel helped me pick it out!"

I nod, trying to gauge Dan's reaction. There's a tension in his jaw, a tightness around his eyes that wasn't there a moment ago.

"She wanted something special for the talent show," I explain gently. "Something that showcases who she's becoming."

Dan nods, but I can see the conflict playing out on his face. He wants to be supportive, wants to celebrate his daughter's growth, but there's a part of him that's not ready to let go of the little girl he's cherished for so long.

"It's a lovely dress," he says finally, his voice strained. "I just... I didn't realize how fast you were growing up, Chloe. It's a lot to take in."

Chloe's smile falters, confusion clouding her eyes. "But Dad, I thought you'd be happy for me. I thought you'd be proud."

Dan closes his eyes for a moment, clearly formulating his response. When he opens them again, there's a tenderness there, a love so fierce it's palpable. "I am proud of you, Chloe. More than you could ever know. It's just... it's hard for me to see you growing up so fast. But that doesn't mean I'm not happy for you, or that I don't support you every step of the way."

He opens his arms, and Chloe rushes into them, burying her face in his chest. I watch as they cling to each other, two hearts navigating the uncharted waters of change and growth.

And in that moment, I understand the depth of Dan's love for his daughter, the sacrifices he's made, continues to make, and the fears he faces as he watches her bloom into the young woman she's destined to become. It's a love that knows no bounds, a love that will guide them through every challenge, every triumph, every bittersweet moment of letting go.

While beautiful, it fills me with an overwhelming feeling of melancholy. I wish, more than anything in the world, that I could have had a dad who loved me as much as Dan loves Chloe.

I watch as Dan gently releases Chloe from his embrace, his eyes glistening with unshed tears. "Why don't you go to your room for a bit, sweetie? Make sure you hang up that dress. I don't want to find it dumped on the floor. I need to talk to Rachel."

Chloe nods, her own eyes brimming with emotion. She casts a glance in my direction, a silent plea for understanding, before trudging up the stairs, her shoulders slumped in defeat.

The silence that follows is heavy, laden with unspoken words and raw emotions. I turn to Dan, my heart aching for both him and Chloe.

"Dan, I know this is hard, but—"

"Do you, Rachel? You're not a parent." His voice is strained. "I don't think you know what it's like to raise a child on your own, to watch them slip away from you little by little, knowing that one day they'll leave and never look back."

Woah! Where's this coming from?

Dan's words hurt, but I take a step closer. I grew up without a dad and would have given the world to have a father like Dan be involved in my life. "No, I don't. But I do know that Chloe needs you to support her, to trust her, to let her grow."

Dan runs a hand through his hair, his eyes searching mine for answers I'm not sure I have. "I want to, Rachel. I want to give her the world, but I'm scared. I'm scared of losing her, of not being enough, of failing her like I failed Rebecca."

The admission hangs in the air, raw and painful. I close the distance, my hand finally finding his, squeezing it gently. "You haven't failed anyone, Dan. From what I've seen, you're an amazing father, and Chloe loves you more than anything in the world. But part of loving her is letting her find her own way, even if it's not the path you would have chosen for her."

He nods, a single tear escaping down his cheek. "I know. I just... I wish I had more time, you know? More time to hold her, to keep her safe, to be her everything."

I smile softly, my vision blurs. "You'll always be her everything, Dan. No matter how old she gets, no matter where life takes her, you'll always be the man who showed her what love looks like, who taught her what it means to be strong and kind and true. But you've got to let her grow up."

"I should go talk to her, apologize for overreacting. Don't go. Please."

I nod. "Take your time."

As soon as he climbs the stairs, I collect my purse and my jacket from the kitchen chair. I'm glad he's gone to apologize to Chloe. And I'm sorry he's still trying to navigate life without Rebecca, but damned if I'm going to hang around to be disrespected again.

EIGHT

♥

The imposing, if slightly tired, brick and tiled facade of Harcourt Foods' headquarters soars before me as I step out of the cab. This time I pause to take it all in, already thinking about which angle we should use in the photo to announce the partnership with Channing Gabriel. My heels click confidently across the well-worn concrete plaza, the spring breeze whipping strands of hair across my face. It's a far cry from the glass and steel office towers I usually visit. But that's one of the reasons I like the company. They're not trying to impress, or pretend to be something they're not—they manufacture frozen food and sell it at an affordable price. This straightforward, no-frills approach is refreshingly honest and nets them hundreds of millions of dollars a year in revenue.

I allow myself a small, triumphant smile as I reach the front doors. Securing a meeting with the patriarch himself, Old Man Harcourt, after one presentation to his product team? I must have really wowed them with my pitch. I like to think I'm good, but boy, if I pull this off, it will be the fastest close. Like, ever. Not to mention winning this account will dwarf Zoe's accomplishments with GreenShoots—hello healthy meat-alternative frozen food, hello even healthier monthly retainer... Hello Rachel Holmes, *partner*.

I try to calm the butterflies in my stomach as I approach the reception desk. This is it—the chance to impress the real decision-maker and seal the deal. All my hard work is about to pay off.

The receptionist flashes me a bright smile, genuinely pleased to see me. "Welcome to Harcourt Foods, Ms. Holmes. You're expected in the executive boardroom."

She escorts me down the hallway and I follow her, my heart rate increasing with each step. When we arrive, she gives me a bright smile and a thumbs up. I pause outside the heavy wooden door to collect myself before entering. I go through my mental checklist, check the buttons on my jacket, adjust the cuffs of my blouse, and push open the door.

Inside, a long mahogany table stretches before me, surrounded by high-back leather chairs. The seats are empty except for one. A man with slicked-back hair and a too-bright smile rises to greet me.

"Ms. Holmes! Pleasure to meet you. I'm Vincent Adler, VP of Marketing." He clasps my hand a little too long, his gaze flickering over me in a way that makes my skin crawl.

I glance around the otherwise vacant room, trying to mask my confusion. "Mr. Adler, I was under the impression I'd be meeting with Mr. Harcourt and the executive board today..."

"Change of plans!" Adler claps his hands together. "The old man got pulled into some emergency golf—I mean, Gulf— oil spill... situation. You know how it is. But lucky for you, it's my opinion that counts around here."

He winks conspiratorially, and I have to physically stop myself from recoiling. This isn't at all how I pictured today going. I force a polite smile as he gestures for me to take a seat.

Adler leans back in his chair, hands behind his head like he's relaxing at his pool in the Hamptons instead of in a corporate office. "So, I hear you've got some big idea to turn us all into a bunch of tofu-eating hippies, eh?"

His dismissive chuckle grates on my nerves. This guy clearly hasn't bothered to even skim my proposal. But I'll be damned if I let his arrogance derail this opportunity. I didn't get where I am, by backing down from a challenge.

I straighten up and meet his gaze head-on, mustering every ounce of professional charm. "Actually, Mr. Adler, plant-based proteins are the fastest growing sector in the food industry. If Harcourt Foods wants to stay relevant, you can't afford to ignore this market..."

I only hope I sound more confident than I feel as I launch into my pitch. All I can do is give this my best shot—even if it means convincing a cocky marketing bro instead of the man actually in charge. I've come too far to let anyone dismiss my vision. Harcourt Foods needs me, whether they realize it yet or not.

"... and that's why partnering with Channing Gabriel on a line of chicken alternatives positions Harcourt Foods perfectly for the future of sustainable eating," I conclude, my voice ringing with conviction as I gesture to the final slide of my presentation.

The boardroom falls silent. I search Adler's face for a reaction. His expression is unreadable, and for a moment, I allow myself to hope that maybe, just maybe, I've gotten through to him.

Then he laughs. A loud, mocking guffaw that echoes off the polished paneled walls.

"Sustainable eating? Come on, sweetheart. People don't want a plate of spinach and quinoa after a hard day at work. Not really. They want real food."

Heat rises to my cheeks at the condescension dripping from his words. *Sweetheart?* Who does this guy think he is? I bite back the retort on the tip of my tongue, reminding myself that losing my cool won't do me any favors.

"With all due respect, Mr. Adler," I say evenly, "the data shows a clear trend towards plant-based options. And it's growing exponentially. Ignoring that shift could mean missing out on establishing your brand as the category leader and with it, a huge opportunity for growth."

He waves a dismissive hand. "Data, *schmata*. I've been in this business longer than you've been alive, missy. I think I know what sells. We don't produce food for the liberal folk of California, we produce real food for working families."

Missy? Seriously? I clench my jaw, my nails digging into my palms as I fight to maintain my composure. I can practically feel my chances of securing this partnership slipping through my fingers with every patronizing word out of Adler's mouth.

I take a deep breath, determined not to let his blatant sexism and narrow-mindedness get the best of me. "Mr. Adler, I strongly believe that Harcourt Foods needs to adapt to changing consumer preferences. If you'll just take a closer look at my proposal..."

But he's already standing up, buttoning his suit jacket with an air of finality. "I think we're done here, Ms. Holmes. Thanks for your... insights, but I think we'll stick to what we know works."

The dismissal stings like a slap. I sit there, stunned, as he strides out of the room without so much as a backward glance. The heavy door closes behind him with a thud, leaving me alone in the cavernous boardroom, my carefully crafted presentation still glowing on the screen.

I slump back in my chair, my chest tight with frustration and humiliation. I can't believe I read the situation so wrong. I thought I had it in the bag. That they'd be begging to innovate.

To partner. To win. Instead, I've been laughed out of the room by a misogynistic dinosaur who can't see past his own ego.

Disappointment settles like a lead weight in my stomach as the reality sinks in. I've blown it. All that work, all that preparation, for nothing. What am I going to tell the team back at CGPR? How can I face them after this epic failure?

I try to gather my composure. I can't let this setback break me. I've faced worse than this and come out swinging.

But even as I give myself the pep talk, I can't shake the nagging sense that this isn't just about Harcourt Foods. It's about everything—my career, my life, my priorities. I feel adrift and it's frightening. Suddenly I'm struck with the thought that if GreenShoots hadn't surprised us with the pitch request, I'd be doing camping things with my sister and her family, and I might even be enjoying it. I just want to retreat to my motel room, close the drapes, and lie on my bed. But first, I have to get out of this damn boardroom with my head held high.

I gather my things and stride out of the boardroom, my chin lifted in defiance even as my heart sinks. I can feel the VP's smug gaze boring into my back as he hovers near reception, but I refuse to give him the satisfaction of seeing me crumble.

As I navigate the wood-paneled corridors of Harcourt Foods' headquarters, my mind races with competing thoughts and emotions. Anger at the VP's dismissive attitude. Frustration at the missed opportunity. And a gnawing sense of self-doubt that I can't quite shake.

I pause in front of a floor-to-ceiling window by reception, staring out at the freeway and the Portland cityscape beyond. The city seems to pulse with energy and possibility, a stark contrast to the suffocating disappointment that engulfs me.

I need to focus on damage control, on finding a way to salvage this mess and prove my worth to Helen and the rest of the agency's executive team.

NINE

Back at the motel, I retreat to my room. I barely have the energy to check the news on my phone. Mount Spurr is still spewing ash and air traffic is still grounded across the United States. It looks like I'll be here for some time to come. Maybe Mom's suggestion to drive the eleven hundred miles to join them wasn't such a bad one.

I stare out the window, watching the rain cascade down the glass in steady rivulets. The gloomy weather perfectly matches my mood. I can't help but wallow in self-pity, feeling utterly alone and beaten. Whatever charm this little family-run motel held has disappeared, along with my humor.

For the first time since arriving, I'm thinking that if I have to be stuck in this city for whoever-knows-how-long, I should really be doing it in five-star comfort, with an on-site spa and room service. It also doesn't help that Dan works here and there's every chance we could bump into each other.

Instead of dissipating, my annoyance with what he said, and implied, has actually increased overnight and is now bordering on rage. No, I'm not a parent, Dan. But I am a woman, and I was once a frightened little girl growing into a teenager. Just like Chloe. Confused, scared, and overwhelmed, as I tried to make sense of the world and my place in it.

There's a reason I don't do 'me time,' because it gets dark, fast. Better to stay busy. Better not to dwell.

Despite all my professional accomplishments, I find myself seriously considering if I am indeed an imposter. It's the only logical explanation. I'm scared to look too deeply at my past successes, because truth be told, maybe it was just a case of right place, right time, and I'm not sure if I'm ready for that sort of hard truth. Of course, I've convinced myself that my ability to win new business was down to my fastidious research, and my obsession with getting into the mindset of my client's customers. But, you know what, maybe it's because the team at Channing Gabriel has built up such a great reputation, that I just have to walk into the room and manage not to fall over, and they will become a client regardless. Maybe they aren't signing up because of me, but in spite of me.

What is the opportunity debit of this supposed success? The long hours, the sacrifices, the missed opportunities for genuine personal connection. I've poured everything into my career, but at what cost? Losing out to Zoe because of an admin snafu, despite the months of groundwork I did to win GreenShoots. Hell, we wouldn't have even been invited into the room to pitch if it hadn't been for my efforts getting Channing Gabriel on their radar. The emptiness inside me grows with each passing minute, and I think for the first time in my life that I might be on the verge of completely losing my shit.

My phone buzzes, jolting me out of my melancholy musings.

It's a text from Dan:

> Hey Rachel, I feel terrible about how things were left last night. Please let me apologize. In person, not by text.

I hesitate, my finger hovering over the screen. Part of me wants to decline, to retreat further into my solitude. I really don't feel like putting a brave face on it all. Not today. But another part of me, the part that is becoming unhinged looking at these four walls, urges me to accept. After all, what do I have to lose? It's not like this week could get any worse.

I type out my reply:

> Sure, why not. Meet you in the lobby in 10?

> Thank you. See you there.

With a sigh, I drag myself off the bed and slip into a pair of flats. I catch a glimpse of my reflection in the mirror—tired eyes, slumped shoulders, a far cry from the polished PR executive I usually present to the world. But right now, I can't muster the energy to put on that mask.

I grab my purse and head out the door, steeling myself for Dan's grand apology. As I step into the elevator, while I firmly believe that everyone deserves a second chance, I can't help but wonder if this is a mistake. But I really do need to get out of the room, and some company, even if it's just an apologetic Dan, is too tempting to resist.

The doors slide open, and I spot Dan waiting in the lobby, his hands shoved into his pockets. He looks up as I approach, offering a tentative smile.

"Hey, thanks for seeing me," he says, his voice tinged with genuine gratitude.

I shrug, trying to appear nonchalant. "Well, it's not like I have anything better to do."

He chuckles softly, and for a moment, the tension between us eases.

"Do you mind if we go outside?" he asks, gesturing towards his car in the parking lot.

Dan opens my door, and I jump into the passenger seat quickly to avoid the rain.

He jogs around the car and drops into his own seat, shutting his door and shutting out the rain that has really started to come down now.

"Listen, Rachel, I wanted to apologize for my behavior last night," he begins, his tone sincere. "I was out of line, and I'm sorry."

I study his face, searching for any hint of insincerity, but all I find is genuine remorse. Slowly, I nod. "I appreciate that, Dan. It's been a tough week for both of us."

He sighs, running a hand through his hair. "Maybe, but that's no excuse. You were a guest in my house, and you were expressing an opinion. I shouldn't have reacted like that. I was out of line, and for that, I'm really sorry."

I shrug, "It's fine. Apology accepted. Water off a duck's back."

But even as I say it, I know it's not entirely true. It felt like a personal attack, and it hurt. It still does.

An awkward silence settles over us.

Dan shifts in his seat, his fingers tapping against the dash. "So, how are you holding up? With the ash cloud and everything?"

Part of me wants to maintain the professional facade, to insist that I'm fine and in control. But something about Dan's earnest expression compels me to be honest.

"It's been challenging," I admit, my voice quieter than I intended. "Today's meeting didn't go very well. I'm not used to being stuck like this, unable to do my job, unable to fix things. I hardly spend any time there, but I actually miss my condo. My stuff, my own bed—I've realized that I'm not good at living out of a small suitcase for more than a day or two."

He nods, understanding flickering in his eyes. "I get that.

It's hard to feel helpless, especially when you're used to being in control."

An awkward silence descends again, and I decide to use the moment to extricate myself from the car.

"I better get going." I search for the handle to open the door.

"Rachel," Dan blurts, "if you're not doing anything, and it sounds like you really don't want to spend any more time than necessary in your room, do you want to come over to the house? I know Chloe would be pleased to see you."

"From sincere apology to emotional blackmail. Smooth."

"She would!"

"I know," I laugh. "I'm teasing. I'd like to see her too."

"Chlo? I'm back. Rachel's here too." Dan shouts up the stairs as we enter the living room.

"Okay, Dad, I'll be down in a minute. Hey, Rachel." Chloe replies.

"Must have homework tonight." Dan opens the refrigerator and pulls out a bottle of craft beer. "Would you like a drink? A beer? Wine?"

"A glass of white would be lovely." With the day I've had, it really would.

As we sip our drinks, the tension dissipates, replaced by a tentative truce. But just as I begin to relax, Dan clears his throat, a sheepish expression on his face.

"Sorry again about last night," he admits, his eyes darting away from mine.

"It's okay," I manage, my voice carefully neutral. "You've apologized, let's move on."

He shrugs, his fingers picking at the label on his beer bottle. "I've gotten so used to making all the decisions since... I think I've confused 'being decisive' with 'I'm always right.' It's been eight years, but I'm still navigating how to cope. You know? I guess I'm so used to being *dad*, I've forgotten who Dan is."

I nod, understanding all too well the feeling of being disconnected from your own life, your own identity.

"It's hard," I say softly, "trying to figure out who the authentic you is, when everything around you is changing."

He meets my gaze, a flicker of surprise and gratitude in his eyes. "Yeah, exactly."

I instinctively reach out, my hand resting lightly on his arm, a gesture of comfort and understanding. "There's no rush. You've been through a lot. Give yourself time to heal, to find your footing again."

Dan takes a long sip of his beer, his eyes distant.

"You know, back when I was on the show, everything seemed so easy. The fame, the success, the adoration... it was like a drug. I got caught up in it all, letting it consume me."

He shakes his head, a rueful smile on his lips. "But I neglected what truly mattered—my family. I was so focused on my career, on chasing that next high, that next paycheck, that I didn't realize how much I was missing out on. And then, when Rebecca died..."

His voice catches, and I squeeze his arm gently, silently encouraging him to continue.

"I wasn't there for her, not the way I should have been. I was too busy, too self-absorbed. Chasing cash, but no idea what for. And now, every day, I carry that guilt with me."

I feel a lump forming in my throat, my heart aching for him, for the pain he's endured.

"Dan," I say softly, "you can't blame yourself. You wanted to be the provider. There's nothing wrong with that. You did the best you could, given the circumstances. And you're here now, for Chloe, being the father she needs. That's what matters."

He nods, blinking back the tears that glisten in his eyes.

"I just... I want to do better, to *be* better. For Chloe, for myself. I want to move on, let the light back into my life, into our lives. I don't know, maybe even date again."

I debate with myself for a moment whether to revisit the conversation, but there are still things left unsaid. Before I can revert to diplomacy, I blurt it out. "You know... moving on doesn't just mean dating again."

Dan's eyes flick toward me, guarded.

I press on. "It means accepting that things change. That *people* change." I glance toward the stairs. "Chloe's growing up. And she will always be your daughter, but she won't always be a child."

His jaw tightens, but he stays quiet.

"You didn't want to hear it last night," I continue gently. "But this is a fragile time for her. She's figuring out who she is, testing boundaries, wanting to prove she's more independent than she really is. Yes, she'll want to do things she's not ready for. Yes, she'll need your rules, your guidance, your advice..." I pause, making sure he's really listening. "But what she will need more than anything is your acceptance."

Dan exhales slowly, his fingers gripping the kitchen countertop just a little tighter. He doesn't argue. Doesn't deflect. Just lets the words settle.

Finally, he nods. "You're right." His voice is low, thoughtful. "I know you are. I just... I don't want her to get hurt."

"She *will* get hurt," I say softly. "That's all part of growing up. It's unavoidable. But if she knows you're there, that there's a safety net, no matter what... That she doesn't have to be afraid to talk to you, that's what really matters."

Dan is quiet for a long moment, staring out the window at

the dark water beyond. Then, with a small, humorless chuckle, he shakes his head. "I think you're right."

I smirk. "I know I'm right."

He huffs a quiet laugh.

I shift slightly. "Okay, serious question. What do you do for fun?"

Dan blinks. "What?"

"For fun," I repeat. "You do know what fun is, right?"

He looks genuinely thrown, like it's the first time anyone's asked him that in years.

"Uh..." He rubs the back of his neck. "I work on the boathouse when I can. I work out after I drop Chloe off at school. I work at the motel." He shrugs. "Other than reading, not a lot."

I frown. "I hear the word *work* a lot. Okay, but what about friends? Hanging out?"

Dan's expression turns slightly rueful. "Yeah... not so much. James and my friends tried for a long time. Kept inviting me out, getting me to go to events, meetups, whatever. Even signed me up to some of those dating sites. I always had an excuse." He sighs. "After a few years... they just stopped asking."

I study him for a moment. The way he says it, there's no bitterness, just a quiet acceptance. But it still makes something in my chest tighten.

"They probably just assumed you needed space," I say carefully.

Dan nods, but his gaze stays distant. "Yeah. Maybe."

Silence lingers again, but this time, I feel it differently.

"You know," I say lightly, nudging his arm, "you could start saying yes."

Dan lets out a small sigh. "Yeah." He looks at me then, a small smirk tugging at the corner of his mouth. "Maybe."

It's not a promise. But it's something I can work with. After today I need a win. Badly.

Not just a work win—a personal one. Something that reminds me I can still make things happen. That I still know how to read people, shape stories, spark momentum.

And I can't help thinking back to that early conversation with Dan. To the way he smiled when he talked about acting like it was a long-lost friend he wasn't sure he had the right to miss.

To the way he brushed it off like it didn't matter anymore —like it shouldn't matter.

But what if it did?

What if I could help him believe in it again? In himself again?

He'd never ask. That much I know. And honestly, that's half the problem. People like Dan—quietly decent, relentlessly selfless—they're so used to putting others first, they forget they ever had a dream of their own.

But I remember.

I saw it. The flicker.

And then, like a spark igniting, an idea takes hold in my mind.

"What if... What if you threw a party? For finishing the boathouse, to celebrate your new start?"

He looks at me, skepticism mingling with curiosity in his expression.

"What kind of party?"

"A housewarming party! A chance to celebrate this new chapter, to surround yourself with people who care about you, who support you. It could be like drawing a line in the sand, marking the beginning of something new and wonderful."

I can see the wheels turning in his head as he considers it, the initial reluctance giving way to a glimmer of possibility. Then, just as quickly, a cloud seems to pass behind his eyes.

"I don't know, Rachel. It's been so long since I've invited anyone over. I don't really have friends anymore."

I lean in closer, my voice filled with conviction.

"That's exactly why you need to do this, Dan. It's time to start living again, to embrace the love and the light that's all around you. This party could be the first step, a chance to heal, to find joy and purpose again. And even if you don't want to do it for you. Do it for Chloe."

He stares at me for a long moment, the conflict playing out across his face. And then, slowly, a smile begins to tug at the corners of his mouth.

"Okay," he says. "Let's do it. Let's throw a party."

And as he clinks his bottle against my wine glass, sealing our pact, I feel a surge of warmth and hope blossoming in my chest. I remember the reruns Mom used to make Claire and I watch when we were kids, shows from the eighties I think, *Highway to Heaven* and *Quantum Leap*. Maybe, just maybe, this unexpected detour in Maine is my *Quantum Leap* moment—leaving a little bit of cheer and happiness with those who need it, before I take my leave and head back to Chicago.

I sip from my glass of wine as I watch Dan's expression shift from hesitation to determination. It's a subtle change, but I can see the glimmer of hope in his eyes, the way his shoulders straighten ever so slightly.

"So, where do we start?" he asks, leaning forward on his elbows. "I haven't exactly been *one of the guys,* lately. I've been hiding out at the house, focusing on Chloe. There's a really good chance that no one will show up."

I can't help but chuckle at his self-deprecating humor. It's endearing.

"Well, first things first, and I'm assuming you don't mind me organizing things, we need to make a guest list. Who are the people you want to surround yourself with, the ones who have been there for you through thick and thin?"

Dan furrows his brow, lost in thought for a moment. "I guess there's my brother, James. He's always had my back. And maybe some of the guys from the boat club, the ones who knew Rebecca..."

His voice trails off, and I can see the pain flicker across his face at the mention of his late wife. Instinctively, I reach out and place my hand on his, giving it a gentle squeeze.

"That's a great start," I say softly, my thumb tracing circles on his skin. "And what about Chloe's friends? I'm sure she'd love to have some of her classmates over for the party, and you could get to know their parents."

Just then, Chloe bounds down the stairs, her face alight with excitement. "Did I hear something about a party?" she asks eagerly.

"Rachel here has convinced me to throw a housewarming," Dan explains, still sounding a bit hesitant.

"A housewarming party? For me?" Chloe practically squeals with delight.

"For us, actually," he corrects.

"Whatever. A party! Oh my gosh, that would be amazing!"

She spins around the room, already bubbling over with eagerness. "We could have a DJ and dancing! And snacks! Ooh, what about a sundae bar?"

Her enthusiasm is infectious, and I can't help but grin. This is exactly the reaction I'd been hoping for.

"See?" I say to Dan, my smile triumphant. "Told you she'd be thrilled."

Dan shakes his head, but I can see a smile tugging at his lips. "Alright, alright. I can see I'm outnumbered here."

"Yes!" Chloe exclaims, rushing over to hug him tightly. "Thank you, thank you, thank you! This is going to be epic. When can we have it?"

As I watch their embrace, a thought occurs to me. "Hey Dan, what kind of budget are we looking at for this shindig?"

He waves a dismissive hand. "Don't worry about that. We'll make it work."

I raise an eyebrow. "I appreciate the sentiment, but parties can add up fast. Why don't we keep it simple? We could do a potluck, have people bring dishes to share. And I can pick up some balloons, streamers, that kind of thing. Doesn't have to be fancy to be fun."

Dan looks at me, a mix of gratitude and something else I can't quite place in his eyes. "I appreciate it. But if we're going to do it, let's do it properly."

"Okay then. Let me get some quotes and put together a plan."

"Whoa, whoa. I'm not expecting you to organize everything. I can manage—"

"Tell me, Dan," I interrupt him, "when was the last time you threw a party? No, scrap that. When was the last time you even attended a party?"

He laughs, "Oh, come on. A keg in the corner, popcorn, beer pong, some sodas for the kids... how hard can it be to organize a few drinks?"

"What you've just described is a fraternity bash. That is *not* a party. Look, trust me on this. Leave it with me and I'll wow you."

"I feel like I should contribute at least."

"You are contributing! You're paying for it. But please, I need this. I need a project to work on, otherwise I'll just be sitting in my motel room having an existential crisis while I wait for the ash cloud to pass."

"Well, okay then. When you put it like that."

"Thank you. But we still need a date. Any birthdays coming up, or significant dates—"

Dan's eyes widen as a thought strikes him. "You know what? Let's do it this weekend. Why wait?"

I nearly drop the pen I'm holding. "This weekend? But it's

Wednesday! We'd need to pull everything together in just a few days and—"

"Exactly," he interrupts, his voice brimming with excitement. "Let's go all out. Hire a caterer, get some live music, the works."

My mind reels at the sudden shift. "Dan, that's a lovely thought, but the expense... I mean, a full-scale party like that could cost a significant amount."

He waves off my concern, his eyes gleaming with determination. "It's fine. Like I said, let's do it properly."

I bite my lip, torn between the desire to create a magical experience for Dan and Chloe and the practical voice in my head screaming about budgets and financial responsibility. "I hear you, but we need to be realistic. You're a single dad, and I know how tough it can be to make ends meet."

Dan glances over to Chloe, who is already on her phone messaging her friends with the news. He leans forward conspiratorially. "I appreciate your concern. I really do. But I've got this covered. Trust me."

The sincerity in his voice gives me confidence, but I can't quite shake the nagging worry. "I do trust you, Dan. I just don't want you to overextend yourself for the sake of one party."

He grins, a mischievous glint in his eye. "Who says it's just one party? Maybe I'm planning on making this an annual tradition."

Dan reaches into his pocket and pulls out a sleek black credit card. He scribbles a figure on a scrap of paper and slides them both across the table towards me.

"What's this?"

"The budget for the party," he says, as if it's the most natural thing in the world. "Whatever you need to make this perfect. I just don't like to talk about money in front of Chloe."

I stare at the figure on the paper, my heart pounding. It's more than I would have ever imagined spending on a housewarming party. More than I would have thought Dan could afford.

"Dan, this is... Are you sure about this? It's a lot of money."

He leans forward, his eyes locking with mine. "I made a lot during my time on the show—more than I knew what to do with at the time. I invested some of it, and I've been careful since. It's not an issue."

A faint smile plays on his lips, and I catch the flicker of pride in his eyes. It's clear he's not just throwing money at the problem—he's thought it through.

Reassured, I reach for the card, my fingers brushing against his, a jolt of what feels like electricity running through me. I glance up, wondering if he feels it too.

But he's already moving on, reaching for his phone. "Right," he says, pulling out a pen and notepad from a kitchen drawer. "I'm going to write down some contact numbers. My guest list. I'll also write down anyone I think might be useful. I think I have a few caterers and suppliers I used when we first bought the house, but I'll warn you now, some of these numbers might be dead now."

Dan tops my glass up and good to his word, he copies out the names and numbers for me.

"Okay, first things first. Theme. I'm thinking 'Enchanted Forest.' We can transform your backyard into a magical woodland wonderland."

I close my eyes, picturing it. Twinkling lights strung up in the trees, garlands of greenery, maybe even a few whimsical toadstools scattered about.

"I love it," Dan says, his voice soft. "It's perfect."

As Dan scribbles down more numbers, I lean back in my chair, running a finger over the rim of my wineglass. It feels good to be planning something, to have a project that requires creativity and focus. I know I'm doing this for Chloe—she deserves a magical night, something to celebrate. And I'm doing it for Dan, too—helping him open up to his friends and neighbors again.

But there's another part of me that's desperate for this to work, and I'm not sure it's entirely altruistic. Maybe it's because the idea of being useful, of doing something tangible, keeps the gnawing sense of failure at bay. An elaborate distraction. Easier to plan a party than to sit in that motel room, dissecting every moment from today's meeting. Wondering if I'm as good as I thought. Or worse—realizing I've been bluffing all along. Or even worse, realizing that maybe I've been bluffing my way through my entire career.

I shake off the thought, focusing on the task at hand. Organizing this party gives me purpose—it feels like something I can actually control, unlike the ash cloud or the Harcourt deal or the way my entire life feels suspended, stuck in some sort of limbo. If I can pull this off, if I can make it beautiful and memorable and perfect for Chloe, maybe I can prove to myself that I'm still good at something.

"Hey, you okay?" Dan's voice cuts through my thoughts, and I realize I've been staring blankly at the notepad.

I muster a smile and nod. "Yeah, just thinking through ideas. I've got this covered."

He gives me a warm, appreciative smile, and something in my chest loosens just a little. I'm not going to let my own insecurities ruin this. Not for them. And not for me.

TEN

———— ♥ ————————

I drive myself to Dan's in the big red beast and opt for quite a circuitous route, convincing myself that I'm sightseeing, when the truth is, I just really love driving an enormous pickup. I am officially converted.

I pull up to Dan's house, the engine rumbling like a small earthquake as I shift into park. It's ridiculous—practically a monster truck compared to my sleek city car back home—but at this point, I've just accepted that Maine and I have very different ideas about appropriate transportation.

Dan steps out onto the porch as I kill the engine, arms crossed, eyebrows raised. "Compensating for something?"

I smirk, hopping down from the driver's seat—seriously, this thing requires climbing—and shut the door with a solid *thunk*. "Yes. For the absolute lack of functional rental cars in this state."

He whistles low, eyeing the truck. "You planning on hauling lumber after the party? Maybe joining a construction crew?"

I toss my keys in the air and catch them. "Actually, I was

thinking of starting a side hustle in competitive mudding. Think I could pull it off?"

Dan tilts his head, pretending to consider. "I don't know. You might need to swap out the heels for work boots first."

I glance down at my ankle boots and shrug. "Fashionable and functional. I'm a woman of many talents."

He chuckles, stepping forward to grab the bags from my hands. "Come on, city girl. Let's get you inside before you start scaring the locals."

I follow him up the steps, grinning. "You are aware you're one of the locals, right?"

"Yeah," he calls over his shoulder, "which is why I'm speaking from experience."

I shake my head, amused, as he pushes open the door and steps aside to let me in. The house smells like fresh wood and coffee, and something about it—about being here—feels oddly... easy. Familiar, even.

Which is a dangerous feeling.

I shake it off, dropping my keys onto the counter.

"Alright. Let's plan a party."

"So," he says, leaning against the fridge, "what's left to do? I can help."

I pause, hands hovering over the checklist. I can feel his restlessness, the way his eyes keep flicking toward the backyard, where the half-painted boathouse sits waiting.

I smirk. "You really want to help with party prep?"

He shrugs, pushing off the fridge. "I don't mind."

I arch an eyebrow. "You don't mind, or you'd rather be outside putting another coat of paint on the boathouse?"

Dan scoffs. "Do you think it needs it?"

I cross my arms, tilting my head. "You clearly do, the way you're looking at it..." I let the sentence hang, teasing.

His mouth twitches, like he wants to argue but knows I've got him. He glances out the window, just for a second.

I sigh dramatically, waving him off. "Go. Paint. Bond with your structure. I can handle the rest."

Dan hesitates. "You sure?"

I gesture to the neatly arranged decorations, which all need to be hanged. "I've got this. Besides, you'll probably just get in the way."

He rolls his eyes but doesn't argue. "Fine. But if you need anything—"

"I won't," I cut in.

He points a finger at me as he backs toward the door. "If you change your mind—"

"I won't," I repeat, grinning.

He huffs out a laugh and finally gives in. "Alright, alright. Yell if you need me."

I watch as he heads outside, already pulling his hoodie over his head like he's been waiting all morning to get back to work. The second he steps onto the dock, his shoulders relax, and I shake my head.

Yeah. He really wants the boathouse to shine.

At ten on the dot, a delivery driver arrives with the printed invitations we'll use for everyone who lives locally. I stare at the colorful array splayed across the kitchen table, my mind buzzing with possibilities. Dan's housewarming party is the perfect opportunity to orchestrate his big acting comeback announcement.

He may not know it yet, but this is exactly what he needs.

The gold-embossed invitations feel suitably fancy for announcing a major life-changing event. They're perfect.

I grab my favorite pen, the one I usually reserve for signing client engagement contracts, and start jotting down ideas for the invitation wording. It has to be just the right blend of intriguing and mysterious, enough to pique people's curiosity without giving away the surprise.

"You are cordially invited to The Maine Event, a housewarming soirée, celebrating new beginnings and exciting revelations."

I read it aloud, tapping the pen against my chin. "Hmm, not bad."

Dan may be hesitant at first, but I know deep down he's been longing to revive his acting career. He just needs a little nudge in the right direction.

I gather up the chosen invitations, envisioning the look of surprise and gratitude on Dan's face when he realizes what I've done for him. Sure, it's a bit unconventional to make such a big decision without consulting him, but sometimes people need a push—especially when they're standing on the edge of something great, and refusing to take the leap.

As I stuff the invitations into crisp white envelopes, anticipation builds in my chest. This party isn't just about Dan's acting comeback; it's about showing him that he has someone in his corner, cheering him on and believing in his dreams.

I seal the last envelope with a flourish, a smile playing at the corners of my lips.

Better to beg for forgiveness than asking for permission, right?

Well.

Here goes nothing.

I tuck the invitations into my purse, my fingers lingering for a moment on the soft flap of the final envelope—like part of me knows I'm crossing some kind of invisible line. But I've made peace with it. Dan might not see it now, but he will.

Sometimes, we need to believe for people, when they can't do it themselves—just until they remember how.

The Portland Tribune office is abuzz with activity as I step through the glass doors, a stack of invitations tucked discreetly in my purse.

The air is thick with the scent of fresh coffee and printer ink, the clack of keyboards filling the space as reporters talk rapidly into phones or hunch over their desks. I scan the room, mentally cataloging the energy. Newsrooms are a lot like PR agencies—organized chaos, fueled by caffeine and looming deadlines.

I approach the receptionist's desk, shoulders back, confidence dialed to maximum PR mode.

This isn't just a party.

It's a pivot.

And it starts now.

"Hi there," I say, flashing my most approachable but professional smile. "I was hoping to speak with someone about an upcoming event. It's quite exclusive, and I think your readers would be very interested."

The receptionist, a young woman with a sleek bob and inquisitive eyes, leans forward slightly. "Oh. What kind of event are we talking about?"

I lower my voice conspiratorially, like I'm letting her in on a massive scoop. "Let's just say it involves a beloved local celebrity making a major announcement. I can't reveal too much yet, but trust me, it's going to be the talk of the town."

Her eyebrows shoot up, and I can practically see the wheels turning in her head.

"Intriguing!" she says, grabbing a notepad. "What kind of announcement?

"Something that'll have everyone talking." I let the pause stretch. "A new chapter. A return. Maybe even... a redemption story."

She exhales, clearly hooked. "Let me see if our entertainment editor is available. One sec."

As she picks up the phone, I allow myself a small, satisfied smile. The seed has been planted, and I can already sense the buzz starting to build.

With the newspaper piece set in motion, I shift gears and set off on my next mission—delivering the invitations to Dan's old friends, the ones he's been so good at avoiding all these years.

I head back to Biddeford in the big red beast, this time taking the time to drive through town.

Not because I have to.

Just because...

Okay, fine—I love this truck. I'm officially converted.

There's something weirdly empowering about sitting up high, feeling the power of the engine beneath me, watching the quaint Maine scenery roll past.

Biddeford isn't big or flashy, but there's something charming about it.

It's a town with history, with character, with people who have known each other for decades.

Unlike Chicago, where everything moves at breakneck speed, where people's faces blur together, where even the friendships can feel... transactional.

I pull up outside the first house on my list—Karl's—a modest two-story home with a front porch swing and an old Labrador watching me from the steps

I step out, invitation in hand, and approach the door. I know these people don't expect me.

Hell, they don't know me at all.

But I know they mean something to Dan. His old crew, the ones who tried to pull him back into the world after his wife died.

The ones he let slip away.

I knock twice. The door swings open to reveal a broad-shouldered man in his late thirties, his brow furrowing as he takes me in.

"Can I help you?"

"Hi." I smile, extending the envelope. "I'm Rachel. A friend of Dan's. He's hosting a housewarming party, and I wanted to make sure you got an invite."

A pause. His gaze flicks to the truck, back to me.

"You from around here?"

I shake my head. "Just visiting. But I figured Dan's friends might appreciate a chance to catch up with him."

Karl's expression softens slightly. He takes the envelope, turning it over in his hands.

"Haven't seen Dan in a while."

I nod. "Yeah, I get that a lot."

There's a beat. Then, to my surprise, he chuckles, shaking his head.

"Man, always was a stubborn ass. Guess it's time someone dragged him back into civilization."

I grin. "That's the plan."

One down.

I climb back into the beast of a truck, key in the next address into the satnav, and rev the engine.

On to the next stop.

ELEVEN

By the time I get back to the house, the sun is already beginning its lazy descent behind the trees, casting a warm amber glow across the backyard. My heart's still thudding from the whirlwind of the last few hours—tracking down Dan's old friends, delivering the invitations, and alerting the press about the big reveal.

Technically, I didn't lie. I just... didn't tell him. Not yet.

Now, the garden is slowly transforming. The last of the string lights are being untangled, a few folding chairs have already arrived from the supplier and are stacked, ready to be set up tomorrow. There's a buzz of potential in the air and I love it.

The party is happening. Caterers are confirmed, menu finalized—local, fresh, and just upscale enough to impress without making guests feel like they can't relax. I even found an event rental company willing to do a last-minute drop-off and installation of tables and décor tomorrow. Enchanted Forest, as Pinterest promised me.

I stop near the porch, brushing dirt from my hands and surveying the scene with a strange mix of nerves and pride. It's all coming together. I just hope Dan sees it the way I do—as a celebration, not a trap.

As if on cue, the screen door creaks open behind me, and Chloe barrels out, her overnight bag swinging from her arm. Her eyes are wide with excitement, and everything is suddenly moving fast again.

"Dad! Dad!" she calls, weaving between the tables until she reaches Dan, who's busy tidying up the decking. "Sarah just called! Her mom said I can sleep over tonight! Can I go?"

Dan straightens, wiping his hands on his jeans, and glances at me with a crooked smile before turning back to Chloe.

"I don't know, Chloe. It's a school night."

"Sarah's mom will drop me off at school tomorrow with Sarah."

"That's not what I'm worried about. I'm pretty sure the two of you are going to stay up all night gossiping and you'll be exhausted tomorrow."

"I promise, we won't. Anyway, Sarah's mom has a strict lights-out at nine rule."

Dan considers Chloe's request, eyeballing his daughter like a drill sergeant before breaking into a grin.

"OK, then. You all packed?"

Chloe nods enthusiastically. "Yeah! I already got my stuff ready. Her mom's picking me up in ten minutes!"

Dan's brows lift in mild surprise. "Am I that predictable?"

"Yes," Chloe states matter-of-factly.

"You've got your pajamas? Your toothbrush?"

"Yes, Dad," she says with a dramatic eye roll, and I can't help but stifle a laugh.

Dan glances at me with a helpless grin, and I shrug. "Sounds like she's got it covered."

He sighs, feigning defeat. "Okay. Go on, then. Just

remember the rules—be polite, say thank you, and don't stay up all night giggling."

Chloe gives him an exasperated look. "Dad."

He holds up his hands in surrender. "Alright, alright. Go have fun."

She throws her arms around his waist, squeezing tight, and then glances up at me. "Bye, Rachel!"

"Have fun," I reply with a wave.

When she's gone, the yard feels quieter, more spacious somehow. Dan watches her go with a lingering smile, and I catch him running a hand through his hair, like he's not entirely sure what to do with himself now.

I lean against one of the tables, crossing my arms. "You look like a man who just lost his best friend."

He chuckles softly, glancing back at me. "It's weird, you know? I get so used to her being around that when she's not, it feels like the house just... stops."

"She's lucky to have you," I say, and he gives me a faint, almost bashful smile.

After a moment, he clears his throat, shifting his weight. "Hey," he says, a bit more casual, "since I'm unexpectedly kid-free tonight... you want to go grab a drink? There's a place just down by the water—nothing fancy, but they make a mean gin and tonic."

His voice is so nonchalant, but there's a flicker of uncertainty in his eyes, like he's half-expecting me to say no. I smile and tilt my head. "You asking me out, Dan?"

"No!" he blurts. "I mean, I'm asking if you'd like to go out for a drink. I don't know. You're welcome to hang out here, I just thought—"

"Only if I get to pick the playlist in the car."

He barks out a laugh, giving me a sideways glance. "Fine. But if I hear any Top 40 pop nonsense, I'm leaving you on the side of the road to fend for yourself."

Dan unlocks the car with a chirp, and as we slide into the front seats, he glances over at me. "Alright. Your choice of playlist, right? Just remember, this truck doesn't respond well to auto-tuned heartbreak anthems."

I smirk, scrolling through my phone. "Relax. I won't make you suffer through *Taylor's Version* tonight. How do you feel about a bit of Arctic Monkeys?"

He nods in approval. "Okay, you've bought yourself five minutes of respect."

"Five? That's it?" I laugh. "Tough crowd."

The drive winds gently along the riverbank, the sky streaked with the colors of sunset—pink bleeding into indigo, with hints of gold flickering through the trees. There's a peacefulness to it, the kind you don't really get in the city. I lap it up.

Dan's hand rests lazily on the wheel, the other drumming lightly on the door in time with the music. "You know," he says, "it's weird not having Chloe in the back seat giving me grief about my driving. Or asking why the moon's following us."

"She's a smart kid," I say. "And very persuasive. The lights-out-at-nine promise was impressive."

He laughs. "She's a force of nature. But I still second-guessed it. I worry she'll wake up scared or miss home, or... I don't know. I probably overthink everything."

"You do," I say lightly, then catch myself. "But that's not a bad thing. I mean, sure, maybe you're a bit overprotective—"

"Oh, thanks."

"—but it's only because you care so much. She's your whole world. And that's... kind of beautiful."

He goes quiet for a beat. "I just want her to have something solid, you know? Something reliable. Not like... here one day, gone the next."

I nod, watching the trees blur past the window. "She's lucky, Dan. She really is."

It takes me a moment to realize I've fallen quiet, and he glances over. "What?"

I shake my head, offering a small smile. "Nothing. Just... wishing I'd had a dad like you."

He doesn't say anything, but I see his knuckles tighten slightly on the wheel, and he casts me a quick look of something almost like sympathy.

"Was he... not around?" he asks gently.

"Nope," I say, my voice light but clipped. "Died in an industrial accident. Mum was left with two of us under six."

Dan winces. "Sorry."

He doesn't push further, just nods, and turns the music up a notch. We let the song fill the silence.

But I feel it settle inside me—this strange mix of longing and admiration. Watching Dan with Chloe over the past few days, the way he listens to her, makes her laugh, sees her— really sees her—it's something I never experienced myself. And it stirs something I didn't expect. Not envy exactly. More like... hope. That it's possible. That men like that exist. That love can look like that.

As we pull into the gravel lot outside the bar, Dan throws me a sidelong glance. "Just so we're clear," he says, "if you order anything with a little umbrella in it, I'm going to mock you relentlessly."

"I'd expect nothing less," I shoot back. "I'm from Chicago remember, not one of you flaky actor types."

He chuckles. "We'll see about that."

The bar turns out to be a welcoming, slightly nautical spot decorated with old lobster traps and faded maritime flags. It smells like cedar and salt, and the playlist is all early-2010s indie—Foster the People, The Lumineers, a little early Florence.

We grab a booth tucked into the corner, half-shielded by a

tall wooden partition. Dan orders for us—two gin and tonics—then looks at me with a smirk.

"Unless you're the type who'll switch it up and demand an oat milk espresso martini?"

I arch a brow. "Please. What do you take me for? I'm from Chicago. I only do oat milk martinis on long-haul flights or after breakups."

He laughs, low and warm, and I realize this is the most relaxed I've seen him.

The drinks arrive, sweating gently in their glasses. We clink.

"To surprise nights off," I offer.

"And responsible parenting via sleepovers," he adds.

We settle in, the buzz of conversation around us humming pleasantly in the background.

"So," he says, leaning in slightly, "tell me something about you that isn't on LinkedIn."

I blink. "That's a very PR way of asking for secrets."

"Guilty. Come on. Something random. Embarrassing. Like... you used to think narwhals weren't real, or you were in a serious fan club for a boy band."

I smirk. "Easy. I used to write fanfiction for the Powerpuff Girls. Blossoms and heartbreak and dramatic monologues. Eight-year-old me had range."

Dan bursts out laughing. "Wow. I was not ready for that. Powerpuff Girls? That's intense. Which one were you?"

"Bubbles, obviously. But with Blossom's hair accessories."

He places a hand over his heart. "This is the greatest confession I've ever heard in a bar."

"Your turn," I say, pointing my straw at him. Dan leans back in the booth, a crooked grin playing on his lips. "Alright, my first celebrity crush was Avril Lavigne."

I raise my brows. "Sk8er Boi Avril?"

"The one and only." He shrugs, not even pretending to be

embarrassed. "The tie, the eyeliner, the whole 'don't care what you think' vibe? It was a full-blown obsession. I may or may not have tried to learn guitar to impress no one in particular."

I burst out laughing. "Please tell me there's photographic evidence."

"There is. And it's buried deep where no one will ever find it."

"Tragic. The world deserves to see Dan-the-pop-punk-phase."

"You laugh now, but I nailed the 'brooding in a hoodie' look. Some say I peaked in 2004."

"Some being you?"

"Obviously."

We fall into a rhythm after that—exchanging stories, teasing each other about our teenage music tastes, bad fashion choices, our favorite childhood snacks. He tells me about the time he accidentally locked himself out of a theater in full costume and had to scale a fire escape in tights. I tell him about a college pitch meeting where I used the word 'disruption' so many times I gave myself a migraine.

The laughter comes easy, like we've done this a hundred times before.

But it's not just funny. It's comfortable.

Dan listens—not just waits to talk, but actually listens. He asks follow-up questions. Smiles in all the right places. Like he's paying attention to more than just the words.

And I realize, somewhere in the middle of all this, that I'm not used to being this seen. Not without being on. Not without performing. And it's... nice.

Too nice.

So, I flick a peanut at him from the little snack dish on the table. "Still can't believe you were a Black Star."

He catches it and grins. "It was a moment. Don't judge me."

"Oh, I'm absolutely judging you," I tease. "But respectfully."

He leans back in the booth, his gaze resting on me for a beat too long. "You're different when you're not pitching something."

That catches me off guard. "Different how?"

"I don't know," he says, swirling the ice in his glass. "More... you, I guess."

I don't know what to say to that. So, I take a sip and deflect with another question. "This is your hangout, then?"

He shrugs. "Not really. I used to come here when... Well, back when I actually had a social life."

"Before Chloe," I guess, and he nods.

"It's not like I mind," he says quickly, almost defensively. "But yeah. Things are different now. Priorities shift."

I tilt my head, studying him. "You ever think about getting back into acting? Or something else, maybe? You've got this energy that just... belongs in front of people."

He laughs, shaking his head. "Nah. That ship's sailed. But you're not the first person to suggest it."

"What about teaching?" I offer. "I saw you with the kids at the rehearsals. You were great with them."

He glances at me, a little surprised. "You think so?"

I nod. "Totally. You brought out their confidence without making them feel silly or self-conscious. They loved it."

He takes a slow sip of his whiskey, mulling it over. "I like it, helping out at the school, I mean. But teaching means evenings and weekends—prime Chloe time. I'm not sure I'm ready to give that up. Besides, part of me feels like I'd be helping other people's kids at the expense of my own."

I give him a gentle smile. "You're a good dad, you know that?"

He doesn't respond, just gives me a shy sort of grin and swirls the ice in his glass.

"So," he says, shifting gears, "you never really answered my question the other night. What's with the PR obsession? You sure that's your life's calling?"

I smile wryly. "Absolutely. It's more than just work. I love it. I fell into it by accident, to be honest. Interned for the summer after my sophomore year and I knew straight away that's what I wanted to do when I graduated. There's something thrilling about crafting a story, finding the angle that'll hook people. It's like getting into their minds and figuring out what makes them tick. Building awareness. Making connections. I guess I love the challenge of it."

"But does it make you happy?"

The question lingers between us, heavier than I expected. I hesitate.

"Sometimes. It's rewarding when things go right. But it's exhausting, too. Working for a big firm means constantly being available. It never really stops."

He nods, understanding in his eyes. "You know... to do your job well, you kind of have to be something of an actor too. Pitching, convincing, persuading..."

I laugh. "I never thought of it like that."

He grins and picks up his pen from the table, absently sketching on a napkin while I watch him, curiosity piqued.

"What are you doodling?" I ask.

He glances at me and then, almost reluctantly, slides the napkin across the table. Instead of pictures, there are words: *character or actor?*

I look up at him, raising an eyebrow. "What's this?"

He shrugs, giving me that crooked half-smile. "Just something I've been thinking about lately. About... being who people expect, versus being who you really are."

I trace the words with my fingertip, my mind whirring with thoughts. "So... which are you?" I challenge.

His smile turns wistful. "That's what I'm still trying to figure out."

I glance down at the napkin again, considering it. "I think... maybe we're all both. We act because we're supposed to. Because it's what people need from us. But sometimes, we slip out of the role, and that's when we're real."

His gaze lingers on me, like he's seeing me differently, more clearly than before. I don't know what to do with this sudden intensity, so I lift my glass and drain the last of my gin.

"Guess I'm not the only philosopher in the room tonight," he teases.

I roll my eyes but can't help but laugh. "Blame the gin."

"Blame the company," he counters, and there's something almost tender in the way he looks at me.

I reach for the napkin and slip it into my pocket. Something about those words—scrawled in his messy handwriting, passed across a sticky table—hits me in the chest. I don't know why. But it feels like a question I've been avoiding for a long time. One I'm sure I don't have an answer for.

"So, what about the rest of your life, then?" he asks, a teasing glint in his eye. "Are you one of those career women who doesn't believe in relationships, or have you just been fending off a line of suitors?"

I chuckle, leaning back in the booth. "A few blind dates here and there. Usually set up by friends who think they know what I need better than I do."

He grins. "And do they?"

"God, no." I shake my head with a laugh. "They're always nice enough, but never... wow. You know? We'd have a perfectly civil evening, eat something overpriced, laugh at the right moments. Then we both go home and never call each other again."

Dan lifts a brow. "Ghosted?"

"No, it's more mutual apathy." I smile wryly. "Like we both quietly agree to let the whole thing die a dignified death."

He laughs, warm and unguarded. "Well, for what it's worth, I think you're great company."

I raise an eyebrow. "Careful, Dan. Sounds like you're flirting."

He spreads his hands innocently. "Just making an observation."

I tilt my head, studying him. "What about you? Have you dated since...?"

He shakes his head. "Not really. There's been no one serious. No one, period, if I'm honest. Between Chloe and the motel and... everything, it never felt like the right time."

"That's understandable," I say gently. "But... maybe it's time you thought about going on a date. You're good company too. Funny, decent. Not bad on the eyes. Maybe invite a potential special someone to the party."

He smirks. "You're laying it on thick tonight."

"Well, I'm in PR," I grin. "Selling people is my job."

He sobers slightly, tapping the side of his glass. "It's not that I'm closed off to the idea. It's just... Chloe. I don't want to confuse her. She's already had enough upheaval. And what if someone does come along and it gets messy?"

I nod, understanding. "Yeah. My mom dated another teacher from her school once and I tell you, Claire and I were awful about it. Acted up, gave her such a hard time. To this day, I don't know if it came to a natural end, or if we just made it impossible for them. Unforgivable, really. It was years before she tried again."

Dan gives a small smile. "Exactly."

There's a quiet moment between us, not awkward, just thoughtful. Then he lifts his glass again. "But... I promise to consider it."

"Good," I say. "And I promise to go on another blind date...

in, oh, about four months, when I have a free hour in my schedule."

He laughs, shaking his head. "You really know how to romance a guy."

"I aim to impress," I reply, raising my glass to clink against his again.

We step out of the bar and into the crisp night air, the briny scent of the ocean drifting in on the breeze. The streets are quiet, lit by the soft amber glow of the streetlights. I hug my coat tighter around me as Dan unlocks the car.

"That was fun," I say, glancing over at him as we walk. "Thanks for the company."

He casts me a look that's all soft edges and crinkled eyes. "Thanks for saying yes."

We reach the car, and he opens the passenger door for me, his hand hovering for a second like he's debating whether to say something else. I slide in, but he doesn't move right away. Instead, he leans on the frame of the car, looking at me with a kind of quiet thoughtfulness.

"You know," he says slowly, "I don't do this much. Go out. Relax. Talk."

I smile gently. "You could've fooled me."

He shrugs one shoulder. "I guess... it's just easy with you. You get it."

I don't reply right away—just meet his eyes and hold his gaze for a beat too long. And in that moment, something shifts. Not dramatically. Nothing explosive. Just a subtle awareness. A sense that maybe—just maybe—we're more than co-conspirators in a school play or two people stuck in the same small town for very different reasons.

Just... two people who enjoy being around each other. Maybe a little more than they're willing to admit.

Dan clears his throat and straightens up, knocking twice on the car roof before moving around to the driver's side.

"Alright. Homeward bound. This housewarming party isn't going to organize itself."

As he pulls out onto the road, the silence in the car isn't uncomfortable. It's full of everything unsaid.

And for once, I don't feel the need to fill it.

Back at my motel, the glow from the reception area spills onto the lot, and for a moment, neither of us moves. Dan kills the engine and leans back in his seat, exhaling slowly like the night is finally catching up with him.

"Thanks again," he says quietly.

I nod, smiling, though there's a flicker of something deeper beneath it. "Any time."

We say goodnight without fanfare—no lingering looks, no dramatic pauses. Just a simple, warm farewell. But as I enter my room and peel off my jacket, the weight of the evening settles around me like a favorite sweater I didn't know I'd been missing.

It's not just the drinks, or the laughter, or the napkin still tucked into my coat pocket. It's the feeling of having been seen—really seen—for the first time in a while. Dan's questions, his quiet observations, the way he listens without interrupting... it all made me feel like I wasn't just performing, or selling, or spinning something for someone else's benefit.

And I liked it. More than I should.

TWELVE

"Rachel, my tummy hurts," Chloe whimpers, curled up on the couch, still wearing her pajamas, with a small stuffed animal clutched to her chest.

I pause in the midst of hanging a garland, my heart sinking. The party is just hours away, and everything was going so smoothly. I can't let a stomachache derail all my careful planning.

"Oh, sweetie," I say, settling beside her and smoothing her hair. "Where exactly does it hurt?"

Chloe sniffles, her big brown eyes glistening with unshed tears. "My stomach feels all twisty and achy. I don't think I can go to the party."

A pang of concern mixes with a flicker of frustration. I know Chloe's health comes first, but the timing couldn't be worse. I remind myself to prioritize her well-being.

"Chloe, I promise we'll do whatever we need to make you feel better," I assure her, my mind already racing with potential solutions. "Why don't we start with some peppermint tea and see if that helps settle your tummy?"

She nods, a glimmer of hope in her eyes.

As I head to the kitchen to prepare the tea, I can't help but wonder if Chloe's stomachache is more than just physical. The party, the excitement, her friends all coming... It's a lot for a young girl to process. I make a mental note to have a heart-to-heart with her once she's feeling better.

For now, I focus on the task at hand, determined to find a way to make both the party and Chloe's well-being a priority.

I return to Chloe with a steaming mug of peppermint tea, the soothing aroma already bringing a sense of comfort.

"Here you go," I say softly, handing it to her. "Careful, it's hot."

Chloe takes a cautious sip, her face scrunching up as she adjusts to the temperature. "Thanks," she murmurs, her voice small and vulnerable.

I sit on the edge of the couch, gently brushing a stray lock of hair from her face. "Chloe, I know there's a lot going on with the party and everything. It's okay if you're feeling over-whelmed."

She looks up at me, her eyes wide and glistening. "I just... I don't want to let Dad down."

"Oh, Chloe," I whisper, pulling her into a hug. "You could never let your dad down. He loves you more than anything in this world."

She sniffles against my shoulder, her small frame trembling. "I miss Mom," she confesses, her voice barely audible. "She always liked parties with friends. She would have loved this."

I instantly feel terrible. I didn't make the connection. Of course, something like this would bring back all the memories. I hold her tighter, hoping it in some way helps.

"I know, sweetie. And I'm sure she's watching over you, so proud of the amazing girl you've become."

As Chloe's breathing steadies, I wonder if a change of scenery might be what we both need.

"Chloe," I say gently, pulling back to look her in the eyes. "I have an idea. Why don't we…"

Before I can finish my sentence, Dan appears in the doorway, his brow furrowed with worry. "Is everything alright in here?" he asks, his gaze shifting between Chloe and me.

I stand up, giving Chloe's hand a reassuring squeeze. "Chloe wasn't feeling too well. We were just having a little heart-to-heart," I explain, offering Dan a small smile. "I think Chloe's over the worst of it now, aren't you?"

Chloe nods, a brave little smile on her face. "Yeah, Dad. Rachel's tea helped a lot."

Dan's shoulders relax, relief washing over his features.

"Hey, Chloe," I say. "I know just the thing to cheer you up. How about we take a little trip to that diner we first met at, the one with the pancakes with all the trimmings?"

Chloe's eyes widen, a spark of excitement replacing the earlier gloom. "Really? You mean Julie's Diner?"

I nod, grinning. "That's the one!"

"But? But what about the party?"

"Party, *shmarty*, we've got plenty of time. I need you in top shape before the guests arrive, and to be perfectly honest, if I never have to blow up another balloon, it will be too soon!"

Dan laughs, "Sure. I'll drive."

"Actually, Dan," I say as I stand. "If it's okay, this is a girl thing. You'll need to stay to let the caterers in. They're due in forty-five minutes."

"Oh. Right… Well…"

"Please, Dad?" Chloe puts on her best puppy dog eyes. I'm impressed.

"Fine," he says.

"Then it's settled!" I declare, clapping my hands together. "Let's get you dressed, Chloe, and we'll head out for a pancake adventure."

Chloe's earlier malaise seems to melt away as she hurries

to get ready, chattering excitedly about the different pancake toppings she wants to try.

As we step into Julie's Diner, the warm aroma of coffee and sizzling bacon wraps around us like a hug. My mind is immediately taken back to my first night in Portland, of the poor woman who collapsed right here, and of Dan without hesitation dropping to his knees to help. The place is buzzing with the easy hum of morning chatter, the clatter of plates, and the occasional hiss of the griddle. The checkered floors, red leather booths, and gleaming chrome counters give the whole place a kind of timeless charm.

Chloe hesitates at the entrance, biting her lip as she scans the room. It's not like the house, where she knows every corner, or like school, where she blends in. Here, in the real world, she looks uncertain—like a kid trying to navigate a space that suddenly feels too big.

I nudge her lightly with my elbow. "We're getting the booth by the window. I called dibs."

That earns a small smile, and she follows me as we slide into the red leather seats.

Chloe snatches up a menu, her earlier nerves forgotten as she scans the options with the intensity of someone about to make a life-altering decision.

"They have even more choices now!" she says, eyes darting between the different pancake stacks. "Blueberry, chocolate chip, banana... Oooh, but you said I could only have two. But one *has to be* peanut butter, so—"

"Really?" I smirk. "You'd sacrifice one of your options for peanut butter?"

She gasps, scandalized. "Peanut butter is the best! You just don't understand."

I hold my hands up in surrender. "Okay, okay. But be warned, I will think a lot less of you if you don't choose maple syrup as one of the sauces."

Chloe giggles, tapping her chin in thought. "It might be too early for that much sugar. I think I might stick to fruit. Maybe blueberries and kiwi."

"Smart thinking," I say, setting my menu aside. "Why don't you choose for me too, little miss sensible?"

As we wait for our order, I take a sip of coffee and glance at her. "So, tell me something. What's the best thing about being twelve?"

She tilts her head, considering the question. "I was allowed a phone. That's pretty cool. And, I guess... that I get to do more stuff on my own? But also... that kind of makes it harder too."

I nod. "I get that. You're old enough to know what you want, but people still treat you like a kid."

"Exactly!" She leans forward, resting her arms on the table. "Like, I want to do things by myself, but I also want Dad to be there... just in case. But not in a 'hovering' way."

"So... present, but not too present?"

"Yeah." She sighs dramatically. "It's a very delicate balance."

I chuckle. "Sounds exhausting."

She grins. "It really is."

I stir my coffee absentmindedly, watching as she fidgets with a napkin. It's a small thing, but I can tell there's something on her mind.

So, instead of diving in with a heavy-handed question, I nudge her silverware toward her. "Okay, serious question. What's your take on diner forks? Too heavy, or just right?"

Chloe picks one up, turning it over in her hands like she's assessing a precious artifact.

"Hmm... a little heavy. But also sturdy, you know?"

I nod, solemn. "Exactly. You don't want a flimsy fork. Not with pancakes at stake."

She giggles, shaking her head. "You're kind of weird."

"True," I admit, "but you laughed, so technically that makes you weird too."

She huffs, pretending to be outraged, but I see the smile she's trying to fight.

The server drops off our plates, and just like that, everything else melts away.

Chloe digs into her pancakes like she hasn't eaten in days, the earlier stress in her shoulders gone. She takes a huge bite, then lets out an exaggerated groan of happiness.

"Ohhh my gosh. These are so good."

"Better than peanut butter?" I tease.

She chews thoughtfully, then nods. "Probably. But don't tell the peanut butter I said that."

"My lips are sealed."

She grins, licking a piece of kiwi off her thumb. "You're okay, you know that?"

I raise an eyebrow. "Wow. That's the highest honor I've ever received from a twelve-year-old."

She rolls her eyes but laughs, and I can't help but feel... something shift between us.

Like maybe we're not just two people in a diner anymore.

Maybe we're friends.

As we pull into the driveway, I notice Dan waiting for us on the front porch, a concerned expression on his face. He rushes over to the car, pulling Chloe into a tight hug as soon as she steps out.

"Hey, how are you feeling?" he asks, brushing a stray lock of hair from her face.

Chloe beams up at him, her earlier worries now a distant memory. "I'm great, Dad! Really."

Dan's eyes meet mine over Chloe's head, and I see a

mixture of gratitude and surprise there. "Thank you. I was worried we'd have to cancel."

I shrug. "It was my pleasure. She's a great kid."

As we head inside, Chloe chatters excitedly about the party, her enthusiasm levels back up to *psyched*. "I can't wait to see everyone's faces when they find out about your big announcement, Dad!"

Dan freezes, his eyes widening in panic. "Announcement? What announcement?"

I quickly jump in, hoping to smooth over the moment. "Oh, just a little surprise we have planned for later. Nothing to worry about."

Dan looks at me skeptically, but Chloe's excitement is impossible to ignore. "Come on, Dad, it's going to be amazing! Rachel's been working so hard to make this party perfect."

As Dan takes in the genuine joy on his daughter's face, I see his resistance start to crumble. He nods, a small smile tugging at the corners of his mouth.

"Alright, if you're both so excited about it, I guess I can't say no. Let's do this."

I leave them to it in the living room and head out to the backyard. The place has transformed. The tables have all been laid out and dressed, and the catering team has nearly finished constructing the bottle bar—I included it as a reluctant nod to Dan's wish for what essentially was a frat party. Now that it's there, it actually makes complete sense.

"No, no, the ice sculpture needs to go over there, by the punch bowl." I gesture to the corner of the table as I hurry over to the caterer. "And make sure we have enough champagne flutes on every table. I don't want to run out halfway through the toast."

The caterer nods and scurries off to follow my instructions. Dan's yard looks incredible. It's unrecognizable. The fairy lights, strung in a crisscross, from the house all the way down to the boathouse twinkle overhead, casting a warm, magical, glow over the nautical-themed décor, which is going to look even more amazing once the afternoon turns to night. Driftwood centerpieces adorn the tables, accented with seashells and tea light candles. It looks like something straight out of Coastal Living magazine. It's going to be amazing.

The doorbell rings, signaling the arrival of our first guests. I take one last look around the yard, making sure everything is perfect. The decorations, the catering—it's all exactly as I envisioned it.

"I'll get it," Dan calls out, heading towards the front door. I follow close behind, my heart racing with a mixture of nerves and excitement.

As Dan opens the door, we're greeted by a small group of his friends and colleagues, all dressed to the nines. I recognize a few faces from when I delivered the initiations, but most of them are new to me.

"Dan, my man!" One of them exclaims, pulling him into a bear hug. "It's been too long. And who's this?"

I step forward, extending my hand with a confident smile. "Hi, I'm Rachel."

The distant hum of chatter and car doors slamming alerts me that more guests are arriving. I smooth my dress and run a hand through my hair.

Showtime.

"Rachel!" A woman with short silver hair approaches, arms outstretched. "It's so wonderful to finally meet you. I'm Marge, Dan's aunt."

"Marge, hello! I'm so glad you could make it." I return her warm hug, catching a whiff of lavender perfume. "I know Dan will be thrilled to see you."

"Oh, I wouldn't miss this for the world. When I heard

Danny was finally coming out of hiding and hosting a party, I booked my train ticket right away. Even with all those problems with flights, I wouldn't have missed this for the world." She winks conspiratorially. "You know, it's been years since he's let anyone into his life like this. Whatever you're doing, keep it up."

I blush, unsure how to respond. "Oh. We're not actually—"

Luckily, more guests begin filtering in, saving me from having to explain the real nature of my relationship with Dan —which I'm still trying to figure out myself. I greet each one with a smile and a handshake, directing them to the buffet and seating areas.

As the house and yard fill with the buzz of excited chatter, I can't help but marvel at the turnout. People really showed up for Dan. Some drove for hours, probably spent more than they should on gas, and rearranged plans just to be here. That kind of loyalty isn't something you can fake.

I scan the crowd, watching as old friends clap Dan on the back, neighbors bring over freshly baked pies like they've stepped out of a Norman Rockwell painting, and even his brother James looks like he's having a good time.

But what really makes me smile is Chloe's little corner of the party.

The kids have claimed the dock as their own. Chloe stands at the center of it all, the undisputed leader of her mini kingdom, her arms crossed as she issues orders to her assembled friends.

"This is serious, you guys," she says, face scrunched in mock concentration. "We only get one shot at the perfect water balloon ambush."

A chorus of "Right!" and "Yeah!" follows.

One of the boys—tall, lanky, and clearly the strategist of

the group—adjusts his glasses. "So, just to confirm, we hit the grown-ups after they've eaten?"

"Exactly." Chloe nods. "They'll be slow. Full. Vulnerable."

A younger girl, maybe eight, clutches her balloon tightly. "What if they get mad?"

"They won't," Chloe assures her. "We'll target the ones who look like they can take it. My dad? He's fair game."

"Ohhh," the group murmurs, delight flashing in their eyes.

I bite my lip, watching from the sidelines. I should probably intervene. Tell them that dousing the host in freezing cold water at his own party might not be the best idea.

But, honestly?

I'd kind of like to see how it plays out.

Nearby, a small squad of girls sit cross-legged on a picnic blanket, braiding each other's hair and comparing friendship bracelets. Every now and then, they cast sneaky glances toward a different group—the older kids, a collection of too-cool-for-school preteens who are half-heartedly kicking around a soccer ball, pretending they aren't invested in the rest of the party.

Chloe, to my surprise, is bouncing between all three groups like it's the most natural thing in the world.

One second, she's scheming a full-scale water war, the next she's showing off a cool fishtail braid, then, before I even realize she's moved, she's jogging over to the older kids and casually stealing the soccer ball right out from under them.

"Hey!" one of the boys groans. "You can't just take it, Chloe."

She spins the ball on her finger. "Why not? You weren't even using it right."

A competitive glint flickers in his eyes. "Wanna bet?"

"Yeah," Chloe challenges. "Let's make it interesting. If I win, you guys have to join our water balloon ambush."

The boy smirks. "And if I win?"

Chloe pauses, then shrugs. "I dunno. You get to feel proud?"

His friends howl with laughter, and Chloe grins, tossing the ball back toward them. Within moments, they're fully engaged in a scrappy, fast-paced game, shouting insults and making daring passes that narrowly avoid flying off into the river.

I can't help but shake my head.

She's good.

Not just at soccer—but at fitting in everywhere.

I glance at Dan, who's still deep in conversation with an old friend, completely oblivious to the mini-diplomatic empire his daughter is building out here.

Chloe might still be figuring herself out, still growing into who she's going to be, but she's already a force to be reckoned with.

And I don't think she even realizes it yet.

The caterer catches my eye and gives me a thumbs up, signaling that everything is in place. I nod back, scanning the yard for Dan. The ice sculpture glistens, the champagne is chilled, and the guests are mingling happily. Perfect.

I weave my way through the crowd, pleased to see everyone has a drink and a smile. The energy is electric, a testament to the impact Dan has had on so many lives, and a clear sign that this party is long overdue.

I spot Chloe by the refreshment table, her eyes wide as she takes in the elaborate spread. I make my way over to her, snagging a couple of canapés en route.

"Having fun?" I ask, handing her a napkin.

She nods enthusiastically, her mouth full of mini quiche. "This is amazing, Rachel! Best. Party. Ever."

As if on cue, the boathouse door swings open, and Dan steps out, waving at everyone to join him.

"Come on, everyone." Chloe shouts, "Dad's got something to show you!"

The guests make their way down to the dock and join Dan at the boathouse.

I hang back, content to observe from the sidelines. This is Dan's moment, and I don't want to intrude. But as the crowd parts, his gaze finds mine, and he mouths a silent "Thank you."

I nod and raise my glass to him.

Dan clears his throat, and the last few murmurs die down.

"Thank you all for coming," he begins, his voice slightly hoarse with emotion. "I know it hasn't been easy, with the flights and all, but it means the world to me—to us—that so many of you are here."

He glances at Chloe, who leaves her friends and joins him, and I feel a lump form in my throat. The love between them is so strong, so pure.

"As some of you know, and probably most of you don't," Dan continues, "I've been working on a little project these past few months. Well, years really. It's something that's very close to my heart, and I'm excited to finally share it with you."

Dan takes a deep breath, then steps aside, revealing a large white sheet. "Without further ado, I present to you... the boathouse."

With a flourish, he yanks the sheet away, and there's a collective gasp from the crowd. The interior of the boathouse is stunning, a perfect blend of rustic charm and modern elegance. The polished wooden beams inside gleam under the array of subtle uplights, and the soft red exterior seems to glow against the backdrop of the river.

I feel a swell of emotion as I take in the details—the nautical-themed decor, the large windows that offer an incredible view of the water. It's clear that Dan has poured his heart and soul into this project, and the result is nothing short of spectacular.

As the guests surge forward to get a closer look, I let them pass, happy to hang back and let them have this moment with Dan and Chloe.

Chloe's voice breaks through my thoughts, and I turn to see her standing beside me, her eyes shining with tears.

"It's beautiful," she says, her gaze fixed on the boathouse. "It's like a little piece of Mom, right here with us."

I nod, my own throat tightening with emotion. "Your dad did an amazing job," I say softly, placing a hand on her shoulder. "Your mom would be so proud."

Chloe leans into my touch, a watery smile spreading across her face. "I can't believe how much work he's done on it. I thought he'd just swept the floor and gave it a fresh coat of paint, but it's like... it's like he brought her back to life, just for a moment.

As I stand there with Chloe, watching as Dan shows the guests around the boathouse, I can't help but feel a pang of longing. The love that Dan and Rebecca shared, the love that still shines through in every detail of this beautiful space... it's the kind of love I've always dreamed of. For all the success I've achieved, for all the lives I've touched through my work, there's still a hole in my heart that nothing seems to fill.

I mentally shake the thought away. This isn't the time for self-pity. This is a time for celebration, for honoring the love that Dan and Rebecca shared, the love that lives on in Chloe.

I squeeze Chloe's shoulder, giving her a warm smile. "Come on," I say, nodding towards the boathouse. "Let's go check it out."

Together, we make our way towards the structure, the laughter and chatter of the guests washing over us like a warm breeze. And as we step inside, taking in the incredible details, the loving touches that Dan has poured into every nook and cranny, my breath catches.

The walls are adorned with photographs capturing cherished moments from his life with Rebecca, each one telling a story of love, laughter, and adventure. A worn leather jacket hangs on a hook, a testament to Rebecca's free spirit, while a collection of seashells arranged on a shelf speaks of lazy afternoons spent combing the beach together.

The guests are equally enthralled, their voices a mixture of awe and nostalgia as they explore the space.

"Remember when Rebecca wore this to our college graduation?" one woman asks, pointing to a large-brimmed sunhat hanging on the wall. "She was the life of the party that day."

"And look at this," another guest chimes in, holding up a well-worn book. "Dan, wasn't this the poetry collection you gave her on your first anniversary?"

Dan nods, a wistful smile playing on his lips. "She carried that book with her everywhere. Said it was like having a piece of me with her, no matter where she went."

As I listen to the stories and memories being shared, I feel a sense of warmth spreading through my chest. It's clear that Rebecca was more than just Dan's wife—she was a beacon of light in the lives of everyone who knew her. And though she may be gone, her presence still lingers in every carefully chosen memento, every lovingly told tale.

I find myself drawn to a particular photograph, one that shows Dan and Rebecca on their wedding day. They're gazing into each other's eyes, their faces alight with the kind of joy that comes from knowing you've found your soulmate. It's a look I've never seen on Dan's face before. It suits him.

"They were so cute together, weren't they?" Chloe says softly, coming to stand beside me.

I nod, unable to tear my eyes away from the image. "They really were," I say, my voice thick with emotion. "Your dad... He loved your mom with everything he had. And I can see that love reflected in everything he's done here."

Chloe smiles, leaning her head against my arm. "I'm glad

you're here, Rachel," she says. "I know it means a lot to my dad to have you with us today."

I wrap an arm around her, giving her a gentle squeeze. "There's nowhere else I'd rather be," I say, and I mean it with every fiber of my being.

THIRTEEN

The warm glow of string lights illuminates the garden path as Dan and I slip away from the chatter of the guests who have now migrated into the house. A gentle breeze carries the sweet scent of honeysuckle, and crickets serenade us from the shadows. I'm grateful for a moment of respite with him.

We walk side by side, our shoulders almost touching, until the boathouse comes into view at the water's edge. In the moonlight, it looks like something out of a painting—rustic wooden beams, large windows reflecting silvery ripples, a freshly painted exterior that will protect it from salt and age for years to come.

Dan goes inside and I follow, pleased to have the chance to see it properly.

"Dan, this is absolutely beautiful," I say, running my hand along the smooth, wooden, paneled walls. "You renovated it all yourself."

He nods, a wistful smile playing at his lips as he pulls the large swing doors closed. "It was her sanctuary. She loved being out on the water, feeling the wind in her hair." His voice is tinged with both fondness and sorrow.

"I can see why. It's so peaceful." I turn to face him. "You've done an amazing job."

Dan's eyes meet mine, glistening with emotion in the low light. "Thanks. That means a lot." He takes a shaky breath. "I wanted to have somewhere to feel closer to her. To remember our time together."

I reach out and give his hand a gentle squeeze, hoping the gesture conveys my understanding and support. We stand there for a moment, hand in hand, the lapping of gentle waves the only sound.

Being here with Dan, in this place he created to honor his late wife, I feel a deep sense of connection, empathy, and there's something else too—a spark, an undeniable pull between us. I know I should probably ignore it, but right now, it's the most alive I've felt in a long time.

Dan turns to face me, his hand still in mine. In the moonlight, I can see the flicker of something in his eyes—longing, curiosity, a hint of guilt. "You know, I can't help but think that you and Rebecca would have gotten along so well. She had that same drive, that same passion for her work that you do."

I smile softly, feeling a warmth spreading through my chest at his words. "Really? What was she like?"

"Brilliant, for one. Always coming up with creative ideas, seeing possibilities where others didn't. And kind, so incredibly kind." His voice is wistful, but there's a note of pride too.

"She was an artist," Dan continues, his gaze softening as he looks out over the yard. "Not the paint-on-canvas kind. More... eclectic. She did graphic design for ad agencies, but on the side, she'd make these incredible mixed-media collages. Old photographs, bits of newspaper, fabric scraps—she'd blend them into something beautiful. She'd spend hours in here. It was her studio."

I picture it for a moment—a studio bathed in warm light, Rebecca hunched over her worktable, bits and pieces scattered around her, totally engrossed in the transformation of chaos into art. I can almost feel the energy of it, like creativity itself is something you can touch.

Dan smiles, a little nostalgic, a little sad. "She had this way of looking at the world that made everything seem connected, like every random object had a story just waiting to be uncovered. It's why her work was so good. Her clients loved her because she'd take these half-baked ideas and somehow turn them into something that made people feel something. She didn't just make things look pretty—she made them... matter."

I can't help but smile at that. "She sounds like she was really talented."

"She was," he agrees. "And completely hopeless with technology." He laughs, a low, fond sound. "We used to joke that if her laptop so much as beeped at her, she'd just give up and go make coffee until I could fix it. She once deleted an entire client presentation by accidentally pressing one button. Panicked, she called me on set, convinced she'd ruined her career."

I chuckle. "Did you manage to save it?"

"Of course. Took me about five minutes to restore it from the recycle bin. But she was so relieved you'd have thought I'd just performed open-heart surgery." He shakes his head, clearly amused by the memory. "She bought me a ridiculous 'Tech Genius' mug the next day as a thank-you. Still have it somewhere."

His eyes turn distant again, and I can tell he's wrestling with the ache of her absence.

I hesitate, not wanting to intrude, but I can't help asking, "Was it hard for her to balance work and being a mom?"

Dan nods slowly. "Yeah, sometimes. She loved being with Chloe, but creating was like life itself for her. I used to worry she was spreading herself too thin, trying to be everything to everyone. It didn't help that I was away so much. But she never saw it that way. To her, creating wasn't just a job—it was part of who she was. Even on the hardest days, she'd always find time to sketch something or pull a few colors together on a mood board. She didn't like feeling stagnant, like she wasn't moving forward."

I can't help but relate to that—always needing to be moving, producing, achieving.

"Sounds familiar," I say with a wry smile.

He glances at me and smirks. "Yeah, I thought you might get that."

I nod, feeling a little more connected to the woman I never got to meet. "She sounds incredible."

"She was," he agrees, his voice quieter now. "And stubborn. God, was she stubborn. Once she got an idea in her head, nothing could make her change it. One time she decided she was going to build Chloe a treehouse—even though she'd never built so much as a birdhouse before. I offered to help, but she insisted it was something she needed to do herself. Three months later, it was done—slightly crooked and nowhere near as high off the ground as she planned, but Chloe adored it."

I can't help but laugh at the mental image. "Sounds like she was determined."

Dan's smile turns soft and a little sad. "Yeah. She always said that just because something's hard doesn't mean it's not worth doing."

There's a lump in my throat that I can't quite swallow. I reach out, placing a hand on his arm.

"She sounds amazing. Chloe's lucky to have had a mom like that."

He glances down at my hand, and for a moment I think he might pull away, but he doesn't.

"Yeah," he says softly. "And I guess that's why it scares me, sometimes. How fast she's growing up. I don't want to... I don't know... let her down. Or make her feel like she's alone."

"You won't," I say gently. "You're doing great with her. Really. And I think Rebecca would be proud of you. I wish I could have met her."

"Me too." His thumb gently traces circles on the back of my hand, sending a shiver up my arm. "But in a way, I feel like she brought you here, to this moment. Is that crazy?"

My heart skips a beat at his words, at the implication behind them. "No, not crazy at all."

Dan takes a step closer, his other hand coming up to tuck a stray strand of hair behind my ear. His touch lingers, his fingertips grazing my cheek.

"Rachel, I..." His eyes search mine.

The air feels electric, charged with unspoken desire. I know we're on the edge of something big, something that could change everything. And even though a part of me is terrified, I don't want to run from it anymore.

Dan's hand cups my cheek, his thumb brushing over my lips. I lean into his touch, my eyes fluttering closed for a moment. When I open them again, he's so close I can feel his breath on my skin.

"Tell me to stop," he whispers, his voice rough with emotion.

Instead, I move toward him, pressing my lips to his in a passionate kiss. Dan responds immediately, his arms wrapping around me, pulling me flush against him. I melt into the embrace, losing myself in the sensation of his mouth moving against mine.

The kiss deepens, growing more urgent. My hands slide into his hair, fingers tangling in the dark strands. Dan's hands roam my back, his touch leaving trails of heat through the fabric of my blouse. I arch into him, craving more contact, more of him.

We stumble backwards until my back hits the wall of the boathouse. Dan's lips leave mine to blaze a trail down my neck, his teeth grazing my pulse point. I gasp, my head falling back to give him better access.

Fumbling fingers work at the buttons of my blouse, and then it's falling open, exposing my lace-clad breasts. Dan's hands skim up my ribcage, cupping me through the delicate fabric. I moan, the sound lost in another searing kiss.

He reaches behind me, unclasping my bra with deft fingers. It joins my blouse on the floor, leaving me bare before him. For a moment, he just stares, his gaze heated and reverent.

"You're so beautiful," he says, before dipping his head to place open-mouthed kisses along my collarbone, my shoulder.

I'm lost in a haze of sensation, my world narrowed down to Dan's hands and mouth on my skin. Nothing else exists outside of this moment, this connection blazing between us. I want to drown in it, surrender completely to the desire coursing through my veins.

I slip my hands beneath his shirt, exploring the planes of his back, the flexing muscles. I want to touch every inch of him, map his body with my fingertips—to be the cause of more of those shudders. Dan groans against my skin as my nails rake lightly down his spine.

We're a tangle of desperate touches and heated kisses, years of pent-up longing pouring out of us. The intensity is overwhelming, and exhilarating. I've never wanted anyone the way I want him right now.

Dan's hands skim lower, toying with the hem of my skirt. I whimper, arching into him, silently begging for more. His fingers raise the fabric and...

I reach for Dan's belt, fumbling with the buckle in my haste. He pulls back just enough to help, undoing his pants and letting them drop to the floor. I can see the evidence of his arousal straining against his boxers, and my mouth goes dry.

With shaking hands, I hook my fingers in the waistband

and tug, freeing him. He hisses as I wrap my fingers around him, giving an experimental stroke. The velvety smooth skin is hot against my palm, and I marvel at the weight of him in my hand.

"Rachel," he gasps, his hips jerking involuntarily as I stroke him again, firmer this time.

Emboldened by his reaction, I find a rhythm, reveling in the soft groans and muttered praises falling from his lips. He feels incredible, and knowing that I'm the one making him feel this way is intoxicating.

Dan's hands grip my hips, his fingers digging into my skin as he tries to maintain control. I can tell he's close to the edge, his breathing ragged and his muscles taut. Part of me wants to push him over, to watch him come undone at my touch.

But then he's stepping back, gently removing my hand. His chest heaves as he tries to calm himself, and confusion washes over me. *Did I do something wrong?*

"Dan?" I question, my voice small and uncertain.

He shakes his head, running a hand through his hair. "We can't. Not here."

Understanding dawns as I take in our surroundings—the boathouse, Rebecca's haven. Guilt churns in my stomach as the reality of what we were about to do crashes over me. *What was I thinking, letting things go this far in a place that means so much to him?*

"I'm sorry," I say, tears pricking at my eyes. "I wasn't thinking."

Dan cups my face, his thumbs brushing over my cheekbones. "Don't apologize. I want this, Rachel. I want you. But not like this. You deserve better. Not here... not now."

His words break my heart. I know he's trying to put me first. I know he means it. But I was completely lost in the moment. Why wasn't he?

I reach for my discarded top, suddenly feeling exposed and

vulnerable. Clutching it to my chest, I try to regain some semblance of composure. The silence stretches between us, thick with unspoken emotions and lingering desire.

Dan clears his throat, about to say something, when a voice cuts through the tension.

"Dad? Are you out here?"

It's Chloe, calling from the backdoor of the house. The sound of her voice jolts us back to reality, reminding us of the party going on inside. Our responsibilities as hosts come crashing down on us, and we share a look of understanding tinged with regret.

I quickly slip my top back on, fumbling with the buttons as my fingers tremble. Dan adjusts his clothes, trying to erase the evidence of our heated encounter. We both know we can't ignore Chloe's call, but part of me wishes we could stay here, cocooned in this moment, forever.

"I'll be right there, sweetheart!" Dan calls back, his voice strained.

He turns to me, apology written all over his face. "Rachel, I..."

I shake my head, forcing a smile. "It's okay, Dan. We should get back. People will be wondering where we are."

He nods, but the longing in his eyes tells me this isn't over. We've opened a door that can't be easily closed, and the implications both thrill and terrify me.

As we make our way back to the house, I can't help but feel a pang of disappointment. We were so close, so ready to take that leap, and now we're back to square one. But I know Dan's right. We can't rush this, not when there's so much at stake.

We pause at the backdoor, taking a moment to collect ourselves. Dan reaches out, giving my hand a gentle squeeze. It's a silent promise, a reassurance that this isn't the end.

Then he's pulling away, plastering on a smile as he steps inside to greet his guests.

I smooth down my clothes and tuck a stray lock of hair behind my ear, steeling myself for the rest of the evening. I know I'll have to put on a brave face, to pretend like my world hasn't just been turned upside down.

The sounds of laughter and chatter from the party drift through the open backdoor, a stark contrast to the intimate moment Dan and I just shared.

As I step into the kitchen, I'm greeted by the sight of Dan, ever the gracious host, offering drinks to a small group of guests. He catches my eye across the room, and for a fleeting moment, the mask slips. I see the same longing, the same unspoken desire that I feel mirrored in his gaze.

But then someone cracks a joke, and the moment is gone. Dan laughs along with the others, the perfect picture of a care-free, charming host.

I, on the other hand, feel like I'm navigating uncharted waters. Every smile, every laugh feels forced, a poor imitation of the genuine emotions coursing through me. I'm acutely aware of Dan's presence, of the way his eyes linger on me when he thinks no one's looking.

I pour myself a glass of wine and take a sip, letting the rich, fruity flavor linger on my tongue as I survey the room. The guests have thinned out, but those who are left are still thoroughly enjoying themselves, with laughter and chatter filling the air. I spot Chloe across the room, her face lit up with excitement as she shows off her new dance moves to a group of admiring adults.

There's a commotion near the front door catches my attention. A man with a camera slung around his neck pushes his way past whoever opened the door, followed closely by a woman clutching a notepad. My stomach sinks. I had completely forgotten about the big announcement.

Dan's face hardens as the journalist bombards him with questions. "Mr. Rhodes, are the rumors true? Are you making a comeback to acting?"

"I'm not answering any questions," Dan says curtly, trying to shepherd the reporters out of his house. But the persistent reporter wedges her foot in the doorjamb.

"The public has a right to know," she insists. "Are you planning to leave Maine and return to Hollywood?"

Anger flashes in Dan's eyes. "This is a private gathering. You need to leave, now."

Confused by the hostile exchange, I approach Dan and the unwelcome guests. Why is he so upset by a little media attention? This could be great publicity for his career.

I touch Dan's arm lightly. "Why don't we just answer a few questions? It couldn't hurt, right?"

Dan pulls away, his jaw clenched. "Rachel, please stay out of this."

Undeterred, I turn to the reporter with a bright smile. "Hi there! I'm Rachel Holmes, Dan's PR consultant. While we appreciate your interest, this is a private event for friends and family. If you'd like to schedule an interview, I'd be happy to arrange something later."

"Actually, we were invited," the greasy-haired photographer waves an invitation in the air before he snaps a few shots of me and Dan, the flash blinding us momentarily. Dan shields his face, his frustration palpable.

"No interviews," he snaps. "I want you both to leave. Now. This is private property."

I try to smooth things over, maintaining my professional composure. "As I mentioned, we're not answering questions today. Please respect Mr. Rhodes' privacy and leave the premises."

The reporter scowls but finally relents. "Fine. But this isn't over. The public deserves to know what's really going on with Dan Rhodes."

As they reluctantly depart, I close the door and turn to Dan, perplexed by his reaction. Why is he so resistant to the idea of relaunching his career? I only want to help him reach his full potential.

But the look on Dan's face stops me cold.

"Where did they get that invitation?" Dan asks, with a mix of anger, hurt, and disappointment.

My heart sinks as I realize I may have overstepped. "I only wanted to help—"

Dan brushes past me without a word, leaving me standing alone in the hall, my mind reeling. I thought I was doing the right thing, but now I'm not so sure. I need to find a way to fix this, to make things right. But first, I need to understand why Dan is so opposed to returning to the spotlight. I really thought he'd turned a corner agreeing to this party.

Deflated, I wander into the living room, feeling like an outsider. The once lively atmosphere now feels stifling, and I can't shake the sense that all eyes are on me. I carry on past them to the stairs and head up to take a moment to collect my thoughts.

As I sink down onto the top step, my head in my hands, someone asks Alexa to play some music, and moments later the buzz of conversation resumes and the party's back on.

I sit there on the steps, my heart pounding in my chest, trying to make sense of how the night unraveled so quickly. Just an hour ago, everything felt perfect—Dan and I, tangled up in the warmth of the boathouse, so close to crossing that line I've been teetering on since the moment I met him. But now, the party that was supposed to be his big comeback has turned into a circus, and I'm the one responsible. I thought I was giving him back his purpose, his passion, but all I did was drag him back into the spotlight he never wanted to face again.

My stomach twists with guilt and frustration. I was so sure I knew what was best for him—so sure that I could make it right. But now all I can think about is the hurt in his eyes, the way he looked at me like I'd betrayed him. The noise of the party filters back through the air, but it feels distant—like it belongs to someone else's life. All I know is that I've made a complete mess of everything, and for once in my life, I have no idea how to fix it.

I remain at the top of the stairs long after the party has found its rhythm again—unnoticed and unmissed. The truth is, it's never enough to just coast. I've always needed to be doing something—something meaningful. I think that's why Chicago never felt quite right, even when I was successful. Sure, I was good at my job—great, even. But making money for clients and seeing campaigns hit their targets didn't feel like it mattered enough. I wanted more. I wanted to do something that left a mark.

Maybe that's why I latched onto helping Dan—because it felt like I could really make a difference, like I could help him reclaim the life he deserved. Only I didn't stop to think if that's what he wanted. I was too busy trying to prove that I wasn't just some high-powered career woman who could only solve problems with a press release and a social media campaign. I wanted to show him I could be more than that—someone who actually makes things better, not just more efficient.

Try this for an impact assessment—a document that's required after every PR engagement—I've bulldozed right through his boundaries and made a mess of it all. I didn't listen. I didn't ask. I just assumed I knew best, because that's what I do. I charge in, convinced I'm saving the day, without stopping to think if anyone actually needs saving. And now, instead of helping Dan move forward, I've dragged him back into the one place he was trying to leave behind.

Thank goodness for small mercies—I'm relieved Chloe

took herself off to bed a while ago and won't see me like this. No one seems to have noticed my absence, sitting here, elbows on my knees, chin resting on my hands. Out of sight, out of mind...

It's probably for the best. I wouldn't even know what to say if someone did come up. I'm stuck in this awful limbo between wanting to run and hide and needing to do something—anything—to fix the colossal mess I've made. I thought I was being clever, orchestrating Dan's big comeback like I was launching a new chip brand in the Midwest. But all I did was bulldoze through his boundaries and make it all about what I thought was best.

The worst part is, I wasn't thinking about him. Not really. I was too wrapped up in proving to myself that I could make something good happen here. That I could do something right. I wanted to give him back his purpose, his pride... but I didn't stop to consider whether it was what he actually wanted.

Now I'm stuck here, hollow and aching, wondering how I managed to destroy the one good thing I've had since I landed in this state. I drag my hands down my face, trying to shake off the sting of tears, when I hear voices drifting up from the kitchen.

It's Dan and James, engaged in a heated conversation. I know I shouldn't listen, but I can't help but overhear snippets of their exchange.

"She had no right, no right at all," Dan says, his voice tight with anger. "Coming in here, trying to manage my life, my career. She doesn't understand."

His brother's voice is more measured. "I'm sure she meant well, Dan. She's just trying to help."

"Help?" Dan scoffs. "By pushing me back into the spotlight? By disregarding my wishes, my privacy? No, that's not help. That's her trying to control everything, thinking she knows best.

"It's not just about protecting Chloe, James," Dan says. "It's about not getting sucked back into that world. You know what it's like—the endless scrutiny, the expectations, the way people pick you apart just because you exist. I promised myself I wouldn't let Chloe grow up in the shadow of that. We've built something good here—quiet, stable. I'm not risking that just because Rachel thinks I need to feel like a star again. I don't want to have every aspect of my life in the public domain. I'm done with all that."

Each word feels like a punch to the gut. Is that really how he sees me? As some sort of controlling, manipulative pain in the ass?

I hug my knees to my chest, fighting back tears. I never meant to hurt Dan or overstep my bounds. I only wanted to support him, to get him out of his funk, to help him see the possibilities that lie ahead. But in my eagerness to help, I've lost sight of what really matters: Dan's happiness, his autonomy, his right to make his own choices.

As their conversation continues, I realize I can't bear to hear any more. Quietly, I slip back down the stairs and out the front door, desperate for some air. The cool breeze does little to soothe my troubled heart as I walk aimlessly down the driveway, wondering how I could have been so blind, so insensitive to Dan's true feelings.

I need to make this right, to find a way to apologize and rebuild the trust I've so carelessly shattered. But first, I need to take a long, hard look at myself and my motivations. Because if I can't be a friend without turning everything into business, then perhaps I have no business being in his life at all.

As I near the end of the driveway, I spot the journalist and photographer huddled together, reviewing the photos they'd taken earlier.

"...run with this one, Rhodes losing his cool," the photographer says, flipping through the images on his camera. "Definitely caught him at his worst."

The journalist nods, scribbling furiously in her notepad. "This is gold. We'll run with the angle of the fallen star, the has-been who can't handle the pressure of a comeback. 'Dan Rhodes: Anger Issues and a Career in Shambles.' It's perfect."

My heart sinks as I realize the gravity of the situation. Not only have I jeopardized my relationship with Dan, but I've also inadvertently fueled a media frenzy that could destroy his reputation and any chance he has at a peaceful life with Chloe.

I can't let this happen. I won't let my mistakes ruin Dan's future.

With renewed determination, I approach the journalist and photographer, clearing my throat to get their attention. They look up, surprised to see me standing there.

"Excuse me," I say, my voice steady despite the butterflies in my stomach. "I think there's been a misunderstanding."

The journalist arches an eyebrow, her pen poised above her notepad. "Oh? And what might that be?"

I choose my words carefully. "Dan Rhodes isn't some washed-up actor with anger issues. He's a devoted father who's been through an unimaginable loss. He's a man who's trying to do right by his daughter, to give her the love and stability she needs."

The photographer lowers his camera, a flicker of uncertainty crossing his face. "But the photos... the way he reacted..."

"He reacted like any protective father would when his privacy is invaded," I counter, my voice growing stronger with each word. "He's not interested in fame or a comeback. He just wants to be left alone to raise his daughter in peace."

The journalist studies me for a long moment, her expression unreadable. "And why should we believe you? What's your stake in all this?"

I meet her gaze head-on, my resolve unwavering. "Because I care about Dan and Chloe, and I made a mistake inviting you. It wasn't my call to make, and I can't bear to think I was responsible for a sensationalized headline. If you have any shred of decency, you'll respect their privacy and let them be."

A heavy silence falls, broken only by the distant sound of laughter from the house. Finally, the journalist sighs, tucking her notepad into her bag.

"Fine," she says, her tone clipped. "We'll drop the story. But you'd better hope Rhodes appreciates what you've done for him."

With that, she unlocks her car and the two of them get it in. I watch them put on their seatbelts, my heart pounding in my chest as the weight of my actions settles upon me.

"Actually," I rap my knuckles on the passenger window of the car. There's a hesitation before it rolls down. "I've had a few glasses of wine, any chance of a lift into Biddeford if it's on your way?"

"Things that bad back in the house?" The journalist chews on her bottom lip.

"Yeah."

"Sure. Jump in. Excuse the mess."

I slide into the backseat, my heart still racing from the confrontation. The leather seat feels cool against my skin as I buckle up, trying to hold back my tears.

"You sure you don't want to join us for a drink?" the journalist asks, glancing at me in the rearview mirror. "Might help take the edge off."

I shake my head, mustering a weak smile. "Thanks, but I think I need some time alone to process everything."

The photographer shrugs, fiddling with his camera. "Suit yourself."

"Where do you need to go?"

"The White Pines Motel."

"I know it," the journalist says as she presses the ignition.

As the car pulls away from the curb, I lean my head against the window, watching the twinkling lights of the house fade into the distance. The gentle hum of the engine fills the silence, and I find myself lost in thought, replaying the events of the evening in my mind.

Winding through the dark, tree-lined roads, I come to a sobering conclusion: I need to focus on my own goals and aspirations, and leave the messy business of relationships behind. Every time I've opened myself up to the possibility of something more, I've ended up hurt, disappointed, and alone. I just don't seem to be able to play nice with others.

Better to stick to the things I can control, like bringing in a huge account for Channing Gabriel.

The car pulls up to the motel, and I thank the journalist and photographer for the ride. As I make my way to my room, a wave of determination washes over me. I unlock the door, step inside, kick off my shoes, and just flop onto the bed, completely and utterly exhausted.

FOURTEEN

A gentle knock on the door pulls me from my thoughts. I sit up, wiping at my cheeks, before heading over to open it. When I do, I'm greeted by Chloe's beaming face, and the sight of her —so bright and excited—nearly undoes me.

"Rachel!" she chirps, practically bouncing on the spot. "Dad said we could come by and say thanks for the party! It was amazing! Everyone's talking about how cool it was."

Before I can respond, she barrels past me into the room, full of energy and enthusiasm, and I spot Dan hovering awkwardly in the doorway, hands shoved in his pockets. His gaze meets mine for just a second before he looks away, clearly still angry—or at least still processing his anger. My stomach tightens.

"Hey," I manage, trying to sound normal. "You're... both here?"

"Yeah," Dan mutters. "James might have had one too many last night, so I'm working a shift. Chloe wanted to come by to say thanks. I figured... it wouldn't hurt."

Chloe's already investigating the room like it's a treasure hunt, picking up my hairbrush and putting it down again.

"Look how many pictures are on the group chat?" she squeals, holding her phone near my face. "Everyone loved the decorations and the food. And Dad's friends kept saying how great it was to see him. It was like... the best party ever in the history of parties."

I force a smile, even though guilt prickles at my skin like tiny needles. "I'm glad you and your friends had a good time."

Dan just shrugs, his face unreadable. "We, uh... didn't mean to interrupt. Just... wanted to pass on our thanks."

Chloe's looking at me with such innocent excitement that it hurts.

"Can we hang out today?" she asks, eyes wide and hopeful. "Dad's gonna be working for ages, and I'm bored. Thought maybe we could go somewhere? Just us?"

My heart sinks. I hadn't exactly planned on being social today—especially not after last night's disaster—but I can't bring myself to turn her down. I glance at Dan, uncertain, and he just shrugs again, like he's leaving the decision up to me.

"Chloe, I'm not sure—" I start, but she cuts me off, flopping onto the bed and giving me those wide, pleading eyes that I swear could crack granite.

"Please? I promise we'll stay out of trouble. I just really want to hang out with you. I thought... after the party, we'd get to do something fun together."

I swallow the lump in my throat, desperately trying to balance my own shame with not letting her down. "I don't know, Chloe," I hedge, glancing at Dan. "I... I left my rental car at your house last night. We'd need to go get it."

Dan clears his throat. "If you could, that would actually be doing me a huge favor. There's not much for her to do here. If you don't mind taking an Uber. Just... head to the house, and hang out there if you want. I'll finish up here and join you later."

Chloe's face lights up like a fireworks display, and she's on her feet in a heartbeat, practically bouncing on her toes. "Yes! Thank you, Dad! Thank you, Rachel!"

Dan and I exchange a glance, and for just a second, I think I see something other than anger in his expression—maybe a hint of regret. Or maybe it's just exhaustion. Either way, it's gone before I can figure it out.

"Just be safe," he says, voice gruff. "And don't leave the house without me, okay?"

"Yes, Dad," Chloe chirps, already dragging me toward the door.

I grab my purse and give Dan a small nod as we pass. "Thanks," I say, and he just nods back without meeting my eyes.

Chloe chatters non-stop as we walk down the motel hallway, already planning out the day like it's some kind of grand adventure. I can't help but smile, even as my heart feels heavy with the weight of how badly I screwed everything up.

Maybe spending the day with Chloe will help. Maybe I'll get my head straight. And maybe—just maybe—I'll figure out a way to make things right with Dan.

The Uber drops us off at Dan's house, and Chloe immediately skips ahead, her energy practically bouncing off the ground. I follow a little more cautiously, taking in the house that's quickly becoming familiar—despite how little I actually belong here. The yard looks pristine, the tables, seating, and decorations from the party all packed away, like nothing ever happened.

I can still see the ghost of last night—how perfect it all seemed before everything fell apart. I force myself to push the memory aside and focus on Chloe, who's already on the porch, waving me over with impatient enthusiasm.

"Come on, Rachel!" she calls. "What do you want to do first?"

I smile at her eagerness, trying to muster up the same level of excitement. "It's your day, Chloe. You decide."

Her face lights up like it's Christmas morning. "Can we take the boat out?" she asks, practically bouncing on her toes.

My stomach drops. "Oh... I don't know. Your dad didn't say anything about boats."

Chloe doesn't even seem to notice my hesitation. "It'll be fine. Dad taught me how to row, and we always wear life jackets. I'll show you!"

I should put my foot down, insist on staying on dry land, but the excitement in her eyes makes me hesitate. I don't want to be another adult who's taking away Chloe's agency and always saying no, who's too afraid of messing up to take a risk. I've done that my whole life—shying away from anything that might blow up in my face. But Chloe's counting on me to say yes, to just go with it, for once.

Before I can come up with another excuse, she's already dashing toward the boathouse, leaving me no choice but to follow. Maybe it's worth letting my guard down. Just this once.

As we get closer, I can't help but feel a twinge of something raw in my chest. The morning sun streams through the wide, open doorway, catching on the fresh coat of deep red paint and bouncing off the water beyond. It's beautiful.

But stepping inside is like taking a punch to the gut. It's here, right here, that I thought maybe—just maybe—everything was going to be okay. Where Dan's hands on my skin felt like the start of something incredible. Where his mouth on mine made my head spin and my heart pound. And just an hour later, it all fell apart.

I swallow the lump in my throat and force myself to focus on Chloe, who's already darting ahead, completely oblivious to the storm raging inside me.

"Look!" she says, beaming as she points to the small rowboat hanging from a winch a foot above the water, newly painted and practically gleaming. "Dad and I worked on it for weeks! He let me paint it. Isn't it awesome?"

I move further into the boathouse to take a closer look. It was covered with streamers and party decorations last night and, well, I thought it was part of the decoration rather than an actual working boat—plus my focus was on something else entirely. It's a simple little thing, nothing fancy, but the wood is sanded smooth, and the paint job is immaculate. White with a deep blue trim, and hanging from a hook on the bow, a wooden nameplate is painted in careful, bold script: Rebecca.

I pause, feeling a pang of something bittersweet. "Rebecca," I murmur. "Named after your mom."

Chloe nods, her fingers grazing the painted letters with a kind of reverence. "Yeah. Dad named it after her when we fixed it up. It used to be all broken down and sad-looking, but he said giving it her name would make it beautiful again."

My throat tightens, and I glance away, not wanting her to see the way my eyes are stinging.

"It looks beautiful," I reassure her. "You did an amazing job. I love the name too."

She glances at me, a little shy now, her fingers tracing the neat lettering. "Mom loved the water... She always wanted to go sailing, but Dad never got around to fixing the old boat until... well, after."

The words hang heavy in the air, and I feel a pang of sadness on her behalf. I didn't know Rebecca, but I know the kind of impact loss can have on a family.

"Your dad seems like he's really doing his best," I say gently. "You must be proud of him."

Chloe nods, but she's not smiling anymore. "He tries so hard to be both parents at once. He thinks I don't notice, but I do. Sometimes he overdoes it, you know? Like, trying to bake fancy cupcakes for my school bake sale when I just wanted plain ones. Or fixing my hair in these perfect braids that don't even look like me." She shrugs, giving me a sideways glance. "I don't want him to think he's not enough. But... sometimes, I just wish he'd let me do some things myself."

I bite back the lump in my throat, touched by how perceptive she is. "You're a smart kid, Chloe. And you're right—he's trying his best. But maybe it's okay to tell him that you can handle some things on your own."

She thinks about it, her little forehead creasing in thought. "Maybe. It's just... I don't want to make him sad. He gets that look sometimes, like he's trying not to cry when he thinks I can't see."

I swallow, wishing I had the right words. "You know what? Your dad's lucky to have you. You're brave, and you're thoughtful, and you care about him. Not every kid would understand that. You're a pretty amazing team."

Her smile returns, tentative but real. "You really think so?"

"Absolutely."

Chloe brightens a little, and I can see the tension ease from her shoulders. She glances at me with a spark of curiosity. "You don't have kids, do you?"

"No," I admit, trying to keep my tone light. "I barely remember to water my plants, let alone take care of another human being."

She giggles at that, and the sound lifts the mood like a ray of sunshine through a dusty window. "Well, you're pretty cool. You'd probably be a good mom if you ever wanted to be."

The unexpected compliment hits me square in the chest, and I'm not entirely sure why.

I muster a smile and ruffle her hair. "Thanks, Chloe. That means a lot."

Chloe doesn't seem to notice my turmoil. She's too busy running her hands over the oars, making sure everything is in place. "It's totally safe," she reassures me, pulling out life jackets from a wooden crate and holding one up with a flourish. "Let's go out on the river. We've got all the safety gear."

I force a smile, trying to match her enthusiasm, but my insides feel twisted up and uncomfortable. It's not just the thought of going out on the water, although that doesn't exactly thrill me either. It's more the lingering echo of last night—of Dan's touch and his anger and my own crushing guilt.

Chloe notices my hesitation and frowns. "You don't like boats?"

I clear my throat, trying to sound casual. "It's not that. I just... I don't really like being out on the water. I'm more of a... solid ground kind of person."

She cocks her head, like she's trying to figure out how anyone could possibly feel that way.

"But it's fun! And it's not scary. We could just go out for a few minutes. Just over to that buoy and back. You'll see, it's easy."

I bite my lip, torn between telling her no and not wanting to disappoint her. Chloe's been through enough, and the last thing I want is to be another person in her life who lets her down. Besides, what's the point of playing it safe all the time? Maybe it's time to take a chance, even on something small. Maybe I need to push myself out of my comfort zone—rock the boat a little.

I nod. "Alright. Let's do it."

Chloe's face lights up with pure delight, and she practically bounces as she fastens the life jackets on both of us.

"You'll see," she promises. "It's super fun."

Chloe winds the winch a few turns, and the boat lowers into the water. She hops in with the grace of someone who's done this a hundred times, while I take a little more time to gingerly lower myself onto the bench seat, gripping the sides.

She giggles. "You look like you're bracing for a hurricane."

"I just don't want to tip us over before we even start," I mumble, trying to find my balance.

Once we're settled, Chloe picks up the oars and gives me a reassuring smile. "See? Totally easy. You just have to find your sea legs."

The boat skims out of the boathouse with a soft push, and I feel my heart race a little as the gentle waves rock us. But Chloe's movements are steady and confident, and slowly—much to my surprise—I relax.

"See?" Chloe says proudly. "You're not gonna puke or anything, are you?"

I laugh, more at myself than anything else. "No. I think I'm okay."

She grins and dips the oars into the water, finding a rhythm that sends us gliding towards the buoy. I let myself relax a little, the tension in my shoulders easing as the boat rocks gently under us. There's something peaceful about it—something calming that I didn't expect. Maybe it's Chloe's confidence. Or maybe it's just that being out here feels like a break from reality—a bubble of calm away from all the mess I've made.

Chloe looks at me, her face thoughtful. "You're good at this," she says.

I arch a brow. "Good at what? Sitting still and not freaking out?"

She giggles. "No, just... going along with things. Not everybody does that. Some people just say no right away without even trying."

Her words hit a little deeper than I expect, and I wonder if that's what I've been doing my whole life—saying no to anything that seemed risky or uncomfortable. Always playing it safe. Always doing the sensible thing. Maybe I've missed out on a lot because of that.

"Yeah," I say softly, more to myself than to her. "I guess it's about time I learned to just... go with it."

Chloe smiles, satisfied, and dips the oars again, steering us smoothly forward. I close my eyes for a moment, just breathing in the fresh air and letting the sound of the river fill my ears.

The rhythm of the oars cutting through the water becomes almost soothing, and I allow myself to just... be. The river stretches out around us, calm and quiet, and for the first time in a while, I feel like I can actually slow down. No deadlines. No pitches. No pressure to prove myself. Just... being here.

As the boat glides further from the shore, Chloe hums to herself—a melody I don't recognize, but it's soft and sweet, and it suits the mood perfectly.

"You know," I say, trying to keep my tone light, "you're pretty brave, taking me out on a boat when I'm totally useless at this."

Chloe giggles again. "You're not useless. You just needed a little push. Besides, you didn't freak out, so that's pretty cool."

I smile at that. Maybe she's right. Maybe I've spent so long convincing myself I couldn't handle certain things that I never bothered to actually try.

"Next time," I say, glancing around at the stillness of the water, "I'll take the oars. Deal?"

Chloe smirks. "Why not start now?"

"What?"

"Take this," she says, handing me an oar. "It's just like riding a bike. Well, a bike on water."

"That's not as reassuring as you think," I mutter, but I take the oar, trying to mimic Chloe's grip.

She shows me the basics—how to row, how to steer, how to work with the current instead of against it. To my surprise, I catch on quickly, the motions feeling natural and fluid.

As we approach the buoy, the rhythmic splashing of the oars and the gentle rocking of the boat lull me into a sense of tranquility. My fears start to melt away, replaced by a growing sense of exhilaration.

"You're a natural!" Chloe exclaims, as I manage to turn the boat at will with a deft twist of my oar.

I feel a flush of pride at her praise. Out here, with the vastness of the water around us and the fresh breeze on my face, I feel a lightness I haven't known in years. It's as if the weight of my responsibilities, my guilt, my self-doubt—it all stays on shore, leaving me free and unburdened.

"This is amazing," I say, tilting my head back. "I feel like I could row forever."

"I knew you'd love it! Just wait until you see where we're going."

She points ahead, and I follow her gaze to a distant structure perched on a rocky outcrop on the other side of the river.

"Wait. Hold on. We agreed to the buoy and back. That was the deal."

"It's just a little further." She points. "In fact, it's less distance than going back to the house."

I turn and realize she's right, we're more than halfway across the river already. What's a little further now that we're here?

"What's there?"

"You'll see." She grins.

As we draw closer, I make out the distinctive shape of a small lighthouse, the white paint long peeled off, and the structure now covered in creepers.

"That's the old lighthouse," Chloe explains, a wistful note entering her voice. "Mom and I used to row out here all the time. It was our special place."

My heart clenches every time Chloe mentions her mom. I can't begin to imagine the hole her loss has left in her life—in Dan's life.

As we approach the base of the lighthouse, Chloe guides

me towards a small, rocky beach. As soon as the bow of the boat hits the sand, Chloe hops out, and then turns, offering me her hand as I step over the bow and back onto terra firma. We pull the boat onto the shore, and make our way up a winding path to the lighthouse door.

Chloe produces a key from her pocket and unlocks the door. "Dad still keeps it maintained," she says softly. "For Mom."

Inside, the musty smell of old stone and sea air envelops us. We climb the spiral stairs, our footsteps echoing in the narrow space, until we emerge onto the gallery deck at the top.

The view is incredible. From this vantage point, the river stretches out in both directions, melting into the horizon. The breeze is stronger up here, whipping my hair around my face.

Chloe leans against the railing, her eyes distant. "Sometimes, when I miss her, I come out here with Dad and I feel closer to her somehow. Like she's still here with me."

Impulsively, I wrap an arm around her shoulders, pulling her close. "She is, Chloe. She's always with you."

We stand there for a long moment, watching the sunlight dance on the swell, each lost in our own thoughts.

"We should probably head back," I say reluctantly, glancing at my watch. "Your dad will be finished with work soon."

Chloe nods, her wistful expression morphing into a mischievous grin. "Race you to the boat!"

She takes off down the stairs, her laughter echoing behind her. I shake my head, a smile tugging at my lips, and follow at a more sedate pace. By the time I reach the bottom, she's already pushed the boat back into the water.

I settle into my seat, grasping the oars. The wood is warm and smooth beneath my hands, the movements already feeling more natural, more instinctive. We glide out into the river, the lighthouse receding behind us.

Chloe trails her fingers in the water, creating tiny ripples that spread out in our wake. "I wish we could stay out here forever," she sighs.

"Me too," I admit, surprising myself with the truth of it. Out here, with the sun on my face and the breeze in my hair, the stresses and pressures of my life in Chicago feel a million miles away.

Lost in thought, I don't notice Chloe's hand sneaking toward the surface of the river until it's too late. She scoops up a handful of water, flinging it toward me with a gleeful laugh.

"Oh, it's on!" I sputter, retaliating with a splash of my own.

Our laughter mingles with the sound of the swell lapping against the prow as we engage in an all-out water fight, the boat rocking gently beneath us. For a precious few minutes, we're just two friends, playing and joking, without a care in the world.

But the moment is shattered by a sudden, sickening crunch. I freeze, my heart lodging in my throat, as I see water beginning to seep through a jagged crack in the hull.

"Rachel?" Chloe's voice is small and scared. "What's happening?"

"I don't know!"

I let go of the oars and cup my hands, trying to scoop up handfuls of water to throw back into the river.

I swallow hard, trying to quell the rising panic. The boat is sinking, the crack widening before my eyes, water pouring in faster than I can bail it out.

"We're going to be okay," I manage, my voice sounding far calmer than I feel. "Just hold on to me, alright?"

Chloe nods, her face pale, her eyes wide and trusting. I pull her close, my mind racing, searching for a solution, a way out. But the shore is too far, the water too cold, and the boat is sinking fast.

As the water laps at our ankles, as the boat begins to tilt

beneath us, all I can do is hold Chloe tighter and pray that help will come, before it's too late.

"Chloe, check your life vest! Hurry!" I shout. My hands tremble as I check the straps and clasps of my own vest, the urgency making my movements clumsy.

Chloe scrambles to the back of the boat, nearly losing her footing on the slippery floor.

"I'm scared, Rachel," she whimpers, her voice quivering.

"I know, sweetie. But we're going to be alright." I try to infuse my words with a confidence I don't feel. The icy water is now up to our shins, the boat groaning and listing heavily to one side. "We're going to have to jump into the water, okay? On the count of three."

Chloe nods, her face a mask of fear and determination. She grips my hand tightly, her small fingers icy cold. I try to calm the frantic pounding of my heart.

"One... two... three!"

We leap from the sinking boat, plunging into the frigid water. The shock steals my breath, the cold seizing my muscles. For a terrifying moment, I'm disoriented, unsure which way is up. But then my life vest buoys me to the surface, and I break through, gasping and sputtering.

"Chloe!" I call out, my voice raw with fear. "Chloe, where are you?"

A small hand grabs mine, and I nearly sob with relief. Chloe clings to me, her teeth chattering, her face ghostly pale. Behind us, the boat slips under the surface, leaving only ripples in its wake.

We bob in the water, adrenaline and fear coursing through our veins. The shore in either direction seems impossibly far away, the water stretching out in an endless expanse. But we're alive. We're together. And somehow, someway, we've got to move. Got to make it to land.

I wrap my arm around Chloe, holding her close. "Just hold

on to me," I say, my voice shaking. "We're going to be okay. I promise."

And as we float there, two small figures in the vast, unforgiving river, I can only hope that it's a promise I can keep.

I kick my legs, adjusting to accommodate Chloe, and head for the shore. But as hard as I kick, we don't seem to be going forward.

If anything, we're going sideways.

It seems the current has other ideas and continues its relentless pursuit towards the ocean. I roll onto my back, and, using the buoyancy of the life preserver, drag Chloe over so that she can hold me around the chest. Switching to froggy style, I feel like I have more power behind each kick.

Stroke. Stroke. Stroke. I remember the words from my swimming lessons all those years ago. The teacher's simple instructions were shouted down to all the students in the water. But that was a swimming pool, temperature controlled, without tides, without any movement whatsoever except the occasional splash from another student whose kick was too high. This is a real, angry, unstoppable river.

The water laps against our faces, cold and relentless. Each swell sends a fresh shiver through my body, my teeth chattering uncontrollably. Chloe's grip around my neck is like a vise, her fingernails digging into my skin. But I welcome the pain, the physical anchor to reality.

"Help!" I scream, my voice hoarse and desperate. "Someone, please help us!"

But there's no response, no sign of anyone nearby. I keep kicking, putting every ounce of effort into it, but the river remains silent, indifferent to our plight. I strain my ears, hoping to hear the distant hum of a boat motor or the shouts of a search party. But there's nothing.

Why would there be? No one knows we're out here.

Chloe whimpers, her face pressed against my shoulder.

"What if no one finds us?" she whispers, her voice small and fragile.

I swallow hard, trying to ignore the icy tendrils of fear squeezing my heart. "They will," I say, infusing my voice with a conviction I don't feel. "Your dad... He'll realize something's wrong when we don't come back. He'll come looking for us."

But even as the words leave my mouth, I can't help but wonder... What if he doesn't think he needs to hurry back because Chloe is being looked after?

Ha. *Looked after.* Yeah, the first time I'm the responsible adult for a child, and this is the result.

No. I can't think like that. Not now. Not when Chloe needs me to be strong.

I force a smile, brushing a strand of wet hair from Chloe's face. "Hey, sing that song you did at rehearsals."

"Now?"

"Yeah, I really liked it."

Her lips are chattering. "I'm not sure I can remember the words."

"Try," I suggest, my voice gentle. "It'll help pass the time until help arrives."

For a moment, Chloe hesitates. But then, softly at first, she begins to sing. Her voice is tremulous and uncertain, the notes wavering in the air. But gradually, it grows stronger, more confident. The melody wraps around us like a blanket, a fragile shield against the cold and the fear.

And as I listen, my heart swells with a fierce, protective love. I may not be sure of much right now—not my career, not my future, not even my own identity. But one thing I know with absolute certainty: I will do whatever it takes to keep this precious girl safe.

FIFTEEN

My limbs are numb. The frigid water doesn't feel as cold, which I know isn't a good sign. I struggle to keep Chloe's head above the waves. And my own. Panic threatens to overwhelm me. I force it down. I have to be strong for Chloe.

"Just hold on to me," I tell her, my voice shaking. "We're going to be okay."

Chloe's little hands cling to my neck, her breath coming in short gasps. I can feel her shivering against me. The poor thing must be terrified.

I look around wildly, trying to get my bearings. I can't make out the lighthouse anymore. But I think I can make out a dock, similar to Dan's, there a cruiser moored blocking the view of the house. If we can just make it there...

A sharp crack makes me jump. Chloe's flailing leg has hit something—the nameplate from the boat. *Rebecca.* The letters glint accusingly as it bobs on the surface.

"Chloe, grab that!" I shout over the wind. "It'll help you float!"

Together we lunge for it. I manage to snag a corner and shove it under Chloe's arm. She grips it like a lifeline.

I'm running out of energy. It doesn't feel like I have anything left in the tank. I. Must. Press. On.

I will myself to stay calm. One kick at a time. That's all I can focus on. One kick, then another. Ignore the burning in my muscles. Block out the cold seeping into my bones. Just swim.

Chloe whimpers and I hug her closer to me. "Your dad will find us," I promise, praying it's true. "He'll be looking for us. We just have to make it to shore."

I squint into the fading light, gauging the distance to the dock. Too far, but we have no choice. Gulping air, I start kicking for land, Chloe a trembling weight against my chest.

Please let us make it, I beg silently. *Please. Dan, where are you? We need you. Chloe needs you.*

I grit my teeth and keep swimming.

The swell is more violent now. They're small waves really. But their size is irrelevant. They're slapping against my face as I struggle to keep my head above water.

"Keep kicking, sweetie," I urge, trying to sound calm despite the panic clawing at my throat. "You're doing great. We're going to be okay."

But even as I say the words, doubt gnaws at me. The shore seems impossibly distant, a mirage shimmering in the gathering dusk. My arms and legs feel like lead, each stroke an agony of effort.

Chloe's grip on the nameplate slips and she cries out in alarm. "Just let it go!" I tell her, tightening my hold. "Just hold to me."

She nods, her face pale and pinched. She's so young, so vulnerable.

I have to save her. Nothing else matters. Not the pain, not the weariness, not the fear. Chloe is all that matters.

With a burst of determination, I renew my efforts, pulling Chloe further on top of me. "Kick your legs," I tell her, demonstrating. "Like you're riding a bicycle. Hard as you can, okay?"

She obeys wordlessly, her small sneakers beating a rhythm against the water. I join her, propelling us inches at a time towards safety.

It's grueling work, fighting the currents that want to drag us under. The water stings my eyes. My lungs burn with every gasp.

But slow stroke by slow stroke, kick by labored kick, the dock creeps closer. I fixate on it, pouring every ounce of fading strength into reaching it.

Just a little farther. Keep going. Don't stop. For Chloe.

I'm not sure how long we flounder together, suspended between hope and dread. Time loses meaning beyond the ragged rhythm of our movements and the drumming of my pulse in my ears.

There's only the cold. The currents. Chloe. The distant dock. And the single, unrelenting thought: We have to make it.

We have to.

A frantic yell from Chloe jolts me out of my semi-delirious struggle.

"Dad!" she screams, her voice ragged. "Dad! Help us!"

I turn my head, following her gaze, and nearly weep with relief at the sight of Dan's car driving slowly along the coastal path. He jumps out, scanning the water, looking for us.

Hope surges through me, electrifying me. I join my voice with Chloe's, shouting his name with what little strength I have left. "Dan! Dan, we're here! Help!"

At first, he doesn't seem to hear us, striding back towards his car, about to drive off. A knot of anguish twists in my chest. He can't leave. Not now. Not when we're so close...

"Dad!" Chloe shrieks again, desperation etched into the single syllable.

Finally, miraculously, his head snaps towards the water. I see the moment he registers our plight, his body going rigid with shock. Then he's running, sprinting towards the bank of the river with a speed that would put an Olympian to shame.

He doesn't hesitate for an instant when he reaches the edge, kicking off his shoes and shrugging out of his jacket in one fluid motion. His phone and wallet hit the ground a split second before he dives into the water, cleaving the surface in a clean arc.

I nearly sob with relief as he swims towards us with powerful strokes, closing the distance in heartbeats. Moments later, his strong arms are around us, holding us up as he treads water.

"I've got you," he says roughly, his eyes wild with fear and relief. "I've got you both. You're okay."

He checks Chloe over frantically, searching for any sign of injury. She clings to him, small hands clutching his shirt. Satisfied that she's unharmed, he turns his attention to me.

"Are you alright?" he demands, his grip on my arm almost bruising.

I manage a shaky nod, too overwhelmed to form words. He seems to understand, pulling me closer until our foreheads touch, all three of us tangled together in a desperate embrace.

Gently, he pries Chloe off his chest and settles her on his back. "Hold on tight, kiddo," he instructs. "Like when you were little, remember?"

She obeys, looping her arms around his neck and burying her face between his shoulder blades. With his hands free, Dan reaches for me, guiding my arms around his waist.

"Hang on to me," he orders softly. "I'll get us to shore. Just hang on, Rach."

I do, clinging to him like a lifeline as he strikes out for the shore, his strong body cutting through the water with determined grace. The solid warmth of him against me is an anchor, a promise of safety amidst the lingering chaos.

As we near the bank of the river, I let my eyes drift closed, exhaustion crashing over me in relentless waves. I'm dimly aware of Dan hauling us out of the water, of Chloe's small form still clinging to him like a barnacle.

Then somehow, I'm sitting in the backseat of his car, still holding on to Chloe, the distant concerned drone of Dan's voice, and the blessed relief of being alive.

We made it, I think hazily, surrendering at last to the beckoning pull of unconsciousness. *We're alive. We're safe.*

He saved us.

My eyes flutter open to the sight of Dan's face hovering above me, his brow furrowed with concern. "Rachel? Hey, you with me?"

I nod weakly, my eyes opening. Beside me, Chloe is curled into a tight ball, her small frame racked with shivers.

"What were you thinking?" Dan demands, his voice rough with residual fear. "Taking the boat out like that without telling me?"

"I'm sorry," I say, my throat tight. "We just wanted... I thought it would be fun."

"Fun?" He rakes a hand through his hair, frustration emanating from every line of his body. "Rachel, that boat wasn't seaworthy. I'd sanded it, painted it to make it look nice, but I hadn't replaced the waterproofing between the boards. It was just for display."

A sinking feeling settles in my gut as the magnitude of our mistake hits me. "I didn't know," I manage, my voice small.

"You're lucky it wasn't more serious," Dan continues, his tone softening slightly. "All this time, you've been asking me to treat Chloe like a grown-up. Well, look what happens. She's just a child, Rachel."

Tears prick at the corners of my eyes, blurring my vision. He's right, of course. I'd been so focused on giving Chloe the independence I thought she needed that I'd failed to consider the risks.

"I'm sorry," I say again, the words inadequate in the face of what could have been. "I never meant for this to happen."

Dan sighs, the anger draining from his features as he reaches out to brush a strand of wet hair from my forehead. "I know," he says. "But it did. And now we have to deal with it."

He turns to Chloe, gathering her into his arms. She clings to him, her face pale and pinched. "Let's get you both inside," he says, his voice gentle but firm. "We'll get you warmed up, and then we'll talk about this."

I nod, allowing him to help me out of the car.

The warmth of the house envelops us as we step inside, a shocking contrast to the chill that has seeped into my bones. Dan bustles about, grabbing towels and blankets, his movements efficient yet tinged with a lingering tension.

Chloe huddles on the couch, wrapped in a fluffy towel, her eyes distant. I long to comfort her, to assure her that everything will be alright, but the words stick in my throat. How can I make such promises when I've so clearly failed her?

"Get those wet clothes off now," he says.

I accept a towel and a robe from him, and he turns and busies himself with Chloe while I strip, my soaked clothes land on the floor with a soppy thud.

"I'll make some hot chocolate," Dan announces, his voice cutting through the heavy silence. "Chloe, why don't you go up and take a shower? As hot as you can take it."

She nods, sliding off the couch and padding down the hallway in a robe much too big for her. I watch her go, my heart aching with the weight of my mistakes.

Dan returns with two steaming mugs of hot chocolate, setting them down on the coffee table. He settles into one of the dining room chairs across from me, his hands clasped tightly in his lap.

"What were you thinking?" he asks, his voice strained. "Do you have any idea how dangerous that river is?"

I wince, the guilt washing over me anew. "I know. I'm sorry, Dan. I didn't realize the boat wasn't seaworthy. I just wanted to do something special for Chloe, to show her that I care."

"By putting her life at risk?" His tone sharpens, anger flashing in his eyes. "I trusted you with my daughter, Rachel. I thought you understood how important she is to me."

"I do," I insist, leaning forward. "Chloe means the world to me, too. I would never intentionally put her in harm's way."

"But you did." The words hang heavy in the air. "I can't lose her, Rachel. Not like I lost Rebecca. I won't survive it."

My heart clenches at the raw pain in his voice. "I'm so sorry, Dan. I didn't mean to. I thought I was doing the right thing. Clearly it wasn't. I don't know what else to say."

"I know you didn't mean to," he says, his voice softening slightly. "But that doesn't change what happened."

Before I can respond, Chloe comes down the stairs, dressed in warm, dry clothes. She climbs onto the couch beside me, curling into my side. I wrap an arm around her, holding her close.

"I'm sorry, Daddy," she murmurs, her voice small. "I didn't mean to scare you."

Dan's expression softens as he looks at his daughter. He moves to join us on the couch, pulling Chloe into a tight hug. "I know, sweetheart. I'm just glad you're safe."

Over Chloe's head, our eyes meet. I have to look away. The shame. The guilt. The disappointment in myself...

I struggle to my feet, cinching the robe tighter around me. The exhaustion from the swim, the panic, the argument with Dan—it all crashes over me in a suffocating wave. I need to get away, to clear my head. I walk towards the door, each step an effort.

"Rachel, wait." Dan's voice halts me. "You can't leave like this. You're in no shape to go anywhere."

I pause, not turning around. The concern in his tone tugs at my heart, but the sting of his earlier words lingers. "I'll be fine," I mumble, though even I don't believe it.

"I'm really sorry," I say as I open the door and head out of Dan's life and Maine forever.

SIXTEEN

I stare at my plane ticket to Chicago, the departure time blurring before my eyes as I sit at the airport bar. Despite the melodramatic exit from Dan's house, I spent two days in Portland before air traffic was fully operational again. But I got to drown my sorrows in the relative comfort of a five-star hotel in the city center, and got to experience room service three times a day.

"What can I get for you?"

The bartender's voice startles me out of my thoughts. He leans on the polished wood counter, his kind eyes taking in my distress with a look of concern.

I blink rapidly, trying to focus. "Um, I'll have a…" My voice trails off as I glance at the rows of gleaming bottles behind him.

What does it matter what I order? In a few hours, I'll be back in Chicago, back to normality. Back to work. Although, truth be told, I'm not sure it's the life I want anymore.

The bartender waits patiently, his gentle presence somehow soothing in the midst of my turmoil.

I clear my throat. "A vodka cranberry, please."

He nods with an understanding smile. "Coming right up."

As he busies himself preparing my drink, I stare unseeingly at the bustling concourse beyond the bar.

Travelers hurry past, their faces alight with purpose and excitement. Couples stroll hand-in-hand, families wrangle exuberant children. They all seem to know exactly where they're going, their paths laid out clearly before them.

And yet here I sit, my own way forward suddenly as hazy as my reflection in the bar's mirrored backsplash. I thought I had it all figured out—climb the corporate ladder, focus on my career, prove myself in a cutthroat industry where success is the only currency that matters.

And somehow, I brought that mindset here—to Maine. Trying to prove that I could make things better for Dan and Chloe, that I could fix their lives like some kind of guardian angel. But I wasn't thinking about what they actually needed. I just wanted to feel useful again. To feel like I was doing something worthwhile. And instead, I nearly got Chloe killed.

"Here you go." The bartender slides my drink across to me, the bright red liquid sloshing gently. "Anything else I can get for you?"

I wrap my fingers around the cool glass, anchoring myself in its solidity. "No, thank you. I'm... I'm good."

Am I, though? Am I really ready to walk away from everything these past weeks have awakened in me? The connection, the belonging, the sense that I could be part of something real?

My stomach twists, and I take a fortifying sip of my drink. It burns going down, a welcome distraction from the ache in my heart. I'll be fine. I have to be. This is the path I chose long ago, and I can't just abandon it because of a few weeks of... What, exactly?

A fantasy, that's what. A lovely dream that has no place in the harsh light of reality. Rachel Holmes doesn't get distracted by small-town charms and cozy family parties. She doesn't let her guard down, doesn't let herself imagine a different future.

No, Rachel Holmes gets on a plane to Chicago and doesn't look back. Even if every fiber of her being is screaming at her to reconsider. Even if she can't shake the feeling that she's making a terrible mistake.

I can do this. I have to do this. I lift my gaze to the bartender once more.

"Could I get my check, please?"

As I reach into my pocket for my wallet, my fingers brush against something unexpected. Frowning, I pull out a crumpled napkin, my heart stuttering as I recognize the scrawled handwriting. Dan's napkin, the one he'd given me that night at the bar. The night that started... everything.

I smooth it out on the polished surface of the bar, my eyes tracing the words that have become so familiar, so precious.

Character or actor?

Three simple words that had sparked a connection, an understanding. A reminder that beneath the surface, we were both struggling to reconcile our public personas with our true selves.

My vision blurs, and I blink back the tears that threaten to fall. How can a silly little napkin hold so much meaning? How can it make me question everything I thought I knew about myself, about what I want?

I should throw it away. Leave it behind, like I'm leaving behind Maine and all the memories it holds. But as I crumple it in my fist, I can't bring myself to let go. It's a tangible piece of the journey I've been on, a symbol of the person I've become.

Or maybe, the person I've always been, beneath the polished veneer of professionalism and ambition. The person who longs for connection, for a sense of home and family. The person who's been hiding behind the mask of Rachel Holmes, Director of New Business Development, for far too long.

My hand shakes as I tuck the napkin back into my pocket, a talisman against the doubts that swirl within me. I can't go back; can't undo the choices I've made. But maybe, just maybe, I can carry a piece of this experience with me, a reminder of what could be, if I'm brave enough to reach for it.

With a resolute nod, I slide off the barstool, and I make my way towards the boarding gate. Towards Chicago, towards the life I've built, the life I've chosen.

But even as I hand my ticket to the gate agent, even as I step onto the plane, I can feel the weight of the napkin in my pocket, a constant presence, the promise of possibility.

And for the first time in a long time, I allow myself to wonder... What if?

With trembling fingers, I unfold the napkin, my eyes widening as I take in the words scrawled across its surface.

"Character or actor?"

The question stares back at me, a challenge and an invitation all at once.

I can almost hear Dan's voice, that gentle, knowing tone he reserves for moments when he sees right through me. He's asking me to choose, to decide who I want to be. The polished, put-together PR executive, always playing a role? Or the real Rachel, the one who laughs freely, who opens her heart, who dares to dream of a different life?

My thoughts are a tangled web as I stare at the napkin, my vision blurring with unshed tears. A part of me longs to be that person, to shed the armor I've worn for so long and embrace the vulnerability that comes with truly being seen. But another part of me recoils, terrified of the implications, of the upheaval it could bring to the carefully constructed world I've built.

I crumple the napkin in my fist, the paper crinkling under the force of my conflicting emotions. How can a simple question hold so much power, so much potential for change? How can a few words from a man I've known for such a short time make me question everything I thought I wanted?

My heart races as I contemplate the choice before me, the path I've been on for so long, or the uncharted territory that beckons. Can I really let go of the security, the status, the identity I've clung to? Can I risk everything for a chance at something more, something real?

The napkin feels heavy in my hand, a tangible reminder of the decision I face. Character or actor. Authenticity or pretense. Love or ambition.

I try to quiet the warring voices in my head. And in that moment, I realize that maybe, just maybe, I don't have to choose. Maybe I can find a way to be both, to embrace the strength and resilience I've honed as Rachel Holmes while also allowing myself to be vulnerable, to be real.

With a newfound sense of clarity, I slowly uncurl my fingers, and smooth out the crumpled napkin. The words stare back at me, a challenge and an invitation all at once. Character or actor.

I trace the letters with my fingertip, a faint smile tugging at the corners of my mouth as I picture Dan's face, the earnest intensity in his eyes as he posed the question. And in doing so, he offered me a chance to rewrite my story, to create a new narrative that encompasses all the facets of who I am and who I want to be.

As I approach the gate, I feel a newfound sense of clarity and purpose. Each step is deliberate, a physical manifestation of my resolve. The bustling terminal fades into the background, my focus solely on the path ahead.

I pause at the threshold, my hand resting on the ticketing counter. For a moment, I allow myself to look back, not with longing or regret, but with gratitude. The ash cloud, meeting Dan and Chloe, the crumpled napkin—they all played a part in this journey of self-discovery. They were catalysts, pushing me to confront the parts of myself I had long ignored.

I cross the threshold, stepping onto the air bridge. The steady hum of the aircraft engines grows louder, a reminder of the world that awaits me beyond these walls. I feel a flicker of excitement, a sense of anticipation of what lies ahead.

As I step onto the plane, the flight attendant checks my ticket and greets me with a warm smile. "Welcome aboard, Ms. Holmes. We're glad to have you with us today and glad to be flying again."

I return the smile, a genuine one that reaches my eyes. "Thank you. Me too."

And I am. Truly. I settle into my seat, my gaze drifting to the small window beside me. The tarmac stretches out before me, a network of roads leading to countless destinations. But for now, my destination is clear. Chicago. Channing Gabriel. A new chapter in my story.

As the plane begins to taxi, I lean back in my seat, a sense of peace washing over me. The napkin may be gone, but its message lives on, etched into my heart. Character and actor. Two sides of the same coin. Two parts of a whole.

And as the plane lifts off, soaring into the sky, I know that I am ready. Ready to embrace all that I am, all that I can be. Ready to write a new story, one that is uniquely, unapologetically, mine.

The gentle hum of the plane's engines fill my ears as we climb higher into the sky. I gaze out the window, watching as the world below grows smaller and smaller. The buildings, the roads, the trees—they all blur together into a patchwork quilt of colors and shapes.

I find myself thinking about Dan, about the time we shared together. The laughter, the tears, the moments of connection that felt so real, so raw. And I realize that, in a way, he will always be a part of me. A part of my story, a chapter in the book of my life.

But it's a chapter that has come to an end. I messed up. And as much as it hurts, as much as I may want to cling to the past, I know that I have to let it go. I have to move forward, to embrace the future that lies ahead.

I reach into my pocket, my fingers brushing against the smooth surface of my phone. I pull it out, staring at the blank screen for a moment before unlocking it. I open up my email, my eyes scanning the inbox for one particular message.

There it is. The email from Channing Gabriel, confirming my return to work. I click on it, reading the words that I've read a dozen times before. But this time, they feel different. This time, they feel like a promise. A promise of new beginnings, of second chances.

I picture myself walking into the office, head held high, ready to take on whatever challenges come my way. I picture myself thriving, growing, becoming the best version of myself.

And I know that, no matter what happens, I will always have this moment. This moment of clarity of purpose, of pure, unadulterated determination.

The plane continues to soar, carrying me closer and closer to my destination. And as I sit there, my heart full of hope and possibility, I know that I am exactly where I am meant to be.

SEVENTEEN

— ♥ —

FOUR MONTHS LATER

I never imagined getting dressed for a date would feel like assembling battle armor.

I stand in front of my full-length mirror, smoothing the silky fabric of my dress with slightly trembling hands. It's a rich forest green—a color Zoe insisted made my eyes "look expensive"—but tonight, I'm not sure what message I'm trying to send. Confident? Curious? Emotionally available?

I haven't been on a real date in months. Not since Portland. Not since Dan.

That thought catches me off guard, creeping in like an uninvited guest. I shake it off, adjusting the strap of my dress. This isn't about him. This is about me. Moving on. Saying yes to the world again.

The condo is quiet, almost suspiciously so. No urgent emails. No impossible deadlines. No campaign crises demanding immediate triage. Just the low hum of the city outside and the quiet clink of my necklace clasp as I fasten it behind my neck.

I check my phone—my Uber is two minutes away. I grab my bag, slipping on a coat as I glance around my place. Everything is exactly where it should be. Tidy. Organized. Predictable.

It doesn't feel like a home. It feels like a base of operations.

The idea unsettles me, but I push it aside. Tonight isn't about soul-searching. Tonight is about dipping my toe back into the world of dating—and maybe reminding myself that life still exists outside of PR decks, crisis plans, and regret.

I lock the door behind me and head downstairs, the familiar clack of my heels on concrete a strange comfort. The Uber is waiting, its interior glowing softly like a promise of something new.

As the car pulls away from the curb, I catch my reflection in the window—composed, polished, every inch a woman who knows what she wants.

I just wish I knew for certain what that was.

The Uber drops me off at *Nouveau*—his suggestion—the trendy restaurant in the heart of downtown. As I step inside, the lively chatter and clinking of glasses promise an evening to remember. The hostess leads me to a table by the expansive windows, giving me a perfect view of the bustling street below.

I slide into the velvet chair, carefully crossing my legs and unfolding the napkin onto my lap like I've done this a hundred times. But inside, I'm jittery. Not in a bad way, necessarily— just... rusty. I focus on the stylish decor—exposed brick walls, Edison bulbs casting a warm glow, and an eclectic mix of artwork. The hum of conversation fills the air, punctuated by bursts of laughter from nearby tables. I can't help but feel a spark of anticipation. Maybe this is exactly what I need, a chance to connect with someone new and let loose a little.

The truth is, I'm not used to this version of myself anymore. The one who shows up early to dates. The one who gets dressed up for the sake of curiosity, of possibility. For so long, I've only dressed to be taken seriously. Power blazers. Monochrome palettes. Always aiming to disappear into competence.

Tonight, I'm trying something different.

I glance around the restaurant, watching other tables for cues. A couple to my left is halfway through a bottle of wine, hands inching closer between courses. Across the room, someone laughs a little too loudly at something not that funny. First-date nerves, I suspect.

Friends toast with colorful cocktails, and I fidget with the napkin in my lap, trying to quell the butterflies in my stomach. Dating has never been my strong suit, always taking a backseat to my career. But I'm here now, putting myself out there. That counts for something, right?

I glance at my phone, checking the time. He should be here any minute. I take a sip of water, surveying the menu without really reading it. The scent of garlic and herbs waft from the kitchen, mingling with the soft jazz playing overhead. I remind myself that tonight is about being brave. Being spontaneous. Living my best life—or, at the very least, trying to.

Lyle arrives exactly on time, striding confidently into the restaurant with that same cocky charm I remember from the pitch meeting. He looks polished and sharp in a charcoal suit, his hair perfectly styled, and I have to admit—he cleans up well.

As he strides toward me, every eye in the room seems to notice him. He has that energy—like he knows he belongs here.

And just like that, I remember exactly why I initially said no.

"Rachel," he greets me with a grin, holding his arms out like he's about to hug me, but then thinking better of it and offering his hand instead. "You look fantastic."

"Thanks," I say. "You too."

He chuckles, giving me a once-over. "I have to admit, I was pleasantly surprised to get your call. I thought you didn't mix business with pleasure."

I shrug with a smile, although I don't appreciate the lingering look. "Usually, I don't. But I'm trying to change that—being a little more open to... new experiences."

Lyle raises an eyebrow, clearly intrigued, but I get the distinct impression that his mind sunk into the gutter before he consciously dragged it back out.

"I like that. Life's too short to stick to rules anyway."

I laugh lightly, even though I'm not entirely sure I agree with him. "Exactly. Sometimes you just have to go for it."

The waiter appears almost immediately, taking our drink orders while we peruse the menu—a whiskey for him and a glass of Pinot Noir for me.

Once the drinks arrive, Lyle raises his glass, giving me a confident smile. "To new beginnings," he says, and this time I agree wholeheartedly, clinking my glass against his.

"To new beginnings," I echo, taking a sip.

Lyle leans back, clearly comfortable in his element. "You know, I have to say, I respect someone who knows what they want and goes after it. That pitch you gave the other week was killer. You really command a room."

I smile, but there's a part of me that wonders if he means it as a compliment or a strategy. Praise often comes easily from people who expect everything to be transactional.

Still, I take it. I've worked too hard not to. "Thanks," I reply.

He nods appreciatively. "Smart. I've always believed that calculated risks are the only way to get ahead. You've got to be willing to bend the rules when it counts."

There's something slick about the way he says it—like he's not talking about bold ideas, but about cutting corners and justifying it later. It reminds me of a dozen other men I've met in boardrooms and during brunches: driven, yes—but never slowed down by things like ethics or empathy.

"So," I say, steering the conversation, "when you're not flipping burgers, what do you like to do? Hobbies? Passions?"

He gives me a look that's somewhere between amused and horrified. "You're kidding, right? I wouldn't be seen dead in one of our restaurants, in front or behind the counter."

I laugh, but it comes out brittle. He doesn't notice. Or maybe he does and just doesn't care. There's a pride in his voice I can't quite align with. I think of Dan teaching kids how to block scenes, mucking in with AV equipment and lighting, never above anything. There's a dignity in showing up, even when it's messy. Lyle seems allergic to mess—and slumming it with staff.

"Oh," I say, my smile faltering just a touch. "Surely, for market research, or employee satisfaction, you need to—"

He waves a dismissive hand. "I'm a vice president, Lara. My staff deals with the nitty gritty. I'm all about the big picture. As for hobbies, I don't really think there's room for distractions if you want to succeed. I've always said that relationships and personal stuff can wait until you're established. You've got to build your empire first. Then you can enjoy it."

I nod slowly, though everything inside me recoils. I used to think like that. Maybe I still do, sometimes. But hearing it aloud—so clinical, so certain—makes it sound more like a warning than a philosophy.

I nod slowly, but I feel a tightening, like something small and sharp curling behind my ribs.

"That makes sense, I guess... but don't you think there's more to life than just work?"

He chuckles, like I've made a cute joke. "Sure, sure. But I figure once I'm at the top, I'll have plenty of time to relax. Right now, I'm focused on getting there."

His voice fills the space between us like an ad jingle—loud, confident, repetitive. I try to keep pace, but it's like playing tennis with someone who's only practicing their serve.

The conversation seems to be very one-sided. He lists off his career achievements, the big brands he's worked for, followed by a monologue about how he's clawed his way up the corporate ladder. I nod and smile in all the right places, but my mind is elsewhere, wondering why on earth I thought this man was worth my time.

After dinner, he insists on paying the bill—making a show of it, really—before escorting me outside.

He pauses on the sidewalk, turning to face me with that same self-assured smile. "I had a good time," he says, leaning closer. "You really are as impressive as I thought."

I manage a polite smile, but I'm already leaning back, not quite ready to let him close the gap.

There's a moment where he looks like he might go in for a goodnight kiss. Instead of panic, I feel... mild curiosity, like watching someone attempt karaoke in a language they don't speak.

I step back, smiling. It's not awkward, just... expected.

"Thanks for tonight," I say carefully, "but I don't think this is going to work."

His confident expression slips for a fraction of a second before he recovers. "Wait—what? I thought we were having a great time. A fantastic meal. Great restaurant—"

"It was delicious," I say honestly. "It was great, really. But... I just don't think we're on the same wavelength. I'm trying to be more open to new things, but I guess I realized tonight that I'm not looking for the same kind of life you are."

His jaw tightens, and he lets out a short, humorless laugh. "Seriously? You're not even going to give this a chance?"

I shake my head gently. "It's not fair to you to pretend I feel something I don't. You deserve someone who's as driven as you are, who wants the same things."

He scoffs, shoving his hands in his pockets. "You're something else, you know that? Most women would kill to be with a guy like me. Successful. Driven."

I suppress a wince. "I'm sure they would. And I'm sure you'll find someone who matches that ambition. But it's not me."

His face hardens, and for a moment, he looks like he's about to argue, but then he just shakes his head. "Your loss," he mutters, giving me one last, almost contemptuous glance before turning on his heel and striding away.

He walks away like he's made some kind of profound impression. And I suppose he has—just not the one he'd hoped for.

The truth is, I said yes to Lyle because it felt like progress. A grown-up move. I'd been trying to say yes to more things lately—less hesitation, more life. He was charming in meetings, ambitious, maybe a bit slick—but he was interested, and that counted for something, didn't it?

Besides, it wasn't like I was holding out for fireworks. I'd had enough of impossible standards and perfect-on-paper crushes. Maybe what I needed was something different. Grounded. Easy. It's just a shame Lyle is a complete douche.

I watch him go, and then pull my phone from my bag to find a driver. I dipped my toe in the dating pool, and, quite frankly, found it wanting. But at least I put myself out there. And maybe that's progress enough for one night.

The app times out for the fourth time and I give up. *No drivers currently available.* Fantastic. It's about four miles to the Lower West Side. I'm not going to walk it—not in these heels—but I decide to walk in the general direction in the hope that the Friday night rush will die down and I can snag a driver later.

It's been a long time since I spent time downtown. Certainly at night. The city streets bustle with energy as I walk, my heels clicking against the pavement. Neon signs glow, casting a kaleidoscope of colors across the faces of passersby. Laughter and chatter spill from bustling restaurants and bars, the sound mingling with the distant honk of car horns.

Despite the lively atmosphere, I feel strangely disconnected, lost in my own thoughts. The date with Lyle plays on repeat in my mind, each moment dissected and analyzed. On the surface, he was determined, attractive, successful —everything I thought I wanted. So why did it feel so... wrong?

I pause at a crosswalk, waiting for the light to change. A couple walks by, hand in hand, their laughter carrying on the breeze. A pang of longing hits me, so sharp it actually hurts. The last time I laughed like that, the last time I felt that kind of connection with anyone, was with Dan.

The light changes and I move with the crowd, still lost in thought. I've spent so long chasing success, climbing the corporate ladder, that I've neglected what really matters. Friendships, hobbies, love... They've all taken a backseat to my ambition.

But what is success, really, if you have no one to share it with? What's the point of reaching the top if you're alone when you get there? I might have got there with Dan, I really might have. But I messed up.

A gust of wind sends a chill down my spine, and I wrap my coat tighter around myself. The city lights blur as tears prick at my eyes, a sudden rush of emotion taking me by surprise. Did I miss my one opportunity, or is it true what they say, that there's plenty more fish in the sea?

What I do know is, I want more than this. I deserve more than this. More than superficial dates and surface-level connections. I want something real, something meaningful. I want a life that's rich with love and laughter and purpose.

I let the revelation wash over me. It's scary, admitting what

I want. It means being vulnerable, opening myself up to the possibility of being hurt.

But it also means opening myself up to the possibility of something wonderful.

I square my shoulders, a new sense of determination filling me. I may not know exactly what I'm looking for, but I know I won't find it by playing it safe. This evening may have been an unmitigated disaster, but that shouldn't mean try it once and give up. It's time to take a chance, to put myself out there in a way I never have before.

It's time to go after what I really want.

As I turn the corner, lost in thought, a familiar face catches my eye. I stop in my tracks, blinking in disbelief at the massive billboard towering above me.

Dan Rhodes.

He's grinning down at me, his eyes twinkling with that same mischievous charm I remember from our time in Maine. But there's something different about him now, a newfound confidence that radiates from the billboard.

"Tune in to *Heartstrings* this fall," the billboard proclaims, "starring Dan Rhodes."

I stare up at the image, a rush of emotions flooding through me. Surprise, first and foremost. When I'd last seen Dan, he'd been adamant that he had turned his back on acting forever, determined not to miss a moment of Chloe growing up. But now, here he is, larger than life on a billboard for a new sitcom.

Pride swells in my chest, mixed with a bittersweet twinge of regret. I was right. Seeing him up there, it's clear he took my advice to heart. He chose to restart his acting career. He stepped back into the spotlight—and he's shining.

And yet, there's something else too. A frustration I can't quite shake, a sense of missed opportunity and injustice that tugs at my heart. We fell out because I could see what Dan couldn't. Admittedly, I shouldn't have pushed without his consent, but still, he got there eventually. What if he hadn't been so quick to dismiss the idea? What if I'd just... waited? Let it be his decision, in his own time?

My mind flickers back to that napkin, the one he slid across the table with his quiet, knowing smile. Character or actor?

I hadn't answered him then. I don't know if I could answer now. But maybe that was the moment—the fork in the road.

I shake my head, trying to push away the thoughts. It's ridiculous. I barely know the man. Not really. And yet, somehow, seeing him up there on that billboard, I miss... him. Us. Or at least the potential of us.

I linger there, staring up at the billboard, letting the conflicting emotions wash over me. Satisfaction and regret. Longing and resignation. Pride that he found his way. And a quiet ache that I wasn't there to share it. It's a bittersweet mix, one that leaves me feeling strangely raw and exposed.

But as I finally tear my gaze away and continue down the street, I can't help but smile. Because even if Dan Rhodes and I never cross paths again, even if the connection we shared was fleeting, seeing him up there on that billboard gives me hope.

Hope that it's never too late to chase a dream. Hope that, even when life takes us in different directions, the people who touch our lives stay with us, inspiring us to be our best selves.

And most of all, hope that somewhere out there, the kind of love I'm looking for is waiting for me. I just have to be brave enough to go after it.

The streets are alive with the usual Friday night rhythm—music drifting from open doors, laughter echoing down alleys, the clink of glasses and the occasional burst of shouting. It should feel electric. Inviting. But I feel oddly detached from it all, like I'm walking through someone else's life.

My heels echo against the sidewalk as I head towards nothing in particular, and that's when it hits me—how often

I've moved in straight lines. Always knowing the destination. Always chasing the next milestone, the next title, the next "win." My entire life has been one long itinerary, and tonight, for once, I don't have anywhere to be. No deadline. No calendar invite. No obligation.

And I feel... untethered.

But beneath that, something deeper stirs. A question I've never really stopped long enough to ask: If I strip away the career, the hustle, the façade—what's left? Who's left?

I've always thought ambition was what defined me. But maybe I used it to protect myself, to stay busy enough that I didn't have to look too closely at what I might be missing.

And I have been missing something.

Not just a person. Not even Dan. But a version of myself who's curious. Soft. Present. A Rachel who's not performing, not selling a vision, *not an actor*—but just being.

Maybe, for the first time in my adult life, I want to know what it feels like to live without a script.

And the thought terrifies me... but it also thrills me.

And maybe that's the lesson in all of this. That life is full of missed opportunities and paths not taken, but it's also full of new beginnings and second chances. Somewhere out there, my own billboard is waiting. And when I find it, I'll be ready to take center stage and shine.

EIGHTEEN

I stare at the blinking cursor on my laptop screen, trying to muster up some semblance of enthusiasm for Incrediburger's new lower-calorie menu. Based on the early success of their plant-based burger, they've embraced our ideas for diversifying their product offerings further with a new range hitting the shelves as soon as we're done with Thanksgiving.

The campaign is strong, and our art team has done an amazing job with the mockup imagery and taglines, but despite the real business need to get this launched, their decision-making has become glacial.

When I say *their* decision-making, I mean Lyle's.

Lyle didn't take my rejection well at all. He's spent the last two weeks outing himself as a total and complete asshole, and is proving to be a thorn in my side by deliberately delaying and frustrating every email, every sign-off, every meeting... It's petty, pathetic, and predictable.

I may have to remove myself from the account so that we can all get back on track, but it annoys me immensely that I won't be able to work with the rest of the team who's proven to be incredibly professional.

I absently rearrange the succulents on my desk, a futile attempt at bringing life to this sterile space. The pot of zinnias, a gift from Zoe after the GreenShoots pitch, serves as a bittersweet reminder. We won the account, the biggest coup of my career, at Channing Gabriel. But at what cost? Late nights, missed dinners with friends, a perpetually neglected personal life?

As if on cue, my desk phone jolts me out of my rumination. It's Jenna, my assistant.

"Rachel, the partners want to see you in the boardroom. Like, now."

I sit up straighter, pulse quickening. "Did they say what it's about?"

"No, but they said to drop whatever you're doing and head over. Seems urgent."

"Okay, thanks, Jenna. I'll be right there."

I smooth my silk blouse and quickly check my face in a compact. An impromptu summons from the higher-ups rarely bodes well. My mind races with possibilities as I make my way down the hallway. Have I slipped up somehow? Overlooked a crucial detail on the Harcourt account?

I pause outside the imposing mahogany doors, steeling myself. Whatever awaits me on the other side, I'll handle it with the poise and professionalism that got me this far. I turn the polished brass handle, and step inside, ready to face the music.

I step into the boardroom, my heels sinking into the plush carpet. The partners are already assembled, seated around the expansive glass table like a corporate war council. At the head sits Crystal Channing herself, impeccably coiffed and poised, her steely gaze fixed on me.

"Rachel, please have a seat," she says, gesturing to an empty chair.

I settle in, trying to read the room. Tense anticipation

hangs in the air, but there's an undercurrent of something else. Excitement?

"We have some news," Crystal begins, her red-lacquered nails tapping against the table. "GreenShoots has served out their six-month notice period with Overt PR, as of this morning, they're a Channing Gabriel client. It's official."

A wave of relief washes over me, followed by a surge of pride. We did it. Months of grueling work, endless revisions, and cutthroat negotiations have finally paid off.

"Congratulations are in order," chimes in Ethan, the director of accounts. "This is a huge win for the firm, and for you, Rachel."

I nod graciously, but inside I'm puzzled. Surely, they didn't call me in here just to offer congratulations?

Crystal, as if sensing my confusion, leans forward. "We wanted to acknowledge your instrumental role in securing this account. Your strategic vision and tireless dedication laid the groundwork for our success."

"Even if Zoe delivered the final pitch," adds Helen, her tone a mix of praise and something sharper. A reminder, perhaps, that my protégé is nipping at my heels.

"Of course," I reply smoothly. "It was a team effort. I'm just glad we could deliver for the client."

"This account opens up exciting new avenues for Channing Gabriel," says Crystal, her eyes gleaming. "And we have you to thank, Rachel. Your hard work hasn't gone unnoticed."

There it is again, that undercurrent of anticipation. I feel like I'm on the cusp of something big, but I can't quite grasp what it is.

"In fact," Crystal continues, "we've been discussing your future with the firm..."

She slides a document across the table, the Channing Gabriel logo embossed at the top. My heart rate kicks up a notch as I scan the header: Partnership Offer.

The room erupts in applause, a cacophony of congratulations and well-wishes. But the sound seems distant, muffled by the pounding of my own heartbeat in my ears.

A partnership. The pinnacle of achievement in this world of glass and steel, of power suits and boardroom battles. The validation of every late night, every missed weekend, every sacrifice I've made at the altar of my career.

My fingers trace the crisp edges of the document, the weight of it suddenly heavy in my hands. This is everything I've worked for, the logical next step in my meticulously planned trajectory.

So why does a flicker of doubt stir in my chest?

Crystal's voice cuts through my reverie. "This is a momentous day, Rachel. We're thrilled to officially welcome you into the partnership ranks."

She extends a pen, an expectant smile on her lips. "Just sign on the dotted line, and let's make it official."

I stare at the blank space awaiting my signature, the weight of the decision settling on my shoulders. The rational part of me knows this is an incredible opportunity, the culmination of years of hard work and dedication.

But another part, a small, insistent voice I've long ignored, seeds doubts. Is this really what I want? Is this the path to fulfillment, to a life well-lived?

Images flash through my mind: the sterile emptiness of my high-rise apartment, the wilting plant on my desk, a silent testament to my neglect. The missed birthdays, the foregone untaken paid time off, the relationships left to wither on the vine of my ambition.

And then, unbidden, a memory surfaces. The boat house by the river, the warmth of Dan's smile, the sound of Chloe's laughter. That door is certainly closed, but the experience gave me a glimpse of a different life, one where success is measured not in titles and accounts, but in moments of connection and joy.

My hand hovers over the page, the pen suddenly heavy in my grip. The eyes of the partners bore into me, expectant, eager. They see a rising star, a valuable asset to be acquired.

But do they see me? The real Rachel, beneath the polished veneer and the impressive resume?

The seconds tick by, each one an eternity. The air feels charged, the silence thick with anticipation.

I take a deep breath, the scent of leather and high-end cologne filling my lungs. This is it, the moment of truth. The crossroads where I decide the course of my future.

Partnership, or something else entirely? The safe, well-trodden path, or a leap into the unknown?

I close my eyes for a moment, seeking clarity amidst the swirling doubts and desires. And then, with a suddenness that surprises even me, the answer crystallizes.

I know what I have to do.

I open my eyes, meeting Crystal's expectant gaze. The words form on my lips, a declaration and a choice all at once.

"I'm sorry," I say, my voice steady even as my heart races. "But I can't accept this offer."

A ripple of shock passes through the room, faces morphing from anticipation to confusion. Crystal's perfectly manicured brows furrow, her lips parting in disbelief.

"Rachel, I don't understand. This is the opportunity of a lifetime. You've earned this. Maybe you don't fully understand the Partners' profit share program?"

I nod, a smile tugging at the corners of my mouth despite the gravity of the moment. "You're right, I have earned this. And I'm incredibly grateful for the recognition and the faith you've all shown in me."

I pause, gathering my thoughts, choosing my words with care. "But I've also realized that my path, my true fulfillment, lies elsewhere. This job, this life... It's taught me so much. But it's not the end goal. Not anymore."

The partners exchange glances, a mixture of disappointment and grudging respect in their eyes. They know, as I do, that once my mind is made up, there's no changing it.

Crystal leans back in her chair, studying me with a newfound intensity. "And what is your end goal, Rachel? What does your path look like?"

I laugh softly; the sound surprising me with its lightness. "Honestly? I'm not entirely sure yet. But I know it involves more than contracts and campaigns. It's about making a real difference, not just to a bottom line, but to people's lives. It's about finding a balance between work and everything else that matters."

I stand, smoothing my skirt, the fabric a familiar armor that I no longer need.

"Thank you, truly, for everything. For the opportunities, the mentorship, the challenges that have shaped me. But now, it's time for me to shape my own future."

I extend my hand, a final handshake, a gesture of gratitude and farewell.

Crystal takes it, her grip firm, her eyes searching mine.

"You're sure about this?" she asks, one last attempt to sway me. "You're sure you want to quit?"

I nod, my resolve unwavering. "I've never been more certain of anything in my life."

And with that, I turn, my heels clicking against the polished floor as I walk towards the door. Towards a new beginning, a new chapter in the story of Rachel Holmes.

The future is unwritten, a blank page waiting to be filled. And for the first time in a long time, I'm excited to pick up the pen and start writing.

I push open the glass door of the boardroom, stepping out into the familiar buzz of the office. But everything feels different now. The weight of expectation has lifted from my shoulders, replaced by a giddy sense of possibility.

I walk to my desk, my steps lighter, my smile wider. I gather my belongings, the few personal touches I've allowed myself over the years. A framed photo of my sister and her family, a small succulent that's managed to survive my erratic watering schedule, and, of course, my favorite coffee mug, my constant companion through late nights and early mornings.

As I make my way towards the elevator, I feel the eyes of my colleagues on me, curious, questioning. But I don't falter, my head held high, my grin unfaltering.

I step into the elevator. The doors slide shut, cocooning me in a moment of solitude. I lean against the wall, the cool metal a contrast to the warmth blooming in my chest.

The doors ping open, and I step out into the lobby, the sunlight streaming through the high windows, bathing everything in a golden glow. It feels like a sign, a blessing from the universe, a nod to the rightness of my decision.

And then, with a final nod, I turn and walk out of the building for the last time, into the bustling city street, into the future that awaits me, unknown and uncertain, but filled with the promise of something extraordinary.

The sun feels warm on my face as I step onto the sidewalk, a gentle breeze playing with my hair. I pause, closing my eyes, savoring this moment of liberation, of beginnings.

Around me, the city pulses with life—the honk of car horns, the chatter of pedestrians, the distant wail of a siren. But for once, I feel separate from the hustle, the relentless drive that's defined my life for so long.

I open my eyes and start walking, no clear destination in mind, just a need to move, to feel the pavement beneath my feet, to let my thoughts wander.

As I walk, I feel a lightness, a loosening of the knots that have taken up permanent residence in my shoulders. The weight of expectations, of proving myself, of chasing the next achievement—it falls away, leaving me feeling unmoored, but also free.

I pass familiar landmarks—the coffee shop where I've grabbed countless early morning lattes, the dry cleaners where I've dropped off my favorite suits, the gym where I've sweat out my frustrations on the treadmill. They feel like markers of a past life, a Rachel that I'm leaving behind.

As I loop back towards my apartment, the low November sun is already starting to set, painting the sky in streaks of orange and pink. It feels like a promise, a sign of the beauty that's waiting, just beyond the horizon.

I fish my keys out of my pocket, feeling the weight of them in my hand. They represent stability, security, the life I've built. But as I slot the key into the lock, I know that I'm ready to let go, to build something new.

I step into my apartment, the space feeling different somehow, like it belongs to a past version of me. I set my pot plant on the windowsill, a small symbol of growth, of nurturing something beyond myself.

And as I look out at the city skyline, I feel a rush of gratitude, of joy, of pure, unadulterated hope.

NINETEEN

I manage thirty-six hours alone in my condo, rearranging furniture, alphabetizing my books, and giving the whole place, not just a spring clean, but a full four-seasons special before I finally come up for air.

I pull into the driveway of Claire and Richard's house. Before I can even cut the engine, the front door bursts open and two pint-sized blurs come racing across the lawn.

"Aunt Rachel!" Lily and Anna squeal in unison, their faces lit up with glee. Behind them, my sister Claire emerges, her eyes wide with surprise.

"Rach! What are you doing here? I thought you were..." She trails off as the kids tackle me with hugs the moment I step out of the car.

"Hey, munchkins!" I laugh, scooping them up and spinning them around. "I decided to take a little break from work. Surprise!"

Claire arches an eyebrow, but her smile is warm. "Well, this is the best kind of surprise. Come on in, I just made some chocolate milk."

Inside, the house looks the same as always—family photos

covering the walls, the faint scent of Mom's lemon bars in the air.

Before I can call out a greeting, Mom appears in the hallway, wiping her hands on a dishtowel, her face lighting up when she sees me. "Rachel! There you are! I was just saying to Claire I thought I heard your car. You look thin. Are you eating enough?"

I offer her a big smile. "Hi, Mom. I'm fine."

She clucks her tongue, shaking her head like I'm still a teenager with bad eating habits.

"Busy or not, you need to eat properly. You're going to wither away to nothing. Come on, sit down. I have some chicken pot pie warming in the oven and leftover lasagna from yesterday. Or I can make you a grilled cheese? You used to love those."

I shake my head, trying to keep my tone light. "I'm really not hungry, Mom."

She narrows her eyes, scrutinizing me like she's trying to read between the lines of my expression. "Nonsense. You never turn down grilled cheese. I'll just make one and—"

"Mom." I reach out and squeeze her arm gently, giving her a reassuring smile. "Really, I'm fine. I just need... I don't know what I need."

Anna, who was waiting patiently for her turn to talk, tugs on my hand insistently.

"Aunt Rachel, I got a new Barbie! Wanna see?" Her green eyes dance with excitement.

"You bet I do, sweetheart. Lead the way!"

As Anna scampers off, Lily climbs into my lap, chocolate milk mustache and all. "I missed you, Aunt Rachel," she says solemnly.

"I missed you too, sweet pea." I kiss the top of her head, feeling a pang. When was the last time I made time for them like this?

Just then, Anna comes barreling back in, a Disney princess in her hands. "I freeze you!" she growls, making the doll stomp across the table—and straight into Lily's chocolate milk. The cup tips, sending a wave of brown liquid right into my lap.

"Anna!" Claire gasps, but I'm already laughing.

"It's okay, no harm done!" I grab a dish towel to mop up the mess, grinning at my Niece. "I think Elsa just wanted to cool off. It's thirsty work, all that covering the world in ice."

The kids giggle and I catch Claire watching me, a curious expression on her face. I just smile, a strange sense of lightness bubbling up in my chest. Maybe I needed a splash of chocolate milk to remember what matters. And right now, getting down on the floor for an epic princess picnic with the kids is all that matters in the world.

The games don't last too long before the girls want to move on to the next thing. Mom convinces them to do some coloring, and earns some whoops and cheers when she reveals a new pack of crayons and a fairy coloring book for each.

When Mom has settled Lily and Anna in the kitchen, she comes and joins us. She sits down heavily on the couch. As much as she loves seeing her granddaughters, it takes it out of her.

"Listen, there's something I need to tell you," I begin, my voice wavering slightly.

Claire and Mom have concern etched on their faces, and I hurry to reassure them.

"It's nothing bad, I promise. It's just... I quit my job at Channing Gabriel."

There's a moment of stunned silence before they both ask the inevitable, "What?" "When?" and "Why?" My mom reaches across the table to grasp my hand, her brow furrowed with worry.

"Quit? Just like that? But, honey, you loved your job. You worked so hard to get that position."

I nod, swallowing the rising tide of guilt. "Yeah, I did. And I thought I loved it. But... it doesn't feel the same anymore. I felt stuck. Miserable, actually."

Claire tilts her head, studying me. "What happened? I thought Channing Gabriel was your dream gig."

"It was," I say, trying to put words to the knot in my chest. "I just... couldn't do it anymore. I needed to stop."

Mom exchanges a look with Claire before reaching for my hand, and squeezing it gently. "I've been saying for years that you'll work yourself into an early grave. Even when you were little—you'd get so upset if you didn't get a perfect score on a test or mess up your homework. You remember that time you tried to play the piano piece from that school recital, and you wouldn't leave the piano for hours?"

Claire laughs softly. "God, I remember that. Mom practically had to drag you away from it. You were convinced that one wrong note meant you were a failure."

I force a smile. "Yeah, well, not much has changed, apparently."

Mom squeezes my hand again, her eyes soft. "Honey, I know you always wanted to make something of yourself, and I couldn't be prouder of everything you've achieved. But you don't have to prove anything to anyone. Not to us. Not to your bosses. Not even to yourself. Sometimes it's okay to just... be."

I feel the lump in my throat swelling, my chest tight with emotion. "It's not just about work. It's... everything. I don't even know what I want anymore. I thought climbing the ladder was the answer. But now that I'm at the top, and I just feel... empty."

Claire rests a hand on my shoulder. "It's okay to feel lost sometimes. Maybe this break is exactly what you need. Figure out what makes you happy again, not just what looks good on paper."

I nod, the words soaking into me like a balm. "I just don't know where to start."

Mom gives me a reassuring smile. "Start by giving yourself a little grace. You're allowed to change your mind. You're allowed to want different things."

I let out a shaky laugh, wiping a stray tear from my cheek. "I'm just scared. What if I don't figure it out? What if I never find something that makes me feel... enough?"

"You'll figure it out," Claire says firmly. "And who wouldn't want to lie around all day while they figure it out?"

The heaviness in my chest loosens just a little, and I nod, grateful for the support. The girls squeal in delight at the table, before Lily comes running in, proudly holding up her masterpiece—a neon pink fairy with green wings.

"Look, Aunt Rachel!" she calls. "Isn't she pretty?"

I smile, genuinely this time. "She's gorgeous, Lil. You've got real talent."

Claire leans closer, dropping her voice. "You know, I haven't seen you this relaxed in ages. Maybe that's a sign."

I glance at her, considering the idea. "Maybe. It just feels nice to be... here."

The front door opens with a familiar clunk, followed by the thud of work boots and the creak of a grocery bag being set down.

"Smells like chocolate milk and crayons in here," Richard calls out, his voice warm and teasing. "Which means either I've walked into a crime scene, or my daughters are home."

"In the living room," Claire replies.

He rounds the corner, his high-vis vest still slung over one shoulder and smudges of dust on his forearm. When he sees me on the couch, one niece tucked into my side and the other sprawled across the rug with her coloring book, he stops short and breaks into a grin.

"Well, look what the cat dragged in."

"Hi, Richard," I say with a smile, brushing a lock of hair off Lily's forehead. "Hope it's okay I turned up unannounced."

"Okay? You're a walking excuse to skip bath time later. The girls will be thrilled." He drops a kiss on Claire's cheek, then gives my shoulder a quick squeeze on his way to the kitchen. "You staying for dinner? Or, do I have to drive you back to O'Hare for another emergency?"

"I'm really sorry about that."

"You missed a great holiday."

"I know. Next time."

Richard carries the groceries through to the kitchen and then washes his hands. "Claire texted you've quit your job? Good for you."

I blink at him. "That's it? No lecture?"

"What? You think someone who's spent twelve years herding subcontractors and trying not to fall off scaffolding is gonna judge you for quitting a job that made you miserable?" He opens the fridge, grabs a beer, and pops the cap off with one practiced motion. "Nah. Sounds like the sanest thing you've done in years."

"Well, when you put it like that..." I shake my head, smiling. "Thanks."

He plops into the armchair, glancing down at Anna's drawing. "Are these fairies unionized yet? You've got them working pretty hard."

"Dad, look! My unicorn's got six legs." Anna giggles, showing Richard her drawing.

"I used to have six legs," Richard says, pretending to cry. "But your mom made me give up the extras when we got married."

Anna blinks once, then twice, looking at her mom and then her dad, trying to process this outrage. "Why?"

"She said it wouldn't be fair to all the other guys at work. I'd always be able to run the fastest."

Anna considers this and then shakes her head vehemently. "You're telling fibs."

"Am not," Richard says. "They're in the attic with your tail. Come on, I'll show you."

With that, he scoops a giggling Anna into his arms and carries her out of the room.

Lily crawls across the couch, wrapping her arms around my waist. "Can you stay the night, Aunt Rachel?"

"You should," Mom says.

"We could have pancakes tomorrow!"

After meeting Chloe, pancakes have a new place in my heart as the go-to food for big moments, and today certainly measures up as one of my biggest. Lily couldn't have offered a better suggestion. I glance up at Claire. "Only if the kitchen's open for syrup-fueled chaos."

Claire raises an eyebrow. "I'll make the batter, if you flip."

"Deal."

And just like that, I feel folded back into the world and family I used to orbit but never made time for. No expectations. No pressure. Just warmth, laughter, and two chocolate-mustachioed kids who think I hung the moon.

The evening winds down in a slow, syrupy blur of bath bubbles, pajamas with teddy bears, and the ritualistic hunt for Anna's missing sock, which somehow ended up in the toaster. Anna was inconsolable for about twenty minutes when Richard was unable to locate his confiscated legs, or Anna's tail, in the attic—but countless promises to look again properly in the morning eventually placated her.

I follow the girls up the stairs, their little feet thumping like a herd of elephants on the carpeted steps.

"We want you to read the story," Lily announces as we reach the landing. "Daddy always skips pages."

"I do not," Richard calls from downstairs.

I suppress a grin. "Well, lucky for you, I'm wide awake."

The girls scramble into bed, surrounded by a menagerie of stuffed animals. I settle between them with the chosen book—some vibrantly illustrated tale involving magical ponies and glittery maps—and read in my best dramatic voice.

They hang on every word, giggling when I do the accents and gasping at the cliffhangers. By the end, Anna's head is on my shoulder and Lily's hand is wrapped around my pinky like it's her anchor to the waking world.

When I close the book, neither one of them makes a move. They're blinking slowly, drifting.

"Will you be here in the morning?" Lily asks, half-asleep.

"Yeah, sweet pea," I whisper. "I'm sleeping over tonight."

Anna, already snuggled into her blanket cocoon, sighs in contentment. "And you'll make pancakes?"

"If you let me sleep past six," I reply, brushing a strand of hair from her cheek.

Lily giggles faintly. "No promises."

I stay a little while longer, watching their little chests rise and fall, their lashes fluttering gently against soft cheeks. There's something grounding about it—this quiet, this simplicity. It's not just comforting, it's... healing. Like some tiny part of me is rethreading itself, just by being here.

Eventually, I tiptoe out, pulling the door closed with a soft click. Downstairs, Claire is curled up with a blanket and Richard's flicking through TV channels like it's a sport.

"Bedtime success?" she asks.

"Two out of two asleep. I expect a trophy."

She hands me a cup of tea instead, and I accept it like it's gold.

"Guest room's all made up for you," Richard says, not looking away from the screen.

"Thanks, really appreciate it."

As I sit down beside my sister and sip my tea, the tension I didn't even realize I was still carrying begins to melt away.

There's no urgent meeting tomorrow. No ticking clock. Just family. And, for the first time in a while, a night of sleep ahead that might actually feel like rest.

Later, after both Mom and Richard have retreated upstairs and the hum of the dishwasher fills the background, Claire and I are left alone on the sofa, legs tucked under us like teenagers during a sleepover. The house has gone still, save for the occasional creak of settling floorboards and the muffled cough from one of the girls.

Claire hands me a blanket and refills my tea without asking. She's always been like that—quietly perceptive, a master of knowing when to prod and when to just... sit.

We sip in silence for a moment before she speaks.

"So," she says softly, "is this a visit-visit or a I-might-move-into-Mom's-basement visit?"

I chuckle, but it's low and tired. "Somewhere in between."

She raises an eyebrow. "That's not ominous at all."

I sigh, curling tighter under the blanket. "A visit-visit. I just needed to stop. Everything's been moving so fast for so long... and suddenly, I didn't want to chase it anymore."

Claire reaches over, squeezing my hand. "You're allowed to change your mind, Rach. Even now. Especially now."

"I don't even know what I want," I say.

"Then maybe this is the part where you figure it out," she says gently. "Not with a five-year plan or a Pinterest board. Just... by sitting still and listening to yourself for once."

A lump forms in my throat. "That's easier said than done."

She shrugs. "Most good things are."

For a while we sit in silence, the kind only sisters can share. Then she leans her head against mine.

"You'll figure it out. And hey—worst case, sell the condo and move back here with us. I'll make space in the garage for your shoe collection."

I laugh, tears pricking the corners of my eyes. "Thanks, Claire."

An hour later, the house has finally gone still. I pad into the guest room—Claire's old childhood bedroom turned into a cozy catch-all—with a borrowed toothbrush and a mismatched pair of pajamas. The sheets are crisp, the lamp casts a warm glow, and the scent of fabric softener lingers in the air.

I sit on the edge of the bed, brushing a hand along the worn quilt. There's a photo on the wall—Mom, Claire, and me on a windswept beach, hair tangled, arms flung around each other. I don't remember when it was taken, only that we were laughing.

My phone buzzes faintly from my bag across the room. I don't reach for it. Whatever it is, it can wait. For once, everything can wait.

Instead, I lie back and close my eyes, listening to the quiet creaks of a house settling into sleep. There's nowhere I need to be, no one expecting a response, no task to cross off. Just stillness. Presence.

In the hallway, I hear the gentle patter of little feet—one of the girls up for a glass of water or visit to the bathroom. A low murmur, Mom's voice, then silence again. This house, this life, isn't perfect. But it's real. It breathes.

I nestle under the covers. Tomorrow, I'll start figuring out what comes next.

But tonight, I just let myself rest.

TWENTY

I sink into the plush cushions of my couch again, surrounded by a blissful chaos of potato chip bags, candy wrappers, and half-empty soda cans. My fuzzy pink slippers dangle off the edge as I stretch out, reveling in the fact that I don't even know what time it is. And I don't care.

The TV hums in the background, the familiar theme song of my favorite baking show spilling from the speakers like a warm hug. I've been playing catch-up for five straight days—something I used to think only happened to people with "hobbies" or "free time." Apparently, that now includes me.

It's strange. This time last week I couldn't go ten minutes without checking Slack or mentally reworking a pitch. Now I can't even remember the last time I opened my laptop. The sheer stillness of this week—no calls, no back-to-back meetings, no fires to put out—should feel unnatural. And yet, here I am, wrapped in a blanket with unwashed hair and greasy fingers, watching strangers in Britain sweat over sponge layers and crème pâtissière like it's the Wimbledon final.

It's heavenly. And terrifying.

Part of me keeps waiting for the guilt to kick in. For the

creeping dread that I'm falling behind, that I'm losing my edge. But it hasn't come. Not really. Instead, I've started noticing how quiet my brain feels when it's not jammed full of KPIs and click-through rates. I'm not sure I like it. But I also don't hate it.

There's a weird kind of peace in not being needed. No one's asking for my approval. No one's pinging me with "quick questions" that are anything but. For once, I'm just... here. Being. Watching sugar collapse and puff pastry rise and realizing how deeply satisfying it is to root for someone whose biggest problem is whether their Genoise is too dry.

The buttery scent of microwave popcorn mingles with the sweet aroma of the scented candle flickering on the coffee table. My modest Chicago condo feels like a cozy haven, a world away from the sleek glass and steel of the CGPR offices.

I glance down at my oversized 'I 🤍 Bears' t-shirt—originally white, now speckled with a constellation of cheese puff dust—and plaid pajama bottoms that may or may not be held up by sheer willpower. A smear of chocolate decorates my left sleeve. I'm not even mad about it.

If anyone from CGPR could see me now... Rachel Holmes, queen of the PowerPoint pitch, reduced to a feral couch goblin surviving on a diet of sugar and sodium. I haven't worn a bra in five days. My Fitbit buzzed once, presumably to ask if I was still alive. I flipped it off and rolled over.

This is the version of me that HR never warned you about: Snack Gremlin Edition. And honestly? She's kind of thriving.

On-screen, a contestant is attempting an ambitious three-tiered cake decorated with delicate sugar flowers. I lean forward, captivated, as the camera zooms in on their intricate piping work.

"Come on, you got this!" I mutter encouragingly at the TV, reaching for another handful of cheese puffs.

It's amazing how invested I get in these baking journeys,

considering my own culinary skills max out at boiling water and burning toast. There's something soothing about watching people pour their hearts into creating something beautiful and delicious, even if I can't relate.

As the contestant steps back to reveal their finished masterpiece, I let out an appreciative whistle. The judges are equally impressed, showering praise on the baker's creativity and technical prowess.

I smile contentedly, sinking further into the cushions. This is exactly what I needed—a week of doing nothing, some time to recharge, to remember there's more to life than work. Even if that "more" mainly involves binge-watching reality TV and consuming my body weight in junk food.

For now, I'm happy to stay right here in my little bubble of relaxation, soaking up every blissful, responsibility-free moment. The real world can wait until next week, or maybe even next month. This week is all about embracing the art of doing absolutely nothing.

That's not to say I haven't given the future, my future, some serious thought. I stare up at the ceiling and try to imagine going back. Back to the endless calls, the weekends lost to 'urgent' pitch decks, the CEO egos, the last-minute rebrands, the tight smiles, the tighter deadlines.

I love what I do. God help me, I actually love PR. I love crafting a story that cuts through the noise. I love the strategy, the psychology, the dance of it. But, what I've come to realize is, I don't love living on someone else's calendar. I don't love sacrificing every spare minute to prop up brands I don't believe in. I don't love being told to 'lean in' while quietly being leaned on until I crack.

And I'm tired of pretending that I want to climb someone else's ladder. I want to build my own damn house.

It hits me—softly, but all at once.

I don't want another job.

I want freedom.

I want flexibility.

I want clients I choose, hours I set, and the kind of balance that doesn't require me to schedule joy like a boardroom meeting.

I want my own consultancy.

There it is. The truth, clear as glass.

It's terrifying, sure. Risky. Unpredictable. But the thought of what comes next makes me feel alive instead of just... responsible.

Still... the truth is, I don't need to figure it all out today.

The work/life balance doesn't start when I land my first client. It starts now. With the life part.

So, I shuffle into the kitchen to make another bag of popcorn. There are at least four unwatched series calling my name, and frankly, I intend to answer them all.

Just as I'm reaching for the remote to line up the next episode, a shrill ringing shatters the peaceful atmosphere. I groan, tempted to ignore it, but a nagging sense of responsibility propels me off the couch.

Padding across the room, I locate my phone beneath a pile of discarded candy wrappers. The screen flashes with an unfamiliar number with a Maine area code, and I frown, debating whether to answer.

Curiosity wins out. "Hello?" I say tentatively, hoping it's not another telemarketer trying to sell me on a timeshare.

"Ms. Holmes? This is Jonathan Harcourt," a gruff voice responds, and my eyes widen in surprise. "From Harcourt Foods."

"Oh! Um, hello, Mr. Harcourt," I stammer, caught off guard. My mind races, trying to figure out why he'd be calling me directly. "What can I do for you?"

There's a brief pause, and I hear him clear his throat. "I was hoping we could meet, to discuss a potential opportunity."

"Opportunity?" I echo, my curiosity piqued. I absently twirl a strand of hair around my finger, trying to picture what kind of opportunity he could be referring to.

"Yes," he confirms, his tone businesslike yet not unkind. "I have a proposition I think you might find interesting. Are you available to meet in person, say, tomorrow afternoon?"

I glance around my apartment, taking in the snack debris and my less-than-professional attire. The old Rachel would have jumped at the chance, no questions asked. But something about this unexpected call gives me pause.

Still, I can't deny the thrill of anticipation that runs through me at the prospect of a new challenge. Maybe this is the universe's way of telling me it's time to get back in the game.

"Absolutely," I find myself saying, my voice strong and sure. "Just name the time and place, and I'll be there."

As I jot down the details, I feel a renewed sense of purpose coursing through my veins. Whatever this opportunity entails, I'm ready to face it head-on.

Looks like my lazy week just got a whole lot more interesting.

I hang up the phone, my mind reeling with possibilities. *Old Man Harcourt wants to meet with me? Why?*

Suddenly, the cozy cocoon of my apartment feels... off. All week, I've been hiding out, convincing myself that stillness was the same as healing. But standing here, phone still warm in my hand, I feel a jolt of something I haven't felt in a while—curiosity. Maybe even hope.

I don't know what Harcourt wants, but whatever it is, it's *something.* A break in the monotony. A door I hadn't expected to find swinging open.

I toss the remote aside and rise from the couch, my pulse quickening.

Time to get your shit together.

I stand in the middle of my living room, chip bags crackling beneath my slippers like autumn leaves. The TV drones on, blissfully unaware that I've just been offered a lifeline—one that smells faintly of opportunity and stale popcorn.

I gather up the empty snack packages and shove them into the trash with a sigh that's heavier than I expect. Not because playtime's over—but because somewhere in the middle of watching other people whip egg whites into stiff peaks, I forgot what it felt like to care about something.

I glance around the room—wrappers, crumbs, the coffee table littered with the depressing buffet of my burnout. It doesn't look like a woman on vacation. It looks like a woman who quit.

And maybe that's what this call from Harcourt is: a line thrown into deep water. A reminder that I'm not done. That I don't *want* to be done.

I grab the Febreze, take one last look at the snack throne I built—and start wiping it all away.

As I straighten the throw pillows on the couch, I catch a glimpse of my reflection in the TV screen. My hair is a mess, and I'm pretty sure there's a chocolate smudge on my cheek.

"Ugh," I groan, rubbing at the spot. "You're a hot mess, Holmes."

But even as I say it, I can't help but laugh. If Old Man Harcourt could see me now, he'd probably wonder what he's gotten himself into.

As soon as I have booked my ticket, this time triple-checking it's for the right airport, I make my way to the bedroom, flinging open the closet doors. I rifle through hangers, pulling out potential outfit options for tomorrow's meeting. Business casual? Full-on power suit? I hold up a blouse, then toss it aside.

As I continue to sort through my clothes, I feel a sense of

determination settling over me. Whatever this opportunity is, I'm going to make the most of it.

But first, I need to find the perfect outfit. And maybe do something about this bedhead situation.

I finally settle on a sleek navy pantsuit that never fails to make me feel confident. As I lay it out on the bed, my mind races with possibilities. What could Old Man Harcourt want to discuss? The suspense is killing me.

I glance at my phone, half expecting it to ring again with more details. But it remains silent. I'll just have to wait until tomorrow to find out.

I adjust my dress in the hotel mirror one last time, my reflection staring back with the ghost of a smirk. The heels are polished, the hair's behaving, and the fitted dress is doing exactly what it's supposed to—broadcasting competence with a touch of intimidation. My portfolio is tucked under my arm like a weapon.

There's a flicker of nerves in my stomach, sure. But there's something else too—electricity. The kind I haven't felt in weeks.

The cab ride to Harcourt headquarters is short. I step out and look up at the aging façade, and stride confidently into the lobby for the third time.

"Rachel Holmes, here to see Mr. Harcourt," I announce to the receptionist. She nods and gestures for me to take a seat.

Minutes later, a statuesque woman in a crisp white blouse and pencil skirt emerges. "Mr. Harcourt will see you now," she says with a polite smile. "Follow me."

We weave through a labyrinth of hallways until we reach an imposing set of double doors. The brass nameplate reads "J.D. Harcourt, CEO".

Inside, the spacious, wood-paneled corner office is more like a den. Framed magazine covers line one wall, yellowed with age, each featuring the steely-eyed, and much younger, visage of J. D. Harcourt himself.

"Ms. Holmes, a pleasure." His voice booms as he rises from behind the massive mahogany desk. Old Man Harcourt is an imposing figure, tall and broad-shouldered, with a shock of silver hair and piercing blue eyes. His handshake is firm.

"The pleasure is mine, Mr. Harcourt. Though I must admit, your call was somewhat unexpected."

He chuckles, gesturing for me to take a seat. "Straight to the point. I like that." He leans back in his leather chair, steepling his fingers.

"I'm led to understand that you pitched quite a significant pivot to my new product development team some months ago."

I glance around his office—at the decades-old production schematics behind glass—and feel the weight of what the Harcourts have built. Three generations of selling chicken. That's not just a business model; it's a family identity. Sunday dinners, backyard barbecues, kids tearing into chicken nuggets between soccer games. The idea of convincing Old Man Harcourt from that to... well, mushed-up vegetables... it's not just a commercial shift. It's emotional. I have to play this very carefully. There's an opportunity here. Small, I grant you, but he did request a meeting. I can keep it cordial, spend ten minutes with the man and hopefully leave him with a little niggle in the back of his mind to *maybe* consider augmenting his product range... or... I can believe in the data. Believe in the market. Believe in me...

"Most men I know wouldn't last ten minutes in a focus group for this kind of pivot," I say lightly. "If it doesn't moo, cluck, or come with a side of fries, it's met with suspicion."

Harcourt raises an eyebrow, intrigued.

"But," I continue, "even the most traditional meat-eaters

are starting to look sideways at their plates. The truth is, one of the hero ingredients I proposed comes from a fungus—*Fusarium venenatum*, to be exact. It's naturally occurring. It's fermented in a controlled environment and produces myco-protein. Packed with fiber. High in protein. Minimal environmental impact. And if you handle the seasoning right—honestly? It has a better texture than chicken breast."

Harcourt leans back, watching me closely.

"It sounds sci-fi. I get that. But it's also science-forward. And if we frame it properly, it won't feel like heresy. It'll feel like progress that respects the past."

There's a beat of silence. His fingers tap slowly against the folder on the desk. I wonder if I've gone too far.

"I'll be frank, Ms. Holmes. There's been some trouble brewing here at Harcourt Foods."

"Trouble? Of what sort?"

Harcourt sighs heavily. "Seems my VP of marketing had some very lofty ambitions, trying to push me out, position himself to take over."

"I'm sorry to hear that," I say, shaking my head.

"Thank you for your concern. But don't worry, I've put a stop to it."

I nod, processing this information. "I see. Well, I'm glad you were able to handle it. But what does this have to do with me, if I may ask?"

"I find myself in need of someone to take the lead on our rebranding. Do you think that someone could be you?"

My mouth falls open in shock. Harcourt Foods is a S&P 500 company. To be handed the reins on a project of this magnitude is a once-in-a-lifetime opportunity. Questions swirl in my mind—the timeline, the budget, the scope...

He watches me for a moment longer, then leans forward, elbows on the desk.

"Tell me something, Ms. Holmes. If you were sitting in my

chair, what's the first thing you'd do to get this company back on track?"

It's a test. A sharp one. He wants to see if I flinch.

"I'd stop thinking like a commodity," I reply without hesitation. "You've spent fifty years perfecting supply chains and margins. But the future's emotional. People don't just buy food—they buy identity. Aspiration. Belonging."

"And you think a rebrand can give them that?"

"I think a brand that talks like a person and moves like a culture can. And that means, before you do anything, you need to reflect the culture with the products you offer."

He raises an eyebrow, clearly not expecting that answer. "And what exactly does that look like? A TikTok dance with a mushroom cutlet?"

I smile. "Not unless you're doing the dancing. But imagine a campaign that leans into your legacy instead of hiding it. A multi-generational story. 'From family farms to future food.' We remind people that you've always fed American families. Now you're feeding their values too."

He leans back again. "And if the board hates it?"

"They'll come around—once they see the market share shift and the headlines soften."

"You're sure of yourself."

"I'm sure of the work," I say. "And I'm sure of what consumers want, even if they don't know how to articulate it yet."

A slow grin spreads across his face. "You don't bluff, do you?"

"Not unless I have a full house."

He laughs, a low, approving sound. "You know, I used to think legacy meant building something too big to fail."

I pause, not sure if he's talking to me or himself.

"But these days, I wonder if it means knowing when to change course—before the tide takes you with it. My generation built empires on convenience and price. But that's not what my grandkids care about. They ask where the chicken lived, what it ate, whether it was happy."

He lets out a dry laugh, shakes his head.

"I used to roll my eyes. Now I listen."

I nod, quietly moved. It's not a confession, exactly. But it's more than I expected.

He straightens, the moment gone, the CEO mask sliding back into place.

"Harcourt Foods is at a crossroads. We need fresh thinking, bold ideas. The product team showed me a copy of the presentation you delivered, and I think you captured exactly what we need to do if we want to make sure this business not just survives, but thrives, over the coming years."

"I still stand by that. And the data supports—"

"Let's get down to brass tacks. The world is changing, Ms. Holmes. Consumer tastes are changing. 'Healthy' and 'sustainable' are words people like me would prefer to ignore, but the truth is we're having to compete on price to maintain revenues. I've been around long enough to know that will only end one way. Whether we like it or not, plant-based alternatives are the future."

I lean forward, intrigued. "I couldn't agree more, Mr. Harcourt. Embracing plant-based alternatives is a smart move for Harcourt Foods."

He chuckles, shaking his head. "I'll be honest, I don't quite understand it myself. Why anyone would choose to eat something pretending to be chicken when they could have the real thing is beyond me. But I'm not blind to the trends."

I smile, appreciating his candor. "It's a different mindset, for sure. But the demand is undeniable. With the right strategy, Harcourt Foods could position itself as a leader in this space."

Harcourt nods, tapping his finger on the desk. "That's

where you come in. I need a comprehensive rebranding plan, a way to introduce these new products without alienating our core customer base. It's a delicate balance. If I offered you the job to turn this all around, would you accept?"

"Mr. Harcourt, before we go any further, there's something you should know. I'm no longer with Channing Gabriel."

His eyebrows shoot up in surprise. "Oh? What happened?"

I feel a knot forming in my stomach, worrying that this revelation could jeopardize the opportunity. "It was my decision. I felt it was time for a change, to pursue new challenges."

Harcourt studies me for a moment, his expression unreadable. The seconds tick by, and I fight the urge to fidget under his scrutiny.

Finally, he speaks. "Ms. Holmes, I didn't choose you because of your affiliation with Channing Gabriel. I chose you because of the vision you outlined in the presentation. Whether you're with them or not is irrelevant to me. So, would you like to head up our rebrand?"

My heart's racing, but I keep my expression calm.

This is it—the moment I've been chasing for the better part of a decade. Not a promotion, not a pat on the back, but real ownership. A blank slate. A legacy brand on the brink, and I've been asked to catch it mid-fall and turn the whole damn thing into something new. Something better.

And yet... I hesitate.

Not out of fear. Not exactly. But because I know what this kind of opportunity demands. It won't just ask for my time or my brain—it will ask for my soul. That's what it cost me last time. I gave everything I had to CGPR, and when it was over, I was so hollowed out I didn't even notice I'd lost myself.

But then I think of Chloe. Of Dan. Of the people who are trying to live their lives with meaning and heart and connection. I think of the girl who walked away from a secure job, a corner office, and a very generous commission structure, because she finally understood there had to be more.

I want this. Not *despite* everything I've learned—but *because* of it.

This isn't just a step up. It's a pivot. A declaration. I'm building something new. On my own terms.

I straighten my shoulders, and meet Harcourt's stare with one of my own.

"I'm in."

He nods, a hint of a smile on his weathered face. "Good. Now, let's talk strategy. I want to hear your initial thoughts on how we should approach this."

I lean forward, my mind already whirring with possibilities. "Well, Mr. Harcourt, I believe the key is to position Harcourt Foods as a forward-thinking, adaptable company that's in tune with changing consumer preferences. We need to showcase your commitment to offering high-quality, sustainable plant-based options, while still maintaining the integrity of your traditional products."

Harcourt nods, his eyes alight with interest. "Go on."

"To do this effectively," I continue, "I'll need to build a dedicated marketing and PR team and establish a proper office space. This will allow us to create targeted campaigns, engage with influencers in the plant-based community, and execute a comprehensive rebranding strategy."

He leans back in his chair, considering my words. "You don't think you can handle this alone?"

I shake my head, meeting his gaze directly. "Mr. Harcourt, I'm confident in my abilities, but I also recognize the scale of this undertaking. To give Harcourt Foods the attention and resources it deserves, I need a talented team behind me. It's not just about me; it's about setting us up for long-term success."

A slow smile spreads across his face, and he chuckles

softly. "I like the way you think, Ms. Holmes. You're not afraid to ask for what you need. Very well, you have my support. Build your team, find your office. Jody, my PA, will reach out to you regarding the contract and benefits package. Just keep me informed of your progress."

I feel a rush of gratitude and determination. "Absolutely, Mr. Harcourt. Thank you for this opportunity and your trust. I won't let you down."

As we shake hands, I can't help but marvel at the turn of events. I didn't think I'd be out of work for long, but a week? Now here I am, embarking on a new chapter with one of the biggest names in the food industry. It's both thrilling and daunting.

I stride out of his office with my head held high, a newfound spring in my step. The excitement is palpable, coursing through my veins as I make my way towards the elevator. My mind is racing, thinking about the first steps I need to take to get this operation off the ground. Moving my entire life to Maine, assembling a team, finding an office space, developing a strategy—it's a daunting list, but I feel energized and ready to conquer it all.

As I step into the elevator, I catch my reflection in the polished metal doors. There's a sparkle in my eye and a hint of a smile tugging at my lips. It's the look of someone on the brink of something big, and I can hardly contain the anticipation building inside me.

The elevator begins its descent, and I savor this moment of triumph. It's not every day that you walk out of a meeting with a game-changing opportunity like this. I know there will be challenges ahead, but right now, all I can focus on is the exhilaration of embarking on this new journey.

The journey back to the hotel is a blur. My mind is already racing with the next steps. I pull out my phone and start jotting down notes, my fingers flying across the screen. There's so much to do, and I can't afford to waste a single moment.

First things first, I need to find the perfect office space. I pull up a few real estate listings on my phone, scanning through the options. It needs to be somewhere that reflects the innovative and dynamic spirit of the agency I'm building. Somewhere that will inspire creativity and collaboration.

I bookmark a few promising listings and make a mental note to set up some viewings as soon as possible. The sooner I can secure a space, the sooner we can hit the ground running.

As I arrive back at the hotel, I'm practically buzzing with energy. I know there will be long days and late nights ahead, but I'm ready to pour my heart and soul into this new chapter. With a team of brilliant minds by my side and a drive to create something truly exceptional, I have no doubt that we'll make our mark on the industry.

I sit down at the desk in my room, pull out my laptop, and dive headfirst into the whirlwind of planning and preparation. There's no time to waste—I have an agency to build, and I'm determined to make it a resounding success.

The next morning, I find myself standing in front of a charming brick building in the heart of Portland's Old Port district. The sun glints off the large windows, and I can already picture the bustling energy of my team inside.

This could be it—the perfect home for my budding agency.

There's something about this city that just feels right. It's a place where tradition meets innovation, where hard work and creativity go hand in hand. And that's exactly the spirit I want to capture with my agency.

Still, I hesitate.

This space isn't just a logistical decision—it's a declaration. A promise to myself and whoever joins me that this is real.

Permanent. And with that promise comes pressure. What if I'm making a mistake? What if I'm not ready?

I step inside, the old wooden floors creaking faintly beneath my boots. The leasing agent greets me with a warm smile, and we begin touring the space. With each step, I try to silence the doubts and focus on what could be. I envision sleek modern workspaces, collaborative meeting rooms, and a cozy lounge area where we can unwind and brainstorm.

I stop near the largest window and let my hand brush against the brick wall. My mind fills in the blanks—laptops open, sticky notes everywhere, music in the background, a team of smart, funny, driven people who believe in what we're building. It's just a shell now, but I can see it all so clearly. And in that clarity, the fear starts to fade.

This isn't just an office. It's a second chance. A fresh start. A leap of faith.

The leasing agent turns to me, eyebrows raised. "What do you think?"

I pause for a moment longer, letting the weight and the wonder of it all settle.

"It's perfect," I say, a grin spreading across my face. "Let's make it happen." As I sign the lease and shake the agent's hand, I feel a surge of pride and determination. This is it—the first official step in bringing my vision to life. And I know, deep down, that this is just the beginning of an incredible journey.

I step back out onto the cobblestone streets, my heart full of hope and anticipation. The future is wide open, and I can't wait to see where this path will lead. But one thing is for sure— with a talented team by my side and a passion for creating something remarkable, there's no limit to what we can achieve.

I stride into The Maine Mall, my heels clicking against the glossy floor tiles with determined purpose. The familiar scents of pretzels and perfume samples waft through the air as I navigate the bustling corridors. I didn't plan to be here this long—didn't plan to be here at all beyond the meeting with Jonathan Harcourt. But then again, I didn't plan to be launching an agency in Maine either.

I only packed for a few days. One decent pair of heels. Two blouses that could pass for professional if you didn't look too closely. Nothing suitable for the next few weeks of hiring, networking, and staking out the office lease.

Now, I need clothes. The right clothes. A suit that says leadership, not burned-out refugee. A coat that can handle a Maine November. A few pieces that can take me from client meetings to café catch-ups without making me feel like I'm impersonating a grown-up.

Because this is real now. I've said yes. I've leased a building. I'm staying—at least until the agency's up and running. Then I'll go back to Chicago, pack up the rest of my life, and come back for good.

Today is about getting what I need to look the part. Not just for others—but for myself. A uniform for the next chapter. Proof, in fabric and fit, that I'm not just reacting anymore.

I'm building something.

My steps falter as I pass the boutique where Chloe and I had spent a giddy afternoon choosing her dress for the singing competition. The mannequins still wear their dreamy pastel gowns, unchanged, like time hasn't moved on—except, of course, it has. That day feels like it belonged to a different version of myself. One who hadn't yet let Chloe down.

I pause, staring at the window display. She'd twirled in the changing room, all elbows and excitement, and asked me—me —if she looked beautiful. I'd told her yes, and meant it with my whole heart. Then I'd left before I got to see her wear it for real.

A pang hits, unexpectedly. Not guilt exactly. More like... the ache of unfinished business. Of wanting to have been someone she could count on.

I exhale slowly and move on. I can't undo what's already been done. But I can show up better going forward.

I scan the storefronts for something suitable. A chance to reinvent myself, to shed the weight of past regrets and forge a path that allows room for both ambition and genuine human connection.

The mall's lively chatter swirls around me, a symphony of laughter and chiming cell phones. For once, I let myself get swept up in the energizing current, imagining a future where I'm not just an observer of life's vibrant moments, but an active participant. With each step, I feel a flicker of hope, a tentative excitement about what lies ahead.

As I round the corner, a familiar logo catches my eye—a stylized coffee cup emblazoned on a chic storefront. The rich aroma of freshly ground beans beckons, promising a moment of indulgence amidst the day's mission.

"Why not?" I ask myself, a smile tugging at my lips. "A little caffeine never hurt anyone."

The bell above the café door jingles as I step inside, the scent of roasted beans and warm pastries wrapping around me like a hug. Sunlight streams through the wide front windows, casting golden patterns on the wooden floors. A low hum of conversation and clinking spoons fills the space, underscored by the hiss of steaming milk from behind the counter.

The barista greets me with an easy smile, and I order a large cappuccino—extra foam—and a chocolate croissant, telling myself I've earned both. As I wait, I scan the room, my gaze lazily drifting past students glued to their laptops, parents juggling pushchairs and caffeine, and couples trading quiet laughter across tiny tables.

And then, like a jolt of color in a sepia-toned photo, I see her.

Blonde ponytail. Familiar stride. That unmistakable bounce in her step.

Chloe.

She's surrounded by friends, mid-laugh, utterly at ease—and for a moment, the world just... stops. Everything narrows into soft focus, everything else blurring at the edges. There's a split second when I don't know what to do. Whether to call out, or disappear before she sees me.

Then her gaze lifts. Finds mine.

Time suspends. Just for a beat.

And then, her face lights up—pure sunshine breaking through cloud cover. No hesitation. No resentment. Just joy.

My coffee is forgotten. I push through the crowd, heart thudding, as Chloe breaks from her group and runs.

Chloe barrels into my arms, hugging me so tightly it knocks the breath out of me—and I let her. I let her squeeze every ounce of guilt and regret out of my lungs, because it feels just so damn good.

"Rachel!" she says into my shoulder. "I can't believe it's really you!"

I hold her just as fiercely, my arms wrapping around her smaller frame. She still smells like strawberries and shampoo. For a moment, neither of us says anything. There's no need. The hug says it all.

Eventually, she pulls back, still clutching my arms, eyes searching my face with an intensity that startles me. "I was so mad when you left," she says honestly. "And then I was sad. But now I'm just... happy."

Tears threaten. I blink them back with a shaky smile. "I missed you too. So much more than I realized."

She grins. "You look really good, by the way. Chic, but a little rumpled. Very fashion-editor-on-her-day-off."

I laugh. "You're too kind. I've been living out of a suitcase."

"Still," she says, tugging me a little closer, "you're here. That's what matters."

We stand like that for a moment longer, until Chloe finally bounces on her toes with excitement. "Oh! I forgot to tell you —I won my heat! I'm through to the State finals!"

"What?" My mouth drops open. "Chloe, that's incredible! I'm so proud of you."

"It's during Thanksgiving break. Two weeks. You have to come. Please?"

My smile falters for a split second. Chicago looms in the back of my mind—the condo, my things, the inevitable logistics of relocation—but her hopeful eyes pull me back into the present.

"I wouldn't miss it for the world," I say, and mean it.

She lets out a delighted squeal, twirling once in the middle of the café like she's made of joy. Then she stops abruptly, a new idea blooming behind her eyes. "Actually... there's something else."

"Oh?" I brace myself.

"Dad's recording an episode of his new show tomorrow," she reveals, a mischievous glint in her eye. "They film the apartment scenes in front of a live studio audience. You should come! It would be such a fun surprise for him."

The suggestion hangs between us.

It's a perfectly Chloe idea—earnest, hopeful, a little chaotic.

I'm a little thrown at the mention of Dan, and I feel a flutter of nerves in my stomach. The thought of seeing him again is both thrilling and terrifying.

I hesitate. Not because I don't want to see Dan—if anything, that's the problem.

"It might be awkward," I say carefully, my voice lower now. "We didn't exactly part on the best of terms."

Chloe tilts her head. "But you said yes to the finals."

"That's different," I say quickly. "That's about you. That's something I wouldn't miss."

She opens her mouth to argue, but I raise a hand gently. "It's not that I don't want to see him. It's just... I don't think he'll want to see me."

Chloe gives me a sympathetic smile, softer now. "You don't know that."

I offer a half-hearted shrug, not ready to let that thought settle. "Maybe. Or maybe he's just relieved not to have to explain me to his friends and family. I sort of burst into his life, made a mess of things, and left."

She frowns. "That's not how I see it."

"Well, I did announce his acting comeback without telling him, remember? And almost got you killed on a boat."

"Almost." She grins. "But instead, you saved me."

I exhale, torn. "It's just... if I show up, I don't want it to look like I'm trying to wedge myself back in. Or make it about me. I don't want to ambush him."

Chloe steps closer and gently links her arm through mine.

"It's not an ambush. It's a seat in the audience. That's all. You're not storming the stage."

I smile at that, but the nerves don't fully dissipate. There's too much I haven't processed. Too much left unsaid between Dan and me. But maybe, I think, being in the audience is a way of saying something without having to say anything at all.

"Please, Rachel?" Chloe pleads, her eyes wide and imploring. "It would mean so much to me. And I know Dad would love to see you too, even if he won't admit it. He's been moping around ever since you left Biddeford. I think he misses having someone to banter with, you know?"

I sigh, feeling my resolve crumble in the face of Chloe's earnestness. "Alright, alright. I'll come to the live recording."

Chloe lets out a squeal of delight, throwing her arms around me in another exuberant hug. "Thank you, Rachel! This is going to be the best surprise ever!"

Chloe pulls back from the hug, her eyes sparkling with excitement.

"I should probably get back to my friends," she says, glancing over her shoulder at the group of girls waiting nearby. "But tap in your number and I'll text you the details for tomorrow, okay?"

I nod, taking her phone and adding my number to her contacts. "Sounds good, Chlo. And congratulations again on winning the heat. I'm so proud of you."

Chloe beams, her smile as radiant as the sun. "Thanks, Rachel. And I'm really sorry about asking you to go out in the boat with me. You saved my life." She gives me a final squeeze before turning to rejoin her friends, her ponytail bouncing with each step.

I watch her go, my heart swelling with a bittersweet mix of emotions. It's probably a good thing she didn't wait for a response. I probably would have burst out crying. Chloe's already halfway back to her friends when she turns, gives me one last wave, and mouths, *Thank you.*

I nod, managing a small smile.

I return to the café, and I sit back down at my table, my coffee now lukewarm. I find myself replaying Chloe's words in my mind. "'I think he misses having someone to banter with, you know?'"

The thought of Dan missing me, of him feeling the same sense of absence that I've been grappling with, it's both touching and terrifying. *Does he miss me? Has he even thought about me since I left?*

But then I remember the way he looked at me in the boathouse, the intensity in his gaze, the unspoken words that hung in the air between us. The want. The desire. The way my heart raced and my skin tingled, like a current of electricity running through my veins.

Those daydreams are quickly put to rest when I remember how furious he was that we'd taken the boat out. That I had risked his daughter's life and all of this within forty-eight hours of announcing his acting comeback without bothering to ask for his permission first... No, of course he hasn't thought of me since. If he has, it's not with longing or regret... It's with relief that I'm no longer around.

How can I let Chloe down gently? The poor girl doesn't understand why going tomorrow is a terrible idea. How could she?

I take a long sip of coffee, steeling myself. I'll go to the recording. For her. To show up, like I should have done the first time. I'll sit quietly, stay out of the way, and applaud when I'm supposed to.

No expectations. No drama.

TWENTY-TWO

The ride to the studio is a blur of nerves and anticipation. I drum my fingers on the back seat, trying to focus on the first round of interviews I've scheduled for tomorrow, but my mind keeps drifting to thoughts of Dan. Will he be happy to see me? Will he understand that I came at Chloe's request and that I don't want to miss the chance to see him perform?

As the car turns into the lot, the looming façade of the soundstage comes into view, and I feel my pulse quicken. I press a hand to my chest, as if I can calm the fluttering there. I shouldn't be this nervous—this was Chloe's idea. I'm just here to support her. That's all. And yet, the thought of walking into Dan's world, uninvited, unannounced... It feels like trespassing.

I spot Chloe waiting by the entrance, bouncing on her toes with excitement. She waves at me enthusiastically, her grin wide and infectious.

"Rachel! You made it!" she exclaims, pulling me into a tight hug as I approach.

I laugh, returning the embrace with equal fervor. "Of course I did. I wouldn't miss it for the world."

We make our way inside, and are issued audience passes at reception and told to proceed through to the soundstage. Chloe's clearly been here before and navigates the bustling corridors of the studio with ease.

It feels like we're walking in circles, the anticipation of other audience members and the echo of shouted instructions surrounding us like static. It's another world—one built on performance, precision, and perfectly timed emotion. I wonder, briefly, what it must be like to live in this world full-time. Chloe seems to float through it like she belongs. Maybe she does.

Arriving at Soundstage #1, we're ushered through to the bleachers. It's free seating, and Chloe takes my hand and leads me across to two seats that are still empty in the front row. I would have preferred something higher up, hidden away. It's only when we get to the seats, I see a small sticker on each which reads Chloe Rhodes +1. Of course, a benefit for the cast and crew to enable friends and family to see their loved ones at work. But then it hits me that I am the plus one. Not the colleague, not the PR expert, not the careful strategist. Just... Rachel. Someone she chose. And maybe that's who I want to be now—someone people choose, not someone who forces herself into the room.

The place fills up fast; the air is buzzing with energy, the chatter of the audience and the hum of equipment filling the space.

"Dad's going to be so surprised to see you," Chloe says, her eyes twinkling with mischief. "He has no idea you're coming."

My heart skips a beat at the thought, a mix of nerves and excitement coursing through me.

"I'm not sure he's a big fan of my surprises," I say, trying to keep my tone light.

Chloe gives me a knowing look, her smile softening. "Trust me, he'll like this one."

As we settle in our seats, I find myself scanning the stage, searching for any sign of Dan. The minutes seem to stretch on endlessly, each second feeling like an eternity.

I haven't seen a full episode of the show yet, but I found a few trailers and clips online last night. It's a fun show that's billed as a comedy-drama. For once, it's actually true—the dialogue is sharp and very witty, but then the characters find themselves embroiled in high-stakes drama that really tests their relationships. The pilot has a solid 7.8 stars on IMDb, which is very healthy indeed. They're filming the apartment scenes from episode three today, which will air next week.

Chloe grips my hand, her eyes sparkling with anticipation. "This is going to be so cool," she beams. "Dad is so good."

I smile at her enthusiasm, my heart fluttering with a mix of nerves and excitement. I keep telling myself I'm only here to chaperone Chloe. And I am. But I'm also here for my own reasons—I really want to see Dan again, even if it's from a distance.

The house lights dim, and the audience respectfully reduces the volume of their chatter. Everyone who needs to cough, or thinks they might need to cough, tries to get it out at the same time.

The three camera operators swivel their cameras, and in quick succession give a thumbs up to an unseen producer.

The director's voice crackles over the PA system. "Places everyone! Scene four. Take one. And... action!"

The set springs to life, suddenly bathed in warm, inviting light. I recognize the cozy living room from the clips I watched last night—overstuffed couches, family photos on the mantle, even a lazy golden retriever sprawled on the rug.

And there, striding in with two of his castmates, is Dan. My breath catches. He looks good. Really good. The hint of grey at his temples only adds to his charm, and that crooked grin of his still makes my heart skip a beat. Not that I'd ever admit it.

Dan launches into his opening monologue, his rich baritone filling the studio. But then, mid-sentence, his eyes find us in the front row. Those piercing blue eyes lock with mine, and for a moment, the rest of the world falls away. I'm transported back to our—his—housewarming party, the promise of something up against the wall of the boathouse...

But then Chloe squeezes my hand, snapping me back to reality. "He's doing great," she says, her voice filled with pride.

I nod, swallowing hard. "Yeah, he is."

I watch as Dan finds his rhythm again, slipping effortlessly back into character. Still, I can't shake the feeling that something shifted in that moment. Like a spark reigniting...but of anger or something else, I'm not quite sure.

Dan's castmates exchange worried glances as he falters, but being true professionals, they adapt seamlessly. The scene flows on, yet an undercurrent of tension ripples beneath the surface. I can see it in the set of Dan's shoulders, the flicker of his eyes toward us.

Chloe leans forward, hanging on her dad's every word. I'm torn between drinking in the performance and studying Dan himself, searching for clues in the subtext. Is this just acting, or is there something more brewing beneath the scripted lines?

As if in answer, Dan goes off-script. He pauses, scans the audience, and when he speaks again, it's not as his character. It's as himself, raw and unbridled. Whispers ripple through the crew. The cameramen turn in their chairs, trying to catch the eye of a producer. Dan's co-stars exchange quick, confused glances, but they follow his lead. Chloe tenses beside me, her hand a lifeline in mine. I know, without doubt, that this isn't acting anymore.

"Sometimes," he says, his gaze boring into mine, "life gives us second chances. Opportunities to right wrongs, to say the things we were too afraid to say before."

My pulse pounds in my ears. *Is he really doing this? Here, now, in front of cameras and a live studio audience?*

Dan's voice rises, raw and unfiltered. "I've spent the last few months really thinking about what matters in life. About the chances we miss, the people we let slip away." His eyes glisten with unshed tears.

I'm rooted to my seat, unable to move. Unable to breathe.

"I've made mistakes," Dan continues, his voice cracking with emotion. "I've let pride and stubbornness hold me back. I thought it was grief, but it was fear. Fear of the unknown, fear of the possibility of finding happiness with someone else. But standing here, looking out at the two most important people in my life, I realize..." He swallows hard. "I realize it's time to stop running from the truth."

Is he talking about... me? Us?

Dan's voice cracks, but he pushes on, determined. "We can't let fear hold us back. We can't let pride or stubbornness keep us from the people we love. Because in the end, that's all that really matters. The connections we make, the love we share."

Each word cuts and heals in equal measure. I remember the walls I'd built; the times I'd run first. I remember Chloe's hug in the mall. I remember the boathouse. The almost. The never was. The maybe still could be.

Tears are streaming down my face now, but I make no move to wipe them away. Beside me, Chloe is openly crying, her small frame shaking with sobs.

Dan's voice softens, but it carries no less impact. "That's what I intend to do. To hold on to the people I love, to cherish every moment we have together. Because in the end, that's what makes life worth living."

As his words fade away, the studio is utterly silent for a

heartbeat. Then, as one, the audience surges to their feet, applause thundering through the space.

But I barely hear it. All I can see is Dan, his chest heaving, his eyes locked on mine. In that moment, the rest of the world falls away, and it's just us.

Us, and the love that has always been there, waiting for us to be brave enough to embrace it.

Chloe is squeezing my hand so tightly it hurts, but I barely notice. All I can see is Dan, laying his heart bare for all the world to see.

For me to see.

"I love you," he says simply, his eyes shining with unshed tears. "Both of you. And if you'll have me, I promise to spend every day proving it."

I'm frozen, my heart in my throat. I can feel the eyes of the studio audience boring into the back of my head. I'm sitting so still I wonder if my heart has stopped beating. I feel like I'm standing at the edge of something, heart in my throat, terrified to fall.

But haven't I already jumped? I left my job. I started something new. I chose people over power, vulnerability over certainty. And maybe that's what this is. Another leap. But for once, it doesn't feel reckless. It feels real.

I know I'm supposed to do something. To react. But I'm frozen to the spot. I want to move. I do. But I can't. *What if this is just performance? A beautiful lie crafted in a moment of emotion?*

Chloe's fingers tighten on mine. She leans in, whispering, 'He means it.'

And that's all I need.

Slowly, Chloe stands, pulling me with her. She glances at me, a silent question in her eyes. I nod. Not quite sure what I'm signing up for.

Together, we step forward into the light.

Hand in hand, Chloe and I walk onto the set, ignoring the surprised murmurs of the audience and the frantic movements of the production crew. My heart races as we approach Dan, his eyes wide with a mix of hope and trepidation.

We stop just short of him, an arm's length away. For a moment, we simply stare at each other, a thousand unspoken words hanging in the air.

Dan remains standing in the center of the set, his broad shoulders heaving, his face etched with a thousand emotions. Surprise, hope, fear, love... They all flicker across his features in rapid succession.

"Did you mean it?" I ask softly, my voice trembling. "Every word?"

Dan nods, a tear escaping down his cheek. "Every syllable," he says. "I've been a fool, Rachel. I thought I could outrun my feelings, bury them in criticism and excuses. But the truth is..."

He takes a deep breath, his gaze unwavering.

"The truth is, I've been in love with you since the moment we met. And I'm tired of pretending otherwise."

A sob catches in my throat, years of pent-up emotion threatening to overwhelm me. Beside me, Chloe is beaming, her face aglow with joy.

"It's about time, Dad," she says, her tone teasing but her eyes shining with affection. "We've been waiting for you to catch up."

Dan laughs, a sound of pure, unbridled happiness. He opens his arms, and Chloe and I fall into them, the three of us clinging to each other as the audience erupts into whoops and cheers.

I hear the applause like it's underwater, a distant roar that barely registers. The lights above are warm, golden, and suddenly this place doesn't feel like someone else's story. It feels like a stage we've claimed for ourselves. For something unscripted. Something true.

The three of us stand there, holding each other tight, as the studio audience rises to their feet in a standing ovation. There's not a dry eye in the house. The air is charged with an electricity that has nothing to do with the bright stage lights.

In that moment, everything else falls away. The cameras, the crew, the curious onlookers—none of it matters. All that exists is the three of us, finally, blessedly whole.

"I love you," I say into Dan's chest, my tears soaking his shirt. "I love you so much."

He kisses the top of my head, his arms tightening around us. "I love you too," he says. "Both of you. Forever and always."

And there, in the warmth of our embrace, I feel a piece of my heart slot into place. A piece I hadn't even realized was missing.

We have a long road ahead of us, I know. Some hurt and misunderstandings to unpack, wounds to heal and bridges to mend.

But for now, in this perfect, shining moment, none of that matters. All that matters is that we're together.

The director throws his hands up in frustration, his face a mask of disbelief. I catch a glimpse of him gesticulating wildly at the crew, but the cameramen just grin and keep filming, their lenses trained on us like we're the most fascinating thing they've ever seen.

And maybe we are.

Maybe this moment, this raw, unscripted display of love and forgiveness, is the most real thing to ever grace this stage.

For years, I believed success meant sacrifice. That you could either build something or feel something—but never both. But maybe the real work is choosing people, choosing love, even when it's terrifying. Maybe I don't have to choose between being whole and being driven. Maybe the person I'm becoming can be both.

I can see our image playing out on the studio monitors. Will they broadcast this to viewers across the country? The big-city PR exec, wrapped in the arms of a small-town single dad and his precious daughter.

It's not the story I would have written for myself.

But as the audience applause continues, as Dan and Chloe pull back slightly to beam at me with identical watery smiles, I realize it's a better story than I ever could have imagined.

We stand there together, basking in the warmth of the moment. The studio fades away, the audience, the cameras, all of it.

In this instant, there is only us.

The director's voice rises above the commotion, calling for a cut. The spell breaks, reality rushing back in, but the glow of the moment lingers.

I blink, taking in the sea of faces, the applause still reverberating through the studio. Hundreds of eyes are fixed on us, some misty with emotion, others wide with astonishment.

"Well, folks," the Assistant Director chuckles, stepping onto the stage, "that wasn't in the script, but I kind of wish it was."

Laughter ripples through the audience, warm and good-natured. I feel my lips curve into a smile, a bubble of joy expanding in my chest.

"Now if you don't mind, we've got an episode to film."

TWENTY-THREE

♥

The energy inside the Ogunquit Playhouse is electric as Dan and I push through the doors. Crowds of excited parents and kids fill the lobby, chattering and laughing.

"Wow, what a turnout!" Dan says, his eyes wide as he takes it all in. "Chloe is going to be thrilled to have us cheering her on."

I nod, smiling at the thought. "She's worked so hard for this."

As we make our way through the throng to find our seats, I feel my phone buzz in my purse. Fishing it out, I see Jonathan Harcourt's name flash across the screen. My stomach clenches. What could he possibly want now, right when I'm about to watch Chloe's big moment?

I hesitate, my thumb hovering over the answer button. Dan notices and raises an eyebrow questioningly. "Everything okay?"

I hit decline and drop the phone back in my bag. "It's nothing that can't wait. Tonight is about Chloe."

But even as I say it, I feel the ghost of my old instincts twitching. The part of me that never let a call go unanswered.

That measured self-worth in responsiveness and resolution times. For years, I let work infiltrate every corner of my life like a slow leak—until it eroded everything personal I could have built.

Not tonight.

Tonight, I'm not a marketer or a strategist or a brand whisperer. I'm not the woman chasing validation in boardrooms and rebrands. I'm just Rachel. Someone who got lucky enough to be here, on this night, in this seat, about to watch a girl I've come to love do something extraordinary.

It's strange, this sense of wholeness. Foreign, but welcome. Like slipping into a version of myself I didn't realize I'd been missing. One who chooses presence over performance. One who understands that sometimes, the most important deal you ever make... is to simply show up.

And I'm all in.

As we settle into our seats, I look around at the faces of all the other proud parents, grandparents, and siblings. The love and support in this room is palpable.

The lights dim and a hush falls over the audience. The velvet curtains part and a single spotlight illuminates the stage. There, in the center, stands Chloe. She looks so poised and confident, her midnight blue dress shimmering under the lights.

As the first notes of her song fill the theater, I feel Dan's hand find mine, our fingers intertwining. Chloe's voice rings out pure and strong, the melody wrapping around us like a warm embrace.

"She's incredible," Dan says, his voice thick with emotion.

I nod, not trusting myself to speak. Tears prick at the corners of my eyes as I watch Chloe pour her heart into every word, and everything else fades away. The stress of creating a new agency from scratch, the pressure of delivering my very best work for Harcourt Foods, the constant buzz of my phone, the weight of expectations. All that matters is the beautiful, brave girl on that stage and the man beside me.

As Chloe hits the final soaring note, Dan and I leap to our feet, our cheers mingling with the thunderous applause that erupts from the crowd.

Pride surges through me, so fierce and overwhelming that it feels physical. I steal a glance at Dan. His eyes are fixed on Chloe, awe and pride etched into every line of his face. He's not the same man who accidentally burst into my motel room. There's a softness to him now, a peace. And I wonder if he sees the change in me, too. I wonder if he feels it—that subtle but seismic shift in how I see the world.

Once, I would've watched Chloe perform through a lens of performance metrics—how well she projected, how her stage presence might read on video, how the judges might perceive her. Now, all I see is her bravery. The way she stands in front of hundreds of strangers and dares to be seen.

I feel something crack open in me, wide and tender. Because maybe that's what love really is—not a grand gesture or a declaration made in front of a studio audience. Maybe it's this. Sitting beside someone who helps you see what truly matters. Cheering for a girl who trusted you enough to let you into her life.

And just like that, I know—I'm not just here to witness a performance. I'm here to witness a transformation. Hers. Mine. Ours.

"Go, Chloe!" Dan shouts, his face split in a grin that rivals the spotlight.

Chloe takes a bow, her eyes scanning the audience until they land on us. Her smile is radiant, filled with the pure, unbridled joy of a dream realized. In that smile, I see a reflection of the woman she'll become—strong, resilient, chasing her passions with reckless abandon.

I lean into Dan's side, his arm coming to wrap around my shoulders. "Have you come round now about the dress?" I ask.

"I have," he agrees, pressing a kiss to my temple. "You were right. She's not a child anymore. She looks amazing."

"And it doesn't make you nervous?"

"Are you kidding me? I'm terrified."

I turn to face Dan fully, my hand coming up to rest on his chest. His heart beats a steady rhythm beneath my palm, as constant and sure as the man himself. His eyes, so often guarded, sometimes haunted even, are now open and warm, reflecting the stage lights like stars.

"Thank you," I say, my voice barely audible over the ongoing applause. "For inviting me into your life, into Chloe's life. I didn't know how much I needed you both until now."

Dan's hand covers mine, his thumb brushing over my knuckles. "Thank you for being here, for seeing us. For choosing us."

Dan opens his mouth, like he wants to say something more, but instead, he pulls me in closer. The gesture says it all. Safe. Steady. Here.

For a moment, I let myself truly feel it—the gravity of being chosen, of choosing back. It's easy to take for granted that love will be chaotic, like the ones we're told about in movies and novels. But this—this quiet, consistent presence— it's the kind of love that builds a life. That holds you steady when everything else is spinning.

I press my cheek to his shoulder and close my eyes, allowing myself to believe in the simple beauty of this night. The stage lights, the music still echoing in my chest, Chloe's triumph still reverberating through the crowd like thunder.

If I'd answered Harcourt's call, I'd probably be knee-deep in details, talking timelines and deliverables. But I didn't. I'm here. And the version of me that's learning to stay present, to love fully, is more than capable of leading an agency *and* showing up for the people she loves.

I'm not giving up who I was. I'm just making space for who I've become.

As the applause finally begins to die down, Dan and I retake our seats, our hands still entwined. On stage, the emcee steps up to the microphone, ready to announce the next performer. But my attention is solely on the man beside me, on the future that stretches out before us, bright and boundless.

I lean my head on Dan's shoulder, content to bask in the afterglow of Chloe's triumph. Whatever comes next, whatever challenges lie ahead, I know we'll face them together. A family, in every sense of the word.

As the next performer begins their act, I find my mind drifting, reflecting on the winding path that led me here. Just a few months ago, I was consumed by my work, convinced that my career was the only thing that mattered. But now, sitting in this theater, with Dan's hand in mine, I realize how much I've changed.

It's not just about prioritizing personal life over professional ambition, though that's certainly part of it. It's about opening myself up to the possibility of connection, of love, of family. It's about recognizing that there's more to life than the next big client or making partner.

I glance at Dan, his profile illuminated by the soft glow of the stage lights. He catches my gaze and smiles, his eyes crinkling at the corners in that way I've grown to adore. I'm overwhelmed by a sense of gratitude, of wonder at the unexpected turns life can take.

"What are you thinking about?" Dan asks, leaning close so I can hear him over the music.

I shake my head, a soft laugh escaping my lips. "I'm just happy."

I lean my head on his shoulder, taking in the scent of his

cologne, the warmth of his presence. On stage, the performer hits a high note, their voice soaring over the audience. And as the crowd erupts into applause once more, I join in, my heart full to bursting.

When the applause fades, the emcee takes the stage once more, his voice booming through the speakers. "Wasn't that incredible, folks? The talent we've seen tonight is truly outstanding!"

I nod in agreement, my gaze still fixed on the stage. Beside me, Dan leans forward, his elbows resting on his knees as he watches with rapt attention.

As the final performer exits the stage and the applause fades to a hum of conversation, the theater settles into a kind of reverent buzz. People shift in their seats, programs rustle, someone behind us lets out an anxious sigh. I glance around the auditorium, noting the nervous energy vibrating in the air —a mix of anticipation, hope, and pride. This isn't just a school event. For these kids, it's a chance to be seen, to shine.

Dan leans in slightly, his voice low. "Do you think she's nervous right now?"

I smile. "Maybe a little. But she's prepared. She's got that quiet determination—the kind that sneaks up on you and then blows the roof off."

He chuckles. "Wonder where she gets that from."

I roll my eyes, but can't hide my grin.

"And now, the moment we've all been waiting for," the emcee continues, a mischievous glint in his eye. "It's time to announce our winners!"

The tension in the air is palpable, a collective breath held as everyone waits for the verdict. I find myself gripping Dan's hand tighter, my heart racing in my chest. Whatever happens,

Chloe made it to the state finals. A huge achievement and one I hope she is proud of. That said, I think her performance was so good, it deserves more.

"In third place, we have... Mia Johnson from Lewiston High School!"

A petite girl with braided hair bounds onto the stage, her face split in a grin as she accepts her trophy. The crowd cheers, a wave of support and admiration washing over the theater.

"And in second place... Liam Nguyen from Oakridge High School, Bangor!"

A boy in a red bowtie takes the stage, his steps measured and confident. He shakes the emcee's hand, holding his trophy high as the audience applauds.

"And now, the moment of truth. Our first-place winner, who will be moving on to the national competition and representing the great State of Maine in New York City..."

The pause seems to stretch for an eternity, the anticipation building with each passing second. My leg shakes with nervous excitement, my free hand clutching the armrest.

"Chloe Rhodes from Ellesbec High School, Portland!"

The world erupts in a blur of sound and motion. I'm on my feet, cheering until my throat is raw, tears of joy streaming down my face. On stage, Chloe stands tall and proud, her eyes shining as she accepts her trophy and a giant bouquet of flowers.

Dan pulls me into a tight hug, his own cheeks damp with emotion. "She did it, Rachel. She actually did it."

I nod against his shoulder, too choked up to speak. In this moment, everything feels right, everything feels perfect. The future stretches before us, bright and full of promise.

The house lights come up, and the theater buzzes with excited chatter as people begin to file out.

I turn to Dan, my heart still racing with adrenaline. "Let's go congratulate our superstar!"

He grins, his eyes crinkling at the corners. "Lead the way."

We make our way through the crowd, exchanging smiles and high-fives with the other proud parents and supporters. Backstage, it's a whirlwind of activity, with performers rushing to change out of costumes and gather their belongings.

And then, there she is. Chloe, her face flushed with triumph, her trophy clutched tightly to her chest. She spots us and lets out a squeal of delight, running to throw her arms around Dan.

"Dad! Rachel! Did you see? I won!"

Dan lifts her off her feet, spinning her around. "We saw, honey. You were incredible up there. I'm so, so proud of you."

I pull them both into a hug, my voice thick with emotion. "We both are, Chloe. You shone like a star tonight."

She beams at us, her eyes sparkling. "I couldn't have done it without you. Without both of you."

As we walk out into the cool night air, Chloe chattering excitedly about the upcoming nationals, I slip my hand into Dan's. He squeezes it gently, and I feel the warmth of it spread through me—not just through my fingers, but deeper, into the quiet parts of myself that used to feel so uncertain, so incomplete.

There's no fanfare now. No audience watching. Just the three of us under a star-scattered Maine sky, our breath visible in the crisp air, the smell of salt and pine carrying on the wind. Chloe walks a few paces ahead, her trophy swinging by her side, already humming what might be her next song. Dan's arm slips around my waist, and we fall into step without needing to say anything.

And I know, with absolute certainty, that I'm home. Not because of where I am, but because of who I'm with. Love didn't arrive as I expected it to—not loud, not dramatic—but quietly, insistently, until it became the foundation beneath my feet.

We don't need to chase applause. We have something better. We have each other.

Tomorrow will come, full of deadlines and logistics and to-do lists. But tonight, under these stars, I have everything I need.

The
Midnight
Meet-Up
In the ER, they save lives. After hours,
they just might save each other
alia smith

CHAPTER ONE

LILY

"BP's crashing, Dr. Harper," Patty states with all the urgency of someone reciting a grocery list.

My pulse is the only thing in this room that's not flatlining. Blood pools on the table. Monitors screech like they're mocking us. The only thing louder is the buzzing in my skull.

"Then let's stop wasting time," I reply, my voice firm. A clamp waits in my outstretched hand. There's a splash of scarlet, a tremble, and a surgical resident ready to crumble like stale cake. "If you hesitate again, you're out. Focus." If I say it enough, maybe one of us will actually do it.

The resident falters. My instincts kick in before he has a chance to fumble anything else. I snatch the instrument and take control. Methodical. Unforgiving.

"Suction," I snap, shifting my focus to the next step. Hours blur in my mind. Minutes turn into blood-soaked seconds. The patient's chest is open wide—I stare into the wound and wonder which will kill me first, the pressure or the sleep deprivation.

"Clamp, clamp, clamp," I repeat. My vision tunnels as I ignore the chaos around me. The monitors, the blood, the failure, all fade into the background. I locate the source of the bleed, pinpoint its weakness. Hands steady. Mind sharp. Five more seconds and it's over.

The patient's vitals crash lower.

"This should have been done ten minutes ago." Patty, again, as if I'm not aware.

As if I haven't been hyper-aware since I walked into this room. The buzzing in my head is a chainsaw now, drowning out everything but my pulse. No anesthesia needed; I've gone entirely numb on my own.

"We're losing him." A voice, a tremor, a doubt in my ability.

No.

"We are not losing him!"

Focus. Clamp. Focus. Clamp.

My hands blur through a dozen instruments. Scalpel. Forceps. Suture. I don't stop to figure out which. No time for a blood transfusion. No time for their second guessing. I can't lose another patient this week. Not like this. Not because of a surgical resident who can't keep up. I feel my exhaustion taunting me, daring me to fail, and I silence it with precision.

"BP's coming back," Patty says, softer this time.

I stitch a closure, count out three steady breaths, wait for the chest to rise on its own. It does.

"Nice work, Doc."

The silence should be comforting, but it's a reminder of how loud my failures were a minute ago. I survey the bloody battlefield around me, noting the carnage on the operating table and especially on the floor.

"Lucky he didn't bleed out," Patty adds, handing me the chart, calling it like she sees it. "That was a hell of a mess."

"We controlled it," I reply. Her eyes say we both know what "it" is. The word hovers between us like a question.

One crisis down, a hundred more to go. I strip off my gloves and toss them in the trash. "It won't happen again."

"More patients coming in from the same accident. It's gonna be a long one," Patty warns. "You planning to take a break, or you gonna keep working like you've got a death wish?"

I ignore the comment, the concern, the past twenty hours. "If you see an open OR, let me know." I catch the surgical resident's eye. Let him know with a single look that his card is marked. "Don't hesitate again," I remind him as we scrub out.

The hallway is cold and bright, which makes it easier to pretend I'm awake. I can't remember the last time I slept. My feet take me in two directions, toward the family waiting area and toward another twelve-hour shift.

The family sits in a cluster of panic, half-collapsed into chairs with soggy tissues and tear-stained faces. I know the type. The hysterics. The over-thankers. The ones who take and take and take until there's nothing left but sleep deprivation and regret. The patient's wife clutches her daughter's arm, using it as a handkerchief. Her sobs fill the entire room. Her breathing labored.

"He's going to be okay, Mom," the daughter says. She looks sixteen, and not at all convinced by her own words. "They've got this. Right?"

I'm five feet away and they're already fishing for hope.

"Mrs. Martin?" I ask, glancing down at the chart like I didn't memorize it hours ago. Like I don't have every detail tattooed behind my eyes.

The woman lifts her head, puffy and raw, eyes leaking relief. "Oh, God," she says, clutching the daughter harder, searching my face for answers. For more than answers. For reassurance and things I don't have. "Is he okay?"

"The surgery went well," I say instead, falling into a chair across from them. Mrs. Martin scoots closer, ignoring my attempt to keep this clinical. "We found the source of the bleeding and stabilized him." My voice is even. "He's stable in the ICU."

Tears form anew, pooling at the corners of the wife's eyes like the blood on my OR table. "Thank you. Thank you, thank you, thank you." Each word sounds like a sob. Like she's used to disappointment. Like she expected me to fail.

They start to tumble, a dam bursting, a river of relief. The woman throws herself at me with the reckless desperation of a patient in V-fib.

I'm quick to suture. I'm slow to react.

My limbs stiffen. Breathing tightens. I stand like an idiot with her arms squeezing me.

My heart knows exactly how many beats per minute this discomfort is. I don't move. I don't breathe. I don't acknowledge the tightness in my chest. She holds me as if I'm saving her life, but all I feel is failure creeping up my spine.

This is the worst I've done since the appendix incident of 2018. I could never have anticipated how hard the hit would be.

I swallow thickly, run through an emotional checklist and come up blank. I need to say something. Anything. A whole sentence. But all that comes out is, "It's my job."

I'm the least-human human they've ever seen.

Mrs. Martin releases me and collapses into the daughter's arms, where the gratitude feels a little more earned. I retreat instead, rubbing my neck where I still feel the contact. The warmth. The failure.

"You're sure he's okay?" The daughter this time, hopeful and sad and two seconds away from finding out I have nothing to give but medical updates.

"We controlled the bleeding," I repeat, turning clinical on

autopilot. "You can check in with the ICU." The words fill the silence.

"He's stable," I assure them. The subtext: I'm not.

Mrs. Martin cries into the daughter's hair. It's a tender, quiet scene that makes my stomach flip like I've swallowed a virus. It's the kind of connection I can't process, so I dissect it instead. Break it into tiny, manageable parts. I know how close I came to failing them. They don't.

"Thank you," the daughter says. "So much."

I rise and back away, stiff, aware of the mess I've left behind. My spine has more rigor than a cadaver. The family is a blur as I make my exit. Their relief is too loud. It makes me uncomfortable. It makes me feel.

I pretend not to hear.

I pause in the stairwell and let the cold wall bite into my spine, let it remind me that I'm a surgeon, not a failure. There's a small voice in my head that sounds suspiciously like my father, telling me that the difference between the two is paper thin. I shut him out, shut everything out. Echoes from the past twenty-four hours bounce off the walls, wrap around my neck. The uncertainty of everything except my exhaustion.

My body aches like an overworked muscle. My mind is worse, churning with static and blood loss. The adrenaline is gone and I feel every single second of the last shift, twenty hours stacked on top of one another. I let myself slide down the wall, as far as my pride allows, until I'm sitting on the stairs with my head in my hands and the exhaustion catches up with me.

Laughter echoes down the stairwell, muffled and distant and meant for people with lives outside these walls. It's a conversation I'll never be a part of, voices from another world. My mind is heavy, but it never shuts off. It whirs and hums and tells me that rest is for people who don't have anything to prove.

If my parents could see me now, collapsed on the stairs, they'd say I was a disappointment. They'd say I didn't have the grit or the drive. And they'd be right. I don't. Not today. Not like this.

The chill of the concrete floor seeps through my scrubs and into my bones. I close my eyes, but it's a mistake, because all I see are the images I've tried to bury deep: the car accident, the blood, the kid who nearly lost his dad because I'd hesitated.

It won't happen again.

My eyes snap open. The sterile white walls close in. My pulse thuds in my ears.

The wife. The hug. The awkward, strangled words that made me feel more helpless than a failed procedure. Why do people have to make things so damn messy? My chest tightens and I want to bolt, but the fatigue has other plans.

This is why I don't let myself think.

When you hold yourself together with stitches, you start to unravel the moment you stop moving.

The stairwell door creaks open and lets in two junior residents, chipper and laughing like the last shift was a walk in the park. Maybe for them it was. Maybe it always will be. They breeze past me without noticing I'm there. I should be thankful. If they saw me slouched on the stairs, they'd know how close I came to cracking.

I lean my head back and stare at the ceiling, ignoring the throbbing in my skull and the tiny, persistent part of me that says this isn't sustainable.

"Pancakes and waffles?" one of them says, as if he can't believe such things exist.

"Breakfast of champions," the other replies. "Count me in."

I try not to be bitter. I try to convince myself that I don't want that kind of freedom, that kind of detachment. That I've chosen this, and I'd choose it again.

"You coming, Dr. Harper?" One of the residents stops and peers down at me. He must not know me very well. He must not know I'm a ghost, haunting this place without even knowing why anymore.

I'm tempted to snap. I'm tempted to say something cruel, like, "If you have time for breakfast, you're not a real doctor."

But I surprise myself. The hesitation is a foreign feeling, an unfamiliar twinge in my chest.

"Maybe next time," I say. I'm not sure who I am for a moment.

The residents leave and I listen to their footsteps fade, listen to their easy laughter as they push open the stairwell door on a lower floor and disappear into the world. Their happiness is an echo, a hollow sound that rings in my ears and makes me more tired than ever.

I catch my breath, my pulse, my composure. I square my shoulders, push myself to my feet, and shove the fatigue away. This is the way it has to be. This is what it takes.

It's not pretty, but it's stable.

I push open the door and let it close with a decisive clang.

CHAPTER TWO

NOAH

Blood pours like a bad horror flick, an over-the-top fountain of gore. I count six heartbeats on the monitor—each slower than the last—before the guy's done for, and I don't plan on wasting a single one. Not today.

"Noah, we're losing him," shouts Nurse Patty. She's all grit and tough love, which explains why I like her so much.

I cut a glance at the newbie, who's about five seconds away from ruining his scrubs.

"Shouldn't we wait for Dr. Patel?" he says, voice cracking, but I'm already snapping on gloves. "If we wait, he's dead." I'm not the waiting type.

This guy's artery is slashed, his blood forming little red lakes around the wheels of the gurney. We haven't seen a bleeder like this since New Year's Eve—the wound you'd get from whiskey bottles and pool cues, not the more pedestrian stabbings.

Nurse Patty yanks a fresh packet of gauze and shoots me a look that says both, 'you're insane' and 'hurry up.'

"He's crashing, Noah!" she shouts, barking out orders and elbowing the resident to suction.

The monitors tell me I have no room for error. No room for anything but an unsteady pulse and dropping BP. A heart rate that's only memorable because it's tanking fast. It's why I don't think twice about the thoracotomy or how much trouble I'll be in for it. You can't teach instincts like mine, but you can get your ass handed to you for using them. I slice the blade cleanly into his chest and feel a slight shudder as my hand hits the rib cage. Rookie loses more color.

"We're really doing this?" he asks, mostly to himself, while Patty already has her hands over the wound, keeping it steady, keeping it real.

I know better than to answer. I focus. The guy's lungs are in the way, his tissue and muscle resistant and fleshy and fighting. It's like an anatomy textbook come to life in a very R-rated fashion, and the kid looks ready to hurl. I pry the ribs apart. My gloved hand fishes inside like it's searching for the world's worst piñata prize.

It's been a few seconds now. Way too many.

"Nine-zero over forty," calls Patty.

The resident's still holding his breath, and I'm about to punch the air out of him if he doesn't catch it soon. "What now, doc?" Patty prods, no fear, just steel.

"I've got this," I insist. I hope.

The organ's a limp, purplish mass of nothing, and I thumb the artery, feeling where it's knotted and tearing and wanting to give up.

But I'm not the giving-up type.

Then: life.

It flutters under my fingers like a newborn bird. One kick. Two. Then full rhythm, and I swear it's the sweetest damn sound I've ever heard. Better than vinyl. Better than old guitars. A steady *lub-dub* from the ECG that wipes the horror-show clean, and for a moment, there's nothing else but this. The win.

"Pulse is one-ten. Pressure's coming up." The monitor pings alive. Patty's mouth quirks into what passes for a grin, and her satisfaction's almost as good as a thank-you note. "Not bad, doc. For a guy working solo."

I wipe my brow with a bloody wrist, feel the tension and adrenaline in every molecule of my body. "You know me—big on happy endings."

Patty snorts. "Big on something."

Resident regains some color. He's still more frightened than awed, but he'll come around. The rest of the team exhales. The room shifts from panic to relief, collective fear shedding like an old skin. Only the suction unit still wheezes, the wet splatter of blood underfoot like rain. They all saw it. They all saw what happens when I get in too deep and too fast and actually pull it off.

"He's stable. Let's get him to the OR" Patty takes charge, shoving the gurney out the door while the rest of the staff stand around, like we just caught the last ten seconds of the Super Bowl. Most of them still don't know what to say when Noah Carter hijacks a trauma case, and that's just the way I like it.

For now, anyway.

Because my celebrations last about as long as it takes for Dr. Patel to breeze in, take a sweeping glance around the carnage, and fix his stare on me. He's crisp. Unhurried. Puts together the whole situation before I even get a chance to bask.

"Dr. Carter," he says. "A word."

Dr. Ajay Patel's office AC is set so low I can feel it chilling my blood. If my talk with him lasts longer than five minutes, I'm suing for frostbite. The desk is a barren wasteland, and Patel's expressions aren't any better. He doesn't bother with hellos or have-a-seats, just straight to business.

"Dr. Carter," he starts, without preamble, "you do not make that call without an attending present."

He's the king of rule-following, and I can practically feel the protocol manual hurling itself at my head.

"He would have died," I counter, but not loud enough to sound like I have a leg to stand on.

"That's not your decision to make," Patel insists, voice clipped and sterile, like the rest of his damn office. He sits back, arms crossed in a way that makes me cross mine too, purely out of spite. "You are a resident, not a hero."

My jaw twitches. I hope it doesn't look too obvious. "With respect, I did what I thought was necessary."

His eyes bore into me, relentless, like a particularly exhausting CT scan. I'm still trying to thaw out from the frosty reception when he delivers the next blow.

"This is the last time we will have this conversation," he states.

The unsaid—*or else*—floats between us like an iceberg, and I know when I'm about to hit something hard. It takes every ounce of self-control not to roll my eyes or laugh out loud. Not because I don't believe him, but because I do. Patel isn't the kind to bluff. If anything, he's probably insulted that I don't take him more seriously.

"Understood," I say, my words as short and sharp as I can make them.

Patel doesn't respond. His silence speaks volumes, most of which are titled *You Are on Thin Fucking Ice*. I'm out the door and into the corridor before the walls start closing in. My pulse is still racing, still wired from the thrill of diving in headfirst and getting away with it. Almost. The only thing I hate more than getting called out is getting called out when I know I'm right, and it's eating me alive.

"Patel looks pissed," comes a voice from the nurses' station. Marcus Young. My partner in crime, except he never gets caught and never breaks a sweat. He's leaning against the counter, all casual-like, grinning in that way that tells me I'm about to be made fun of. "How bad was it?"

I pull up beside him, trying to match his breezy air, trying to forget the crack in my façade that Patel must have seen.

"Could've been worse."

He shakes his head in mock dismay. "Could've been better. So that's, what, your third warning?"

"Fourth," I correct, like it's a point of pride. "But who's counting?"

Marcus laughs, and it's a solid, reassuring sound, like a warm blanket over all this cold, clinical shit. He hands me a chart to review and claps me on the shoulder.

"You are," he says. "At least, you should be."

I snort, pretending not to care but caring more than I'd ever admit. It's the same argument every time, and Marcus has seen me through enough of them to have the script memorized.

"Patel doesn't want a repeat of last year, man. You're not in New York anymore. Just keep your head down for a while, okay?"

"Where's the fun in that?" I fire back, scanning the chart, scanning his face. He's the only one who ever dares to tell me the truth straight up, even if he knows I won't listen. Especially if he knows I won't listen.

We're in the eye of the storm, nurses running in every direction, clipboards flying, cases stacked up like overdue bills, but Marcus and I stand still in the chaos, anchored.

I shrug it off, or try to. "As long as the patients live, does it really matter?"

Marcus's eyes are sympathetic, but unyielding. He's got the whole perceptive-best-friend thing down to an art.

"Maybe not to you," he replies, "but this place isn't Emerald City, and you're not the Wizard. They play by different rules here."

"Rules, *shmrules*," I retort, feigning bravado, ignoring the tight knot in my chest, the one I never quite shake when someone calls me out on my shit. The one Marcus can see plain as day. "It'll be fine."

He arches an eyebrow. "It always is until it isn't."

I know he means well, but it's more than I can deal with right now. Too much truth, too much realism. I smile, a mask I've perfected over the years.

"You're right, Dad. I'll try not to embarrass the family name."

Marcus laughs again, this time louder. "Too late."

And maybe it is. Maybe it's way past too late. But at least we're still laughing about it.

The sixteen-year-old skater next on the list has the hangdog expression of a guy who's had both his bones and his pride severely broken. I'd put money on the pride being the more painful of the two.

"Dude, I think I broke it," he moans, pointing to the swollen balloon he used to call his hand.

I'm still fresh from my first scolding of the week, but I haven't lost my touch with bedside manner or sarcasm.

"What gave it away?" I ask, studying his chart. "The searing pain or the fact that your wrist looks like a pretzel?"

He glares up at me, the look every teenager saves for adults who don't immediately acknowledge how tragic their situation is. "Oh, you're funny."

"Most people think so," I shoot back, a grin breaking through despite the bruising Patel's lecture left behind. I nudge his arm gently to check the range of motion, and the kid winces in dramatic fashion.

"Am I gonna lose it?" he asks, half-concerned, half-expecting me to tell him he'll never play Xbox again.

"You'll live," I assure him, slipping on a pair of gloves. "But next time, maybe stick to Tony Hawk?"

He doesn't laugh, but I see the corners of his mouth twitch. Another hard-ass cracked, courtesy of Dr. Carter. The room's a different kind of chaos than before, still busy but humming along. This kind, I can handle with my eyes closed. I gently feel the mangled wrist again, then look him straight in the eye.

"Ready?" I say, making sure he knows what's coming.

The teen nods, an act of bravery that lasts all of one second before he shuts his eyes tight.

"Here we go," I tell him, steady hands on the fracture. "Three, two—"

A swift, precise motion. The crack sets everything back in place with a satisfying click.

"Wait, did you—?"

"All done," I confirm, grinning at his confused relief. "It'll hurt like hell for a bit, but you'll get used to it."

I unwrap my gloves, and he watches me, a strange mixture of awe and incredulity. I've seen the look a million times, but it never gets old. There's nothing like impressing a teenage boy, who has never been impressed by anything.

"You did that in, like, five seconds," he says, clearly wondering if I've been juicing.

I lean back against the counter, crossing my arms and enjoying the rare moment of being the good guy, the one no one's yelling at. "Better than spending ten weeks in a cast, huh?"

His eyes meet mine, still full of suspicion and admiration and a little bit of that leftover glare. I slap a temporary splint on and send him off for X-rays.

"Get him checked out and on his way," I tell the nurse,

handing over the chart. "This kid's got a story to tell, and it's not gonna sound believable if we keep him here all day."

The nurse nods, and the teen shoots me a last look as he's wheeled out.

"Thanks, doc," he mumbles, embarrassed and relieved, like most of my patients. Like most of the people in my life.

"No problem," I call after him, even though he's already out of earshot. I don't expect a parade in my honor, but I'd settle for a quiet cup of coffee, just me and the chaos and the dull roar of a trauma ward that never stops being loud.

The desk is stacked with more cases. An elderly woman with hip pain, a middle-aged guy with chest tightness, a toddler with a Lego where Legos should never be. Routine. Comfortable.

It's a fine line, what we do here. Walking the tightrope between urgency and ease, crisis and calm. One minute, I'm literally holding someone's heart in my hands, squeezing it like I want to restart the world, and the next I'm setting bones and cracking jokes and pretending like nothing gets under my skin. Not the work. Not the warnings. Not the way I run from one to the next, hoping this place can keep up with me, hoping I can keep up with myself.

"Dr. Carter, we need you in bay four," calls the nurse, and the respite vanishes, a puff of smoke. A pretty illusion.

"On my way," I say, grabbing the next chart and getting ready to jump back in.

By the time I get to the break room, my entire day has been caffeine-deprived, sarcasm-reliant, and desperately in need of a quiet five minutes. I crack open a drink and find Dr. Lily Harper, an incredible surgeon and reigning ice queen of Emerald Bay, standing by the coffee pot like it just insulted her entire family.

"Of course," she mutters, in that way that tells me I'm

about to get way more enjoyment out of this encounter than she will.

"You seem surprised," I say, leaning casually against the counter. "Night shift coffee is a gamble at best."

Lily's sharp features are drawn in focused irritation, the kind she usually reserves for uncooperative interns. "And yet, somehow, I always lose."

There's a hum of broken air conditioning in the background. I sip my drink, let her think she's ignoring me, which is exactly the opposite of what she's doing.

"Rough night?" I ask, my voice as innocent as I can make it.

She finally looks at me, brown eyes flicking with the intensity of a thousand derailed plans. "I spent the last five hours stitching organs back together. And now, the one thing keeping me going is gone."

"The work or the caffeine?" I quip, knowing full well what she means.

"The caffeine," she states flatly, not missing a beat. I have to admire her dedication. And her stubbornness. It's almost as strong as mine.

"Poor Lily," I say, the mock sympathy dripping from my words as I hold up my half-empty energy drink. "You want half?"

"I'd rather die," she retorts, so fast and deadpan that it nearly knocks me over.

I have to laugh, because it's exactly what I expect from her. Everything I say, she's got a comeback twice as quick, twice as dismissive.

"All right, Doctor," I declare, enjoying the game, enjoying how much it bugs her that she's playing. "Let's make a deal. I'll refill the pot if you admit I'm your favorite ER doc."

She stares at me, unimpressed. "That's a bold assumption."

"I like my odds." I grin, and it's her turn to ignore me,

except we both know she can't. I watch, amused, as she finally grabs the coffee canister and sets to work.

Lily Harper doesn't know how to lose, even at this. She doesn't know how to back down. Not when I corner her like this, and maybe that's why I do it. To see the cracks in her armor, the flashes of real, human irritation.

I'm still smiling as she turns her back, the universal signal for *I'm done with you*, which means it's only a matter of time before she gets pulled back in.

The pot gurgles to life, and she gives it more attention than it deserves, like if she just ignores me enough I'll leave, like she doesn't know I'm staying until she blinks first.

"That all you've got?" I press, loving the stubborn set of her shoulders. Loving the challenge.

"Pretty sure you're late for another heroic rescue," she counters, without looking, without losing the smugness in her tone.

I chuckle, raising my drink in a mock salute. "Catch you later, Lily."

The use of her first name earns me a frown, but it's worth it. Every time. I walk out of the room, energy drink still in hand, and already I'm wondering what she'll say next. Already counting the minutes until I get to bait her again, see that look she saves just for me.

The woman is infuriating. The woman is brilliant. The woman is never, ever going to admit I'm her favorite. But one day, she might. She might even mean it.

SUBSCRIBE TO ALIA'S MAILING LIST
&
RECEIVE YOUR FREE NOVELLA

www.aliasmithbooks.com

ABOUT THE AUTHOR

Alia Smith writes heart-warming romantic comedies filled with wit, charm, and just the right amount of chaos.

When she's not crafting love stories, she can usually be found curled up with a book, getting emotionally invested in reality TV, or attempting to keep Galaxy—her cat and chief muse—from sitting on her keyboard.

She lives in a cosy Oxfordshire home, where she firmly believes that every great romance starts with a good cup of tea.

www.aliasmithbooks.com

 instagram.com/aliasmithbooks

 amazon.com/author/aliasmith

BINGE THE SERIES

AUTHOR'S NOTE

Hi,

Thanks so much for reading *The Maine Event*!

It was a lot of fun to write. I truly hope it was an entertaining read.

If you enjoyed it I would be incredibly grateful if you'd be so kind as to leave a review.

Reviews really help authors for a number of reasons, not least, providing feedback on what readers like and improving visibility of the book on online retail sites.

Thanks in advance and I look forward to reading your thoughts.

Alia xx

www.ingramcontent.com/pod-product-compliance
Lightning Source LLC
Chambersburg PA
CBHW050554190726

48283CB00007B/2131